# OFF THE TRACKS

by AuthorHouse 07/08/2014

8-1-4969-2205-2 (sc)
78-1-4969-2204-5 (e)

y of Congress Control Number: 2014911885

This book is printed on acid-free paper.

# OFF TH

## A Beatnik F...

AuthorHouse™ LLC
1663 Liberty Drive
Bloomington, IN 47403
www.authorhouse.com
Phone: 1-800-839-86

Published

ISBN: 9
ISBN: 9

Libra

A
d

# Constance Hood

authorHOUSE®

# TABLE OF CONTENTS

# DEDICATION

Dr. William O. Westervelt who brought the dream to so many of us

# ACKNOWLEDGEMENTS

Writing this book has been a journey in itself. My mother wanted the stories to be told, but not until after she had left us. My husband, actor Chet Hood, was able to bring dear ones alive again. Early readers Bill Weeks and Joseph Saroufim asked all the right questions. Shirley Ostrander, Peter and Irene Moritz, Ute Jensen, and Jeff Westney were a treasure trove of details. Andee Rebeck remastered the audiotapes from 1961 parties. Special thank yous to Kirsten Westervelt Foster for hours and hours of readings and conversations and Aviva Layton, my editor. Finally my neighbor suggested that I just "Put it out there." Bon Voyage!

# CHAPTER ONE

## New Years' Day 1961

In the gray dawn living room, my brother Jack and I were foraging for party snacks, chips with Uncle John's garlicky bleu cheese dip, cold sweet potato casserole with marshmallows on top, and pizza. New Year's Eve had seen one Mom's blockbuster parties.

Our mother, Eleanor Osborne Schloss, was the only divorcee in Elmira, New York. We had returned from New Mexico in 1956 to settle in her hometown, near her parents and the families of her four brothers. When she arrived, her old friends did not come by grandmother's to wish her a welcome home. Ladies at the church where she had grown up would greet her after a sermon, ask how the children were, and then leave with their families. They never invited us over to play with their kids. But now Mom was teaching art in the Junior High Schools, and she and grandfather had bought a Victorian home to restore. It was a great party house.

Jack tried part of a martini, one without cigarette butts dropped into the glass. I never wanted to try a martini. They smelled nasty and who the heck would put an olive into a beverage? Yechhh! But I did drink a glass of Seneca Indians punch, made with Sloe Gin and orange juice. There was some left in the bottom of mom's crystal bowl. The only problem was, someone had brought pickled beets to the party. A hardboiled egg rested in a cup of sloe gin and an orange slice was dropped into the dish of beets. We steered clear of the beets and settled onto the couch, clearing off a space between the ashtrays to dig into our treats.

My name is Kate, Katrine Schloss. I was in the sixth grade at the school where my mother taught art, and I had received a beautiful white and gold diary for Christmas. Finally it was January 1st, 1961 and I could begin writing.

Mom slept in after parties and today was no different. A quick peek through the hall door had seen her prone, with her long hair draping out between two fluffy pillows. She liked to huddle under her down comforter on the cold gray mornings. The old maid's quarters, which had slept several servants, was now a master bedroom with an enormous brass bed and fringed velvet and satin covers. The seven windows in the room each had lace curtains as well as glass shelves full of tinted bottles and perfume flasks. They did not look out over a backyard. We had searched for two years for a house that had no yard to take care of. Instead, directly beneath her bedroom windows was a stand of lilacs, white, lavender, and rich deep purple, bushes so large that they covered the second story windows. Lilacs had filled the house with scent in May when we had moved in. But in January the snow fell so thickly that my brother and I could jump out of our second story bedroom windows and land in the soft white stuff.

This morning a blizzard had blanketed two sports cars. An MG and an Austin Healy Sprite lay buried under 28 inches of overnight snow. Their owners had wandered off into the darkness with the last guests. I decided to ignore the frozen brilliance, and instead was reading a Richard Halliburton book about exotic adventures in warm places. Halliburton's true story about swimming in the pool in front of the Taj Mahal under a midnight full moon had all the parts of a great story – romance, mystery and a little danger. That last thing I wanted to do was to go out and play or even worse, shovel the sidewalk. So my bushy hair remained uncombed; we couldn't get a comb through it anyway. There was no reason to brush teeth before digging into the snacks and I had no intention of getting dressed, even though I was wearing the ugliest plaid pajamas ever. Each year

Grandmother would give Uncle John pajamas for Christmas, which he refused to wear. He slept in his Jockey shorts. After the first washday the pajamas would end up at our house, where mom could then cut them into nightwear for Jack and me. She didn't put any ruffles or lace on them. Even the buttons were ugly, oversized and booger gray. Mom said that I couldn't have a new nightgown until I began making my bed daily, and that was not going to happen. Forget picking up the odd homemade dresses and skirts. That wouldn't happen either. Apparently I was too tall for little girl's clothes and the wrong shape for ladies clothes. So I only got recut hand me downs fashioned from a bunch of stuff that had been in the attic since the 1940s.

The doorbell rang. "You get it!" "It's your turn." "I don't want to spill my plate."

"Let's flip!" But by then Jack had been tricked. He was already off the couch looking for a coin to toss. The bell rang again. We ignored it. Neither of us wanted to go outside anyway. I also didn't want to open the door to snow flurries and melting mud puddles on the floor because I would be blamed for the mess.

Now we heard thumping on the front porch. Someone in heavy boots was trying to kick away the sticky new snow. "Rats!" The doorbell rang again as I shuffled through the entry hall toward the front door. "What kind of ratfink comes over on Sunday morning?" and opened it. I squinted at a teddy bear of a gentleman, who peered back at me through his thick glasses. My announcement was clear: "The party was yesterday." The heavy storm door closed. The doorbell rang again. This time the man asked, "Is Ellie here? She invited me to come by this morning." "Oh really. What had she been drinking?" "Hi, I'm Louis. You must be Kate. The name suits you."

Louis was balding with thick glasses, and bright eyes that found fun in everything. "May I come in?" he inquired politely.

"Yeah, I guess so. Mom's not up."

"I'm not in a hurry. Good things are worth waiting for. What are you reading?"

"The Book of Marvels, stories about an explorer, but not the old fashioned kind."

"Oh! That was a favorite of mine when I was a boy." He pulled off his glasses again to wipe the fog down. The heated living room made everything steam up. "This upstate winter is quite an adventure too."

"What?"

"Well, I grew up in Los Angeles, California, but I live in Greenwich Village now. Everything here looks like a painting. I can't believe how gorgeous it is up here, the frozen rivers with iced trees, almost like a fancy white cake. There are wind patterns on everything . . ."

"You an artist?"

Louis laughed, "No, but this is so peaceful."

"You haven't shoveled much snow, have you?"

"Your mom and I are going to Watkins Glen today."

"Like heck she is. We go in the summer and she screams because Seneca Lake is so cold. She hates it there." Then I decided to not say any more. If the first date went badly, then he wouldn't bother us again.

*　　*　　*

Mom's room upstairs was completely silent, in a "do not disturb" mode, but Jack had slipped up the backstairs to waken her. He could climb into her big brass bed and ask for a cuddle on Sunday mornings. Mom said that I kicked. "Mommy, there's this guy downstairs. He says you have a date." "What time is it?" Jack looked at the big hand and the little hands on the clock, "I think it's nine and something." "Oh god, honey, go and turn on the bathtub, will you?" Jack trotted down the upstairs hall.

Downstairs, Louis was asking all about the ornate rosewood piano, so I played him a couple things out of my newest book. I had only been taking lessons for a few months, and couldn't play like my friends who had started in the first grade. Then he sat down on the bench, played a few chords and announced, "This needs tuning. Do you have a skate key?" He then removed the top from the old baby grand. He said that you begin at middle C, and he had me hum the notes to scales after that. We didn't need to worry about the D. The pad was shot and it didn't make any noise. Sometimes he hummed and I used my skate key to adjust the pegs. Then mom sauntered downstairs in a dress and a pair of ballet flats. At least she was acting like herself. There was no way she was going hiking with this man. She chain smoked, and hated exercise in any form. But, she did get into his VW Beetle, and he took the convertible top down. The two drove off into the fairytale landscape, headed for Route 14 and Watkins Glen.

*   *   *

That afternoon Uncle John dropped by to pick us up along with the week's laundry. Sunday afternoon was laundry time for our family. Each little group in the extended family of uncles, aunts and cousins had scheduled times to do laundry at Grandmother's house. That way the four smaller families of Osbornes could get by on one set of laundry appliances. Uncle John, the youngest, was a bachelor, so Grandmother took care of him and he helped her out with errands and repairs. Mom was missing in action again, so I got the task of doing five loads of sorting, washing, drying and folding.

Grandmother's house was always full of people, and friends were welcome. Tommy Milunich, a nice neighborhood boy, stopped by. We had been friends since first grade. In fact, we had a wedding when we were seven. It was a splendid affair. Mom sewed a hula hoop into the hem of one of her old party dresses, a white one with ribbons, lace and just a few tiny red flowers in the voile. We had a white wicker baby carriage with a doll in it, and Mt. Zoar street was decorated with yards of gold satin ribbon left from some stage production. Cookies and lemonade were served. Then we continued our friendship without any more reminders of matrimony, and the neighborhood kids quit teasing us about spending time together. This afternoon was a cold one, and at some point Tommy had suggested that the three of us play hide and seek, mainly seeking warm places to hide. First, Jack was supposed to hide. Then Tommy and I went to the coat closet in the front room. Damp woolens and warm furs were hung in the closet, and the space was also crowded with a large safe. Tommy sat down on the safe. "Shhh . . . Remember when we got married?" "Yuh."

5

"Do you know what married people do?"

How the heck would I know that? Grandmother Estelle was not married. She was not divorced either. Grandfather Roy lived across town with someone named Loretta whom grandmother hated. Ellie was not married, and neither was Uncle John. Uncle Bill and Monika were the only married people around, and they tried to keep it to themselves. Being married involved privacy, so how would anyone know about it?

"Um, something about bills I think? But I don't really know what a bill is." Tommy began to giggle. "Here, you have to sit on my lap." "Why?" "Because I'll show you what married people do."

"But I'll hurt you."

I had been too big to play wrestling games with my uncles since I was six. They made me be the fat lady in the neighborhood circus, and now on top of that I was the tallest kid in the class by a good half a head. Tommy was not the second tallest. Tommy sometimes had good ideas, but this didn't seem to be one of them. But friends are friends. Were we still married? How long do you get married for? I tried to sit on Tommy's lap, but I kept slipping off. I found my balance by leaving my feet on the floor while I sat on his lap. His feet did not touch the floor. Then Tommy tried to put his arm around me. "Why are you doing that?" My feet were already on the ground and we had solved the problem with sliding off his lap. "Because that's what married people do. They kiss and stuff."

"Are you serious?" By this time the entire event was like two dogs "wrassling." If you have ever had a 90 pound golden retriever jump on your lap, you would know exactly what this felt like. Tommy was trying to put a 98 pound girl on his lap, and it wasn't working. We started giggling and fell against the closet door, spilling out onto the rug. Tommy dusted himself off and went home. I headed back to the laundry room.

As soon as the last pair of underwear was folded and bagged, mom opened the door with Louis, the guy from Greenwich Village, who was standing behind her with his pipe and beret. Mom looked like a wet mop. Louis had a huge grin on his face.

"Guten Abend Louis! Fancy meeting you here. . . . Looks like you two have gotten pretty wet. I'll take your coats." Uncle Bill greeted Louis warmly, first in German, then in English. A high school German teacher, Bill was one of the most popular educators in town. He had been one of the first exchange students to live for a year in Germany, and now our family was in the fifth or sixth year of hosting exchange students from countries that had been in the war. Bill taught the children of displaced immigrants and German Jews. Several families spoke Yiddish at home, and parents wanted their children to learn formal German. He was a vital link between life in the new country and the old.

The mandatory Sunday evening dinners at Grandmother Osborne's were deceptively normal. Parts of the drama were predictable. Grandmother Estelle, always straight and correct, presided at the end chair that she had occupied since the 1920s. A tall woman with strong features, she kept her right wrist on the table, and her left wrist in her lap. Her large hazel eyes behind the rimless glasses did not miss much. To her right sat Uncle Bill and his wife Monika, with a possible guest space; and to her left Peter and Irene, a young German transplant with his French wife, followed by Mom. Uncle John took the end seat for carving and serving, and my brother and I flanked him. This was for correctional purposes. I liked to play with my food, arranging it on the plate, even sculpting my mashed potatoes and squash into artistic tableaus before devouring them, and Jack slouched at the table, sometimes leaning onto his elbow. He had to have the corner, because he was left handed, and whenever his elbow ended up on the table, Uncle John would grab his arm and "bang!" so hard that the entire table vibrated and the dishes shook in their places.

Grandmother Estelle was well read in foreign affairs, and politics was considered to be appropriate table conversation. With the Cold War heading to a possible series of new European conflicts, things were no longer as simple as America good/Germany bad. Bill led the conversation, offering his viewpoint that we needed to make friends with Germans because the Russians were threatening everyone. "Bruce Olmstead just got released. He's coming home."

Bruce had been part of a crew on a six-seat reconnaissance plane, shot down by the Russians over international waters in July. A local boy from Hoffman Street, he had been in Elmira's daily news as the town prayed for his safe release from Soviet prisons and KGB interrogations.

John, a Korean War Air Force veteran, commented, "Damn that took a long time. There was no way that Bruce flew that klunker into Russian territory. Can't believe we didn't get him out before now." No one at the Elmira Star Gazette had reported on the conditions of his release, and President Eisenhower was leaving office.

"I bet Ike offered to shoot every goddamn Russian plane out of the sky if Olmstead and Powers weren't released."

"You're probably right."

"Hey, did you hear that Krushchev sent President Kennedy a New Year's telegram? He congratulated him on the election, and hoped that we would now enter a new era of peace and understanding."

"Did Kennedy write him back?"

"Yes, he suggested a summit conference."

"That was a waste of telegraph money."

Jack took advantage of the pause in the conversation, "Mommy, how was your hike?" "Oh sweetie, it was just wonderful, like a fairyland. The rocks and waterfalls are all frozen. They looked like castles with their arches and rainbow icicles dazzling in the sun." "Did you go up to the bridge?" I already knew the answer to my dumb question. Mom was terrified of heights. She wouldn't even walk on the creaky boardwalk that spanned the Chemung River.

"Oh yes, we hiked the entire two miles. Some of the cliffs are a hundred feet high and frozen solid. The only sound from the bridge is maybe a little rushing of a stream where it breaks over a rock in the ice. Sweetie, you would have loved it. The frozen willow trees look like a lace veil with diamonds hanging over everything." Louis gazed at Ellie throughout this, and then took her hand. Unfortunately this lovely family scene was disturbed by someone's gagging and coughing into her napkin. Excuse me, I was choking.

Estelle quickly moved the conversation back to world affairs. Despite his misgivings about Russians, Bill predicted that if the

U.S. didn't learn how to make friends and make peace, victory would not be an option. "If we don't make the United Nations into a powerful organization and respect others' thinking, we will just blow ourselves up." Grandmother Estelle ventured, "At church this morning we talked about how important peace will be to our future. Then we took communion, and celebrated how Jesus would have wanted peace, truth and love. The alternative for us will be eternal damnation." Louis entered the conversation,

"Mrs. Osborne, what church do you go to?"

"Oak Street Presbyterian."

"Oh. Is it true that the Presbyterians drink grape juice instead of wine at communion?"

"Well, the wine is a symbol of the blood of Christ, so we use grape juice to symbolize the wine. In what religion were you raised, Louis?"

"Catholic. Communion is a sacrament, and we are drinking the blood of Christ. The communion wafer is the body of Christ."

"Well, you do know that we take bread to symbolize the body of Christ."

"Yes, but you chew your bread as if it were food."

"Aren't we all nourished by his spirit?"

"During communion, Catholics absorb the holy spirit in the bread without chewing it. We believe that the body of Christ is in the wafer. When the wafer dissolves within us, we hope that we have become part of the Christ.

"Oh, how interesting. Peter here was raised Catholic, and we have known a few others. Ellie, would you mind dishing up the sherbet?"

Mom stood, then looked at grandmother.

"I can't, I'm afraid of what it will turn into." Grandmother Estelle began to cough into her napkin, and the brothers roared with laughter. Louis bit his lip. Kate and Ellie dished up the orange sherbet, carefully placing each cut glass dish and spoon in the center of the dessert plate.

Peter Moritz and his wife Irene had been fairly quiet through the meal as Bill expounded on his ideas of how the Germans and French should make peace. Uncle Peter had been one of Bill's "Experiment Brothers" in the 1950s, and had decided to come to the US and to make his life. One day a couple years before, he had been working in his family's stables when a petite and very young French girl came knocking at the barn. She was lost, and her companions had gone on without her. That day she found Peter, and her future. Because Peter was in the process of emigration to the United States, Irene had come to stay in Elmira to be near him. She had planned to stay at Peter's apartment across town. Grandmother announced that there was no way that an unmarried couple would be allowed to cohabit. There needed to be an immediate wedding. This was an interesting proposition for two people who hadn't spent a lot of time together. For one thing, Peter was a German Catholic and Irene was a French Jew. Neither a priest nor a rabbi would consider marrying them to each other. Estelle insisted on a marriage or she would revoke her offer to sponsor Peter's immigration. So, ten days after Irene arrived in the U.S., grandmother's minister conducted the church service. When they notified their families of the happy event, both were disinherited.

Irene spoke French and German. She was a true Parisienne, and wore all black clothes, black tights, and stiletto heels. Aunt Monika and Mom took careful advice from her on how to walk, how to flirt, and how to smoke a cigarette. The three ladies were a hit at the local bars. So, at the end of dinner, Irene stood up. "I go take a douche." Grandmother's spoon clattered on her sherbet dish. Mom and Monika looked at each other, stifling laughter. Why all the women were holding their breath? Apparently, translated literally from the German or French, Irene had said that she was going to take a shower, not wash her bottom. Irene's announcement was simply bathroom protocol for a home with one set of plumbing and eight people.

Louis looked across the table at my brother and me, smiling.

# CHAPTER TWO

## Snow Days

I blinked at the white glare that came through the opened door. There was snow everywhere. Sunshine, Uncle John's dented yellow jeep, was smushed into the drift at the curb. The jeep was a World War II surplus item that grandfather had found in a junkyard in 1946 and then painted schoolbus yellow for safety. "They can see you coming." My uncle still used it sometimes to knock around town, usually when it was too icy for him to drive his motorcycle. His all-night call in show on WENY was a local favorite. He told jokes and wrote really bad poetry that he shared between the songs. He hadn't gone home to bed yet. John's 6′4″ frame filled the door and the size 14 snow boots stepped into the foyer ahead of the gentle giant. He wiped the frost and fog from his thick glasses, and began removing his outdoor clothing in the heated Victorian foyer. He set the sopping wet beret and muffler on the baby grand piano. "Mornin' Missy, morning Buster!"

"Uncle John! Mom, Mom, it's Uncle John!"

Jack skipped up the stairs and woke the sleeping dragon. I could almost see a head pounding with steam coming out of her ears but instead she wrapped her blue silk kimono around her waist and staggered down the curved staircase. "Good Morning, Mommy O! What's happening?" "Dammit John, do you have any idea what time it is?" Our family rule was that there was to be no noise, no games and no loud talking before 9:00 AM. He ignored her comment and began to ramble on about his previous evening, "Well, anyhoo . . . I was coming down the hill from WENY, and I saw this farmer sort of hunched over a ditch, and I stopped to see if he was in trouble or something. The old man was just about to put a rock through the head of this . . ." and he held out a funny little puppy. "I just couldn't stand it Ellie. Wouldn't you love to have a dog?"

By now, we were looking over mom's shoulder. Uncle John was big enough to protect us if Mom went off before she had her coffee. I stared at the brown and black mutt, partly because my glasses were upstairs in my bedroom. He was not cute. I liked collies. Little Jack started petting him. How adorable. "I've named him Bozo," said John casually. He had selected a name from one of Jack's favorite television shows. I looked at Mom as Jack began to beg. "Oh mommy, please? We'll take care of him. Here, I'll get him some water." A groan, or was it a roar, pulsed through Mom. "You mean like your hamsters? You let them loose and we had brown and white mice all over the place last winter." Then she took the puppy and put him inside her kimono to protect him from the cold winds and snow flurries that were blowing across the porch.

Jack grabbed the puppy and began to play with it. He had located a rope in our construction materials and put the end in his mouth. Probably some extension ladder would slip and cause an accident because of this. He and Bozo were tugging on it growling and flopping all over the rug. I located a carton and a doll's baby bottle for the puppy, and made him a little bed near the kitchen stove. I know that it would not be OK if he peed on the rug. The puppy, that is. About Jack I was not so sure.

Obviously this was a morning to make a hangover breakfast for the adults. Uncle John had been teaching me how to cook. In fact, he put a soup ladle in my Christmas stocking. I should have been mad, but I thought it was neat to have a grown up present. He said it was because Mom was always making soup, and then dishing it up with a coffee cup. He didn't give her the ladle, because he figured I would end up being the family cook. I think it was because he never shopped until December 24, and he didn't have a kid's present for me, but he gave us things all the time. He was like that.

So, I marched through the dining room and into the kitchen. The crusty black iron skillet was already on the stove, and there was leftover rice in the fridge. The margarine hadn't been put away. I scrubbed out the skillet, dribbled in a little margarine, and raided the spice cabinet for interesting smelling herbs and some curry powder. Curry was the newest flavor. Once the rice was browning, six eggs were scrambled into the entire mess. There was no bacon. We located the percolator, scrubbed out the residue and began to brew a pot of Maxwell House. How could adults possibly drink that bitter swill? Hot chocolate would have been nice. We didn't have any.

Next to the table was a washtub full of dishes and some sacks of plaster, plumbing supplies, and the box of paintbrushes. We were in the process of restoring the old house, with a lot of guidance from grandfather. The Grove Street kitchen still had its embossed tin ceiling, free standing cabinets for dishes, and gas jets poking out of the walls. We cleared an island on the kitchen counter and set out our plates.

Just a few blocks away, my West Elmira girlfriends were probably sitting on soft wall to wall carpets eating sugar cereal in their pretty Lanz nightgowns—pastel flannels with delicate frills—and watching early morning cartoons on big TV sets. Sugared cereal was not ever on our breakfast menu. It was expensive, and grandmother said it was bad for us. It was really unfortunate to have a grandmother with diabetes. We all had to watch sugar because she had some disease that wasn't catching. We could buy Sugar Corn Pops instead of cookies if we wanted, but there was no way we were giving up the cookies.

There was also no TV at 112 Grove Street. If you wanted cartoons, Ellie would hand you a pencil and paper. The only available entertainment was a record player in a heavy-duty cardboard case, and lots of popular records. "*It was a one eyed, one horned flying purple people eater . . . .*" One advantage to having your uncle run the local radio station was that you got lots of sample 45s and LPs with a never ending supply of songs that were only a few months out of date. OK, some of the records were really old, like jazz and things, but there were some really humorous ones. Jack and I especially liked the "Flight of the Bumblebee" played on a slide trombone. Spike Jones was our absolute favorite.

We loved our funny old house, and we worked on it every weekend. Each week we had something new to show for our creative endeavors. Mom loved it for its flaws. The kitchen was now the last and most difficult part of the renovation process, and Grandfather Roy was in charge. While Jack and I ripped the old linoleum, peeled up the pieces, and scrubbed dozens of corners in the convoluted space, Grandfather designed the cabinetry and counters that he would build and install. Mom was going to paint the tin white, and then have a soft floral pink and lavender kitchen that would go with her rapidly accumulating antiques. She wanted displays of bottles and flowers everywhere. Groceries were not a priority.

One afternoon we had all arrived home from school, and in the center of the kitchen were several boards, and a lot of cabinets. Grandfather Roy had obviously been laboring for days. Jack and I looked at them. "They're green. They'll look awful." Mom glared at me. "Be quiet, and don't you dare say a word to your Grandfather." Jack piped up, "it won't be so bad, pink and green go together." Gently Mom answered him. "Kids, your grandfather is red/green colorblind. He can't tell the difference between the colors. After he hangs the cabinets, we will go ahead and get the pink paint and paint them ourselves." Grandfather's station wagon pulled up in the alley, and his high pitched Yankee whistle signaled his arrival at the back door. He strolled into the kitchen, removed his work cap, and wiped the fog off his glasses. "Hi honey, how do you like the cabinets? I finally got around to it. I thought we would get a handle on this mess here. You've had your things piled up on workbenches and in cartons for months now." Ellie rushed across the kitchen and threw her arms around his neck. "Oh Dad, they're just beautiful. I can't believe you did them so quickly – you must have worked night after night." Roy's brilliant blue eyes twinkled behind his work glasses. "How do you like the color Ellie?" She stepped back, "Dad, it's perfect." Roy gazed at his grown daughter. "You do know it's a primer coat, right? Your pink is still at my shop. I can read labels." Grandfather was funny like that.

But now Mom had a new boyfriend. Would Louis help us with the house? "Oh honey, he doesn't even live in a house himself. He moves a lot. He just has a room in New York City." Does he know how? "Gosh, we have never talked about it. He knows a lot of things, but he might not know how to make stuff." Does he have kids? He does not, but he likes kids. "Is he married?" Jack asked the stupidest questions. "Of course not honey. He is divorced, just like I am." "Does he work?" "He used to be a teacher, like me, only he taught science. I don't think he is working right now."

Our house renovations continued, and grandfather made the third floor into a cute one bedroom apartment. One Monday after school Shirley Ostrander showed up with her guitar and her suitcase, to move into the third floor apartment of our old house. Miss Ostrander was one of the best music teachers ever. She was pretty and knew how to sing and play jazz clarinet. She was from a local farm and was engaged to a man named Ray. At 21, she was only 10 years older than me, but Mom said she could handle her Junior High classes very well. She sure could teach. Over the past summer she had taught me how to make peach and blueberry preserves, and how to assemble a quilt. Jack had learned how to shoot a frog between the eyes, skin a rabbit and drive a tractor. This young woman was going to make a wonderful farmer's wife.

Her dad's farm truck was full of her belongings. Jack followed her up the stairs with a box of Kingston Trio records. She picked up a paint scraper, and began showing my brother and me how to prep surfaces carefully. Before they had just slopped on the colors. Layers of paint and wallpaper had sealed together over the years, and we now learned how to strip down to the plaster and begin with a clean wall. Window putty was manufactured into all varieties of worms and snakes, and then installed to seal the drafts in the house. A powerful new Kirby vacuum system was put to work in every corner of the house, even sucking up the dust out of bed pillows. Salvation

Army findings received new coats of paint and violet corduroy upholstery. Songs filled the house.

> *We're coming, we're coming, our brave little band.*
> *On the right side of temperance we now take our stand.*
> *We don't chew tobacco because we do think*
> *That the people who use it are likely to drink.*
>
> *Away, away with rum by gum,*
> *Rum by gum,*
> *Rum by gum,*
> *Away, away with rum by gum,*
> *The song of the temperance union.*

Shirley was a cook. "Dad butchered a steer this week. This roast is for us." She showed Kate how to crumble and roll the perfect pie crust, slice and macerate the apples, and glaze the top to perfection. Jack began to do his homework at the kitchen table, drooling like a dog.

> *We never eat fruitcake because it has rum.*
> *And one little bite turns a man to a bum.*
> *Now can you imagine a sorrier sight*
> *Than a man eating fruitcake until he gets tight?*
> *Away away with rum by gum . . .*
>
> *We never eat cookies because they have yeast,*
> *And one little crumb turns a man to a beast.*
> *Now can you imagine a greater disgrace*
> *Than a man in the gutter with crumbs on his face?*
> *Away away with rum by gum . . .*

The best of all was when Shirley would pack us up and take us to her parents' Pennsylvania farm for the weekend. Mom would take the bus or train to New York City to see Louis, and we would get two days of fun. Shirley had three sisters who knew how to cook and sew, milk cows, and drive tractors. But her sisters were pretty. I wished I were more like them. I knew Mom was frustrated that her little girl was no beauty. Once she broke a hairbrush over my head because she couldn't get it through the cowlicks. Since then, my hair had always been cut by a men's barber so that we could avoid morning fights about tangles and snarls. Now a copy of *Seventeen Magazine* with a blue-eyed blonde model lay in the bathroom. Shirley taught me how to set my hair in the roller pattern demonstrated inside the magazine, and even showed me how to sleep in the hard bristly rollers. The hair did not really cooperate, but it was improved. Then Mom tried to help. She pulled off my glasses, and made an embarrassing scoop necked blue blouse. They were closer to "a look." I wasn't.

I was still too tall, and my legs were big. Everyone was trying to learn to jump like cheerleaders, and to writhe and squirm in the newest dances. I couldn't even walk gracefully. Clumsy works like this:

"I can't believe you didn't see that curb." Stupid, I can't even see my feet.

"You didn't watch where you were going." No, I slipped on some goo on the floor. "Sorry I dropped you when you jumped off the parallel bars." You were expecting a little kid, weren't you?

The result of all this was that the right foot now had three breaks in it. Foot bones are small, so Uncle John's dance teacher friend suggested we just tape it up and keep my leg up on the couch. By now the foot was all lumpy and flopped outward unless I remembered to pull it in to look nicer. No one is going to dance with someone who has floppy big feet. Might as well take one of the cows from the farm. And since dancing was the first step toward dating and marriage, I already knew my prospects of being a lady were slim to none.

One Saturday Shirley took us out for ice cream. Out of the blue Jack asked Shirley, "My mother is pretty. Why is she divorced?"

"She and your dad couldn't love each other any more."

"Why didn't he love her if she is pretty? Do you know where he is?" Uh oh, Jack was going to ask stupid questions about our father again.

"But you and Ray love each other, right? Your diamond is really pretty." We needed to get off the subject of our dad really quickly. "You are engaged to marry Ray. Do you love him? When will I get to meet him?"

Shirley thought carefully about her answer. "Ray and I have known each other since high school. We have lot of reasons to be together, and I'm sure we will be very happy." I wasn't sure that she had answered my question, but I wasn't sure about the love stuff either.

"Am I going to get divorced?" Shirley's large brown eyes widened as she looked at me. "Oh rabbit, why would you ask that?"

"Because Mom and Grandma Estelle are both divorced, except Grandma isn't really. Why do people get divorced? And didn't grandmother and grandfather love each other once?" "Well, if they get married and it was a mistake, then they get divorced. But your grand parents—they raised five grownups. That took a very long time. I'm not sure what happened there. Your grandmother worked very hard to make her family."

"So if I never ever get married, I won't need to get divorced?" That was a relief. Now I had a plan.

"Will you and Ray live with us after you are married?" Another stupid question from Jack.

Once Monday mornings came around, Shirley was Miss Ostrander again. She exchanged her jeans for neat skirts and blouses with flowers on them. Mom was Mrs. Schloss, the art teacher. She had always worn colorful flowered shirtwaists like the other teachers, but on a recent trip to New York City she came back with a bunch of black leather. She made it into a short skirt and vest. It wouldn't show all the clay and paint in the art room. These days Ellie was up in the mornings singing and pouring cereal. What if she had finally met someone who wanted to be a father for Jack, or maybe even just tolerate us? Louis was smart and funny, and he made people stop picking on me. Even better, he told us that if someone was bullying, it might not even be about you. It might be another problem entirely. I liked that advice a lot better than trying to learn to hit people back. Uncle John's boxing lessons were not going well. Louis wore glasses, and had survived it. Maybe it was OK for men to have glasses. Anyway, his eyes twinkled and he thought we were funny.

What if someone loved our mother and really cared about us kids?

Maybe it was time to rethink our attitudes about mom's boyfriends. We were in no hurry to see her get married. Daddy Herman used to scare me. He spanked us with his leather slippers. First grade was awful. Every morning on the drive to school he would say that my mother was leaving, and I would never ever see her again. I didn't cry while he was explaining all this to me. Then after class started I would throw up or make a mess in my pants like a baby. Finally, their divorce was official and Uncle Bill drove to New Mexico to take all three of us move to New York. All household goods would be divided evenly. The sets of towels and washcloths were piled in the back seat with the three of us. In the car, on the way out of Albuquerque, I threw up all over them, and Bill stopped at the nearest trash bin. Now there was room for all of us in the back seat and I didn't need to touch my little brother. Because we moved in February, there were no Valentines in the new school. When the teacher asked me to read aloud about Dick, Jane, and Spot I kept quiet. The little family stories didn't make any sense, so why bother deciphering the secret code of all those letters and words? Then, in the second grade, Mrs. Johnson found out that I still didn't know how to tell time. She realized that I couldn't see the clock or the letters and signs on the classroom.

The funny thing is, there was nothing wrong with my hearing. I heard everything they were saying. That's why Shirley called me "Rabbit." One day the grownups were all having afternoon coffee in grandmother's dining room while we were playing under the buffet. Mom was really upset that the doctor had announced that I needed glasses. She didn't want her second grader to wear them. "Men seldom make passes at girls who wear glasses." How this could possibly matter? "Oh no, she has those gorgeous turquoise eyes; we can't put glasses over her face. Aunt Monika contributed, "She is already a little withdrawn. All she does is read. She doesn't even like to play outdoors or watch TV. Girls in glasses are social misfits." I wondered about their concerns. I hated sports. People just threw balls around that you couldn't see until you were hit with one. Uncle John suddenly raised his voice. "Withdrawn? A social misfit? Do you realize that she has probably never even seen your face clearly? You try having conversations when you can't really tell what someone thinks or feels." Mom continued, "I just don't have $40 for a pair of glasses for a kid who will just break them." So, after the glasses were fitted, they were for school only. Young ladies do not wear glasses to socialize.

School was a bore. All our friends were across town at the schools near Grandmother Osborne's house. Now, each morning, a taxi came to drive over the bridges and across the railroad tracks. Mom couldn't drive, so she had no time to take us to the nice school in our neighborhood. We did not know anyone in her school but since mother taught there, we needed to be extra good, all the time. Mrs. Holloway, the sixth grade teacher, was a sad little woman who complained about her teenage daughter to the whole class. Luckily, she would often step out into the hall, where she could then complain about her students to any adult who walked by. Did all adults hate their kids? Mrs. Holloway drilled long division, with the same problem demonstration, each day for the entire year. Then she would hand out the mimeographed sheet to the students and the tedium would continue. If you worked too fast, Mrs. Holloway would give you more sheets from her towers of filing cabinets.

Mom's art room was the most exciting place in the new school. It was often filled with teenagers from early morning until the afternoon shadows fell. Mud was flying around on wheels, being grasped and pulled into pots. In the storage room, a group of students was building huge dinosaurs out of paper maché to decorate the gym for a Flintstones themed "Caveman Dance." She bounced from student to student, blonde ponytail swinging down her back, her leather skirt and apron covered with tempera paint and glue. Some days the local florist sent over flowers, older ones not quite good enough for sale. The flowers could be used for drawing and painting. In March as the kids studied about Japan a real Japanese lady came and taught us Ikebana – the Japanese principles of floral arrangement.

It turned out that Mrs. Holloway really did understand a few things about kids. One day she was having a conversation in the hall, with some other adult. "We have been trying to move her into seventh grade since October . . . . reading level . . . . so tall. But they won't allow her in with the older kids." Mr. Diven, the guidance counselor eventually invited Mom to the principal's office for a talk, while I waited in a big wooden chair outside of his door. Was she in trouble? This is where kids went if they were in trouble, and sometimes they might get paddled.

"Ellie, we have known each other a long time – how is your brother? He was such a brilliant student at Southside High."

"Gus, Richard is inventing things for Westinghouse. You know that. My cab comes in 20 minutes – and I have paint and clay to the ceiling of my classroom. Did you want to talk to me about something?"

"We need to talk about Katrine. She has special needs. We have the results of the school wide IQ testing."

"Oh my god – I knew Kate was difficult, but I didn't think she was retarded."

"Calm down Ellie, it's not quite like that. She is further off the standard scale than the most retarded child in this school."

"She can't be — some of those kids can't do anything. My god, we have four classes of them."

"No Ellie, It's the other way around. She has special academic needs. And, you will have to figure out how to finance college for her. It's going to be a real challenge.

"Tell me about it. She challenges everything I say. She questions everything I do, and then she criticizes the way it is done. That's only me. She is even harder on herself."

"Ellie, we have to get something going for her. How about if I work with her? I can drive Kate to the downtown library for books every two weeks.

Mom had the cab driver take us to grandma Estelle's house. Over Grandma's meatloaf, she bragged about the conversation with Mr. Diven. Uncle Bill had his masters degree from Cornell, and was working on a second one. He looked at her – "How high is it? . . . Good god, she's just a girl. Why, that's like putting teats on a bull." Grandmother glared at him, then cleared her throat. I looked at my lap.

Mr. Diven, the counselor, came to Mrs. Holloway's class the next morning, and took me out to the soda shop. Lovell's had a special called a Lucky Mondae – a soda with an ice cream sundae on top. It was my lucky Wednesday. If I could study anything at all, for any amount of time, what would it be? It happened that the diaries found in our "new" old home revealed unpublished details about successful Peary expedition to the North Pole. Ross Marvin, chief engineer of the expedition, had lived in our house. In the diaries he was worried about failure, and about the intent of expedition members to "get him." His writing got really scribbly. Either the harsh conditions of the far north were becoming too much, or there was dissent on the expedition that had never been revealed. Gosh, the unanswered questions – How did the men get along when they knew they could die? Were they crabby or calm? Did they collaborate or compete? Were they heroes? The diaries chronicling of Ross Marvin's breakdown had not been donated to the Historical Society. Notes about his mysterious end were not in the display cases with Marvin's furry Eskimo suit. They never would be, because a neighborhood boy, one that I had a crush on, had stolen the diaries after we showed them off one afternoon. But I remembered what was in them.

Mr. Diven asked really hard questions that usually meant trips to the downtown library or the historical society. There was an international competition for finding the true North. The British and the Norwegians had also been struggling through the ice, looking to place their flags at 90 degrees of latitude. The magnetic north pole keeps shifting, so they were racing toward moving targets. The idea that planet earth had not yet been fully explored was marvelous. No one had learned everything about it. In fact, discoveries about the poles were continuing. Suddenly it made sense when Mr. Diven talked about how clever Uncle Richard was. It turned out that Uncle Richard had been an inventor on the 1958 Polaris expedition, when a submarine was sent deep into the Arctic Ocean. They did not know if the North Pole was land or ocean, and suddenly it mattered. The Polaris crew found out that an ocean ran underneath the pole, bringing Russia and Canada very close together. Uncle Richard had designed a system to insulate electronic wiring for the extreme temperatures so that we could find out. He could tell us all sorts of things about different chemical compounds and their reactions to unknown variables of cold or heat.

Then, Mr. Diven moved on to Thor Hyerdahl and his unique theories of global migration. Hyerdahl believed that very early peoples may have traveled across oceans in handmade craft, and brought their customs from place to place. Since Mom had a minor in art history, she helped me find archaeological evidence and photographs of unexplained mysteries from long ago. So, each day as the classes drilled in their exercises, I sat in the back of the room, occupying two desks with a pile of heavy books. I didn't have to do long division any more, not ever again.

Little brother Jack's ability to annoy and irritate grew exponentially. He was everyone's little darling, talkative and friendly. Couldn't we just sell him, or at least put him in a zoo? Shirley told Jack that hamsters could make babies every four days if you let them play together. So, in the evenings he would start his two hamsters at the top of the third floor stairs, and watch them breed on each step, until the little animals were exhausted. Sure enough, in three weeks "Jimmy" had dropped 15 hamsters into his nest. "Mommy, Mommy, Jimmy is having babies!" Mom looked at the bloody little clumps coming out Jimmy's butt, and suggested we leave him alone for a few days.

Because of Jack's curiosity, nothing in the house worked. Grandfather had given Jack his own set of tools, but he didn't know how to make anything. He needed adult supervision to use a saw or hammer. So, he used his screwdrivers to take everything in the house apart. When he put things back together, there were usually a few pieces left over. We couldn't make waffles or toast, the record player had just one speed now, and the TV snowstorms were worse than the blizzards outside.

After his experiments in biology and physics, Jack directed his attentions to psychology. The hamsters had been a fine introduction into reproduction. One day he placed a squid in the toilet with a little ketchup. I really needed to use the bathroom, but instead, "Mommy! Mommy come here!" I forget who was screaming.

Jack peeked around the corner of the bathroom door.

"Hey Latrine! What's wrong?"

"Something awful has come up through the sewer."

"Can I see it?"

"No, maybe it's a dead baby or something. It's horrible." Jack began to giggle in the hallway. I threw open the door, took two giant steps, and punched him out.

# CHAPTER THREE

## Lemon Trees

*Lemon Tree, very pretty, and the lemon flower is sweet,*
*But the fruit of the poor lemon is impossible to eat.*
*Don't put your faith in love my boy, my father said to me,*
*"I fear you'll find that love is like the lovely lemon tree."*
*Kingston Trio*

When Mom's love life was going well, she was nicer to me. Maybe she was showing her new man what a wonderful mother she was, or maybe she was nicer just because she was happy. Apparently life was sweet and rich if there was a significant man around, and it was foul and bitter when all you have is your kids. Now mother had a nice boyfriend who was interested in everything the family did. He seemed to like us the way we were, and he also liked my silly uncles.

On a Wednesday evening, the kitchen phone rang – a long distance call from New York City. "Mom, Louis is calling!" Shirley and I were washing the pile of dishes from dinner. Mom wiped her hands on the slightly grubby dishtowel, and took the receiver from Jack.

"It's wonderful to hear your voice too. I didn't know how you felt about that crazy group at Sunday dinner. My brothers can really be hard on guys I bring home."

"Um hmm . . . glad you got back to the city safely."

"Oh god, this is so funny. After the other night at dinner, mother thought you were quite the choirboy. You really fooled her. It's a wonder she didn't have a heart spell over you with that story. I have never had a religious boyfriend – even when I met guys in church youth groups. You sounded so different from anyone I've brought to dinner. My brother Bill was choking on his meat loaf."

Suddenly her face was quiet and serious as she listened to him talk. She shooed us kids out of the kitchen, so we went to the dining room and got out the Parcheesi set. We also did not make a sound. I wanted to listen. I gave Jack my special glare, but he was being good. He wanted to listen too.

"So you actually joined a monastery? Why didn't you go back home to your family in San Francisco?"

Mom paused and fiddled with her ponytail, took a deep breath, and began talking again. Jack and I were supposed to leave her alone for adult conversations on the kitchen wall phone. The Parcheesi on the dining room table was evidence of a game in progress, while we listened in on her conversation with Louis. We quit glaring at each other and bickering over the dice as we realized that this was by far the most serious talk we had ever overheard. I didn't even look at the game board, and I was avoiding a glance toward the wall phone in the kitchen. Jack fumbled with the board markers. We settled in for a long conversation. Flies on the wall had nothing on the two of us.

Shirley joined us in the dining room, whispering. "You two! Let your mother have a private conversation. Would you like to come upstairs?"

"No." So she pulled out a game piece and joined us in silent Parcheesi.

". . . umm, what do they do all day in a monastery? Monks don't have jobs, do they? They sure don't have families. What responsibilities do they have? God, today I spent 6 hours with 30 students an hour, located groceries, fed the kids, and checked homework and now I'm picking up a little. Don't tell me you prayed all day long. And, you are way too friendly to have spent years not talking to anyone."

The whole house was silent. Jack and I didn't even fight.

"What do you mean, the whole point is to "not have? Louis, there are some things we must have to . . . to . . . keep comfortable. What about work? Is that why you don't have a job?"

This did not sound good. If he didn't have a job, then? Then what? Would he get a job?

"Somebody supports the monasteries too. I even know that. Good grief, I have just been doing some calligraphy lessons in my sixth grade classes because they are studying the middle ages. Don't even give me some nonsense about how monks live simply – and don't need handouts. They are not self-sufficient."

Mom was exasperated. She was using her quiet "let's be reasonable" voice that we had heard more than once when she and grandmother disagreed. She took a deep breath.

"Louis, the church asks every single member to give 10% of what they have to support its institutions. How is that not a handout? Are you telling me that monasteries don't accept money from the collections?"

"Up Route 14? Of course, I would love to go. And yes, I think Kate would be delighted."

Finally the conversation was back on a familiar track. Usually Ellie talked to men about the time and place of their next date, and shared a joke. She had never, ever discussed the kids with her boyfriends. Sometimes a man would show up to the door, bring a new toy or puzzle, and then she would sweetly ask us in some kindergarten teacher voice to take the puzzle and go upstairs. I hated the dating games, especially my mother's exhaustion and anger when things didn't turn out right. This guy was tricky. Apparently I was going to be delighted by something.

*   *   *

"And, our brothers are our family . . ."

The surprise was that Louis had driven upstate and was taking Mom and me to the monastery where he used to live. It was a quiet place in the hills just up the river from our town. Mom was excited to be with him. I was curious.

The immaculate white walls and dark beams of the monastery were beautiful. It didn't have a lot of pictures to confuse us. When the bell began to ring, it became magical. Mom was not hearing it, she was looking at Louis. Louis really talked to me that day, the way Mr. Diven talked about history, other times, and other places.

Mom wasn't really listening. "OK, I understand that part, but Louis, how did you handle living with all men, with no thoughts of ever meeting a woman again? That seems a little wild – I mean the idea. Of course that works for mother . . . she worries constantly about my chastity and my reputation."

Sometimes mother talked about the weirdest things. She didn't even like cats, but I had heard long lectures from grandmother Estelle about a woman's reputation. Enough of the cats. Louis liked to explain things and I had questions.

"Why do they live away from the city? Can they go to the store? Why do they wear those bathrobes? Is it nice to be able to read all day?"

Louis and I laughed as we went into heated buildings, trying to wipe the condensation from lenses in order to see. At the same time, he listened very carefully to mother.

"Ellie, I found the existence peaceful and freeing. Praying . . . well, it's more like thinking and talking inside yourself, reading what others have found, . . . seeking answers . . . maybe sometimes seeking questions?"

Mom stopped right in the middle of the hall.

"Jeez, talk about trying to find your . . . . just what did you find? How in heaven's name did you go from being a monk to being a beatnik, if that's what you are?"

"Oh, poverty and chastity were fine. I couldn't handle the obedience. Beatniks don't have to obey anyone."

"Do you think prayer works?" Mom had scored the point on this one. Even I knew that prayers were more like a habit, not like a real conversation. I had prayed for lots of things that I didn't get.

"I realized that I wasn't always praying to Jesus or even to God. I was asking for help from . . . understanding from sky, finding a direction in the wind, salvation in a thunderstorm. Once I caught myself praying while I was watching a free throw in a basketball game. I was afraid of the heights that I could never reach. Other times I wrote about the things I was praying for, even . . . Then I realized that all I was doing was escaping. I had somehow escaped my life, but I was still there."

"And being a beatnik is not escaping?"

There was a long pause. "Ellie, I have a surprise for you too. I have taken a job with Amacher Volkswagen in Horseheads, and will be moving upstate. We are going to have time to get to know each other much better."

Louis moved to Elmira and became a regular guest at the Grove Street house. He came in the evenings after work, usually with a festive bottle of wine to offset Ellie's efforts at cooking. He soon learned that Jack and I enjoyed science, and night after night he came through the door with the makings of a science experiment. "How do you get a boiled egg inside of a milk bottle?" The procedure is to carefully set up a kitchen table lab space with a clean glass milk bottle, several strips of paper, matches, and of course the hard-boiled egg. The idea is to light the strips on fire, drop them into the bottle, and then set the egg on top. As the paper burns, it uses up the oxygen and a vacuum forms. Jack was already excited about playing with matches, an interest that had not gone well in the past. "Oooh! Look at the egg wiggle. It's dancing. Wow, the fire is really going now. Why does it stink?" The egg burned up, the paper turned to a mess of ash, and the bottle shattered. So much for science time. We continued in our efforts to tune the piano with a skate key, but no one we knew had a tuning fork. Strings on the piano were adjusted over and over, perhaps for the first time in decades. The tunes sounded funnier from week to week. The piano repair project did not have a good end either, but everyone found out what was inside of one.

\*   \*   \*

Snow Days happen when it is impossible to get the streets cleaned up to let traffic through. The 1961 blizzards went on and on, and Elmira was snowbound for days at a time. The city was immobilized – no schools, no stores, no offices could open. People paid kids a small fortune, like 50 cents, to shovel narrow paths down driveways or across streets. Then, the snowplows came through, and the piles of snow grew to a colossal size, sometimes six to eight feet high. Because it had been plowed, this snow was very dense, and you could cut an igloo into it. Little girls took their dolls, books, and a thermos of hot chocolate to their ice castles. Boys became snow warriors, running over the banks and through the tunnels, playing with their army men. Neighborhood brats would tell us that the atomic bomb had struck New Mexico, and that our father was dead. Jack and I would run screaming into our bomb shelters in the snow.

Jack was a sissy, and terrified of the bullies. At home he had learned that "guns are not good toys for a boy, and football is a good way to get hurt." Uncle Bill was called in. "Kids, Donnie and Alan are not telling the truth. They say those things to upset you. They are mean because their parents talk about your mom being alone. Yes, Nazis were real, and they hurt a lot of people. No, the Nazis can't hurt you now."

Louis was our hero. He was warm and affectionate in a teddy bear way and he loved doing things with us. We no longer were unwanted accessories belonging to an attractive woman. First of all, he explained to Ellie that I could have a chance at a normal life, even if I wasn't like her. I had to laugh. Her life wasn't normal anyway. "This isn't about how pretty Kate may or may not be. You should know that. It's about her life. She deserves an opportunity to live in a world that is greater than 24 inches from her nose. Oh yeah, if she decides to spend a few days with her nose in a book, let her ask hard, disturbing questions, and don't cut her off with some smart answer. She needs to think things through." Louis must have been a wonderful teacher; he knew just how to make learning one of the thrills of life.

Louis' warmth was contagious and we began to thaw out. Jack loved the masculine influence; Louis understood Jack's curiosity. Jack had been surrounded by women – and loved learning how to be a guy. "Why is there light? What makes things fly?" Mom brought home sticks, tissue, glue and string. She was planning a unit on kite making in her art classes. "Let's build insects. Then when we fly them everyone will think the earth is being invaded by giant bugs." So, everyone studied all about the parts of an insect. I designed a butterfly and Jack designed a cockroach. The dining room floor was the only room left with a full sized floor space so it became an art studio. Once the tissue was cut and glued, the sticks and string had to be maneuvered so that the new kite didn't tear. After a week of working every day after school while mother napped, the kites were ready to fly. Snow was melting and the wind was blowing. The knoll in the park would give us a great head start, because the kites were heavy from all the glue and decorations. Nothing flew. We ran across the hill, dragging the big kites behind us. I took great care not to break the gold and purple butterfly. Jack's cockroach was already a damp wad of tissue and broken sticks. So, the kites were put aside, and we spent the afternoon somersaulting down the hill.

\* \* \*

Mom's best friend was Linda, a talented actress originally from New York City. Linda and Ellie had developed a traveling puppet theatre. Recent events in the South had brought the concept of integration to Elmira. Everyone knew the Jews lived west of Hoffman Street unless they were recent immigrants, and the Puerto Ricans and Blacks lived east of State Street. Factory workers lived on the Southside. Neighborhood schools were defined by their populations. Ellie had designed the puppets, "Spots and Stripes," and Linda wrote stories about getting along with people who were different. She and Ellie taught in schools with the Negro and Puerto Rican students, but they lived across the main road through town. My best friend Mel and I spent long hours carefully pasting tiny scraps of tissue into puppet heads.

As an English teacher and a wonderful storyteller, Linda was fascinated by the new poetry that was coming out of Greenwich Village. After all, this town has housed escaped slaves, welcomed Jewish immigrants, and helped all newcomers conform to its standards. "Everyone is entitled to the pursuit of happiness." Children inherited the civic pride of the town where Thomas K.

31

Beecher and Mark Twain had shaped their ideas. Elmira hadn't experienced a shift in consciousness in a hundred years. "We are not part of the prejudices that are tearing the South apart." At the same time community leaders were concerned: "Should we rent to Negroes? The Jewish deli is closed on Saturdays . . . Italians and Greeks smell like garlic . . . . , the Irish drink too much . . . . you know."

The Beatnik movement had captivated the local theatre crowd. After many weekend road trips to New York City, it was time to bring the scene upstate. An old one-room schoolhouse was converted to a coffee house. An abstract artist covered the walls in, umm, designs? Patterns? or was it just markings in paint? I wasn't sure. Mrs. Lofland's kindergarten could have done it. But sometimes everyone would rush to hear a cool jazz artist or some new poetry. Uncle John did some stand up comedy. The adults were acting like bad kids. Mom said that they were breaking all the rules of music, art and poetry. She made me take a look at the precision of calligraphy, and the markings on abstract paintings and compare artistic visions. OK. All the adults were delusional.

Louis had all sorts of ideas about how to break the rules of life. Like, why should bath nights be Wednesdays and Saturdays? Why does everyone find it necessary to own a house or hold down a job? In fact, those things were not hip. Now he had our attention. We loved our funny house. Mom even had plans to paint it purple on the outside. Louis didn't have a house, but Mom wouldn't let him stay with us.

Beatniks lived in an adult world. Men were cats and women were chicks. It was hep to be a cat. I'm not sure if it was good to be a chick or not, but I'm pretty sure that Beatniks didn't have children. Mom made a really good beatnik. Her black leather outfits were a great start and she stopped curling her hair. Lipstick was a non-negotiable. She was going to wear lipstick and earrings no matter what. Meanwhile, there were the details to attend to, like cigarette holders. Linda used colored filters on her cigarettes. Ellie preferred an elegant long holder. Louis smoked a pipe. Elmira's artistes had begun wearing berets, and reading word soup, or as they called it, abstract poetry. Because Mom was an artist, she started using really dark nail polish to accentuate her already long hands. Also, glue and paste did not show under the layers of nail lacquer. The black leather turned out to be a very practical uniform for an art teacher, because paint and clay could be wiped off the leather. Our old metal curlers became part of the findings that students used for building robot sculptures and Telstars.

Suddenly "Spots and Stripes" was no longer radical social commentary, and flowery pink kitchens were on the way out.

\*    \*    \*

*"The flower in the glass peanut bottle formerly in the kitchen crooked to take a place in the light,*
*The closet door opened, because I used it before,*
* it kindly stayed open waiting for me, its' owner.*
*I began to feel my misery in pallet on floor, listening to music, my misery, that's why I want to sing.*
*The room closed down on me, I expected the presence of the Creator,*
*I saw my gray painted walls and ceiling, they contained my room, they contained me.*

. . . .

*They kindly search for growth, the gracious desire to exist of the flowers, my near ecstasy at existing among them."*
*Alan Ginsberg*

\*    \*    \*

On a January afternoon, Mom and Linda were in the dining room, with the round purple table appropriately set with a lace doily and dainty china teacups. Harry Belafonte was on the record player as the teachers relaxed. The "tea" they drank in front of the children was a rum and coke. Mel and I had an emergency, so we had to bother them. We needed to look for Bozo in the dining room.

"Bozo ran off toward the park – why don't you take your sleds and go find him?" Linda suggested calmly.

"Mom! We were drawing him. We don't want to go to the park! He needs to sit still. Besides, our snow clothes are all drippy and cold."

"Well, he's little; he could get lost under all this snow and freeze to death. But, it's your choice I suppose." Mel started to cry and we fled out the front door, screaming for the puppy. Then we ran back inside to get our coats.

Mom was getting up. "This 'tea' needs a little kick." The antique phonograph cabinet in the living room had a secret push-through compartment, and she retrieved the bottle of rum. Bozo scampered out from behind the heavy drapes and jumped up into Linda's warm lap. The tea was just what they needed, a very satisfying drink, and the two ladies exhaled simultaneously – blowing smoke plumes into the air and slouching into their chairs.

Linda leaned forward, "I can't stop thinking about last weekend, the poetry, the stories, and the people we met. They were so unencumbered—free to explore the world. Didn't you love the feeling? Obviously we can't abandon our homes and children, but if we could only do that for a few hours sometimes." Mom started laughing. The idea that Linda was taken with the bare bricks and wads of cobwebs of the Beatnik cellars in New York City was just hilarious. Everything about Linda and her home was immaculate. She was the impeccable wife and mother. Mom tossed back her ponytail, and began to laugh.

"What?"

*I just figured something out!*

"What?"

*I know what to do with my basement.*

"Ellie, what does that have to do with Beatnik poetry?'

*Lets do it.*

"Do what?"

*Have a beatnik party in my basement.*

Linda stared at her. Her home on the hill had recently been done over in all white: furniture, upholstery, and a white carpet with simple modern glass tables and streamlined stainless steel appliances. She lifted her teacup full of rum and laughed.

*   *   *

Our cellar was a set from an Alfred Hitchcock horror movie. It was the one part of the house still untouched by the renovation process. A set of rickety plank steps led down from the kitchen above. Nearly a year after moving into the house, this cellar was still completely black with an impressive collection of cobwebs. Multiple sweepings had not really made it into the magical playhouses that the other kids had, with space to roller skate, a ping pong table or even a second refrigerator full of treats. My attempt to paint a side room pink left the wall looking like someone had thrown up all over it. Jack did not paint his playroom.

The old coal-burning furnace had been converted to gas, but the coal residue had never been cleaned out. The cellar was paved, and its floor sloped and rolled around the furnace to make it easier for shoveling coal. A snarl of massive asbestos pipes was aimed to the twelve rooms above. Colonies of mice and insects inhabited all the dark corners. The first attempt to clean out a couple side rooms to store canned foods and tools was a mess. Before stepping into the cellar, it was necessary to don protective clothing, which included wet bandannas over the faces of children and adults, long sleeves, and sturdy boots or shoes. The bandannas went black in minutes, making everyone look like robbers. We sneezed soot for days, which attracted unwanted attention from classmates at school.

The Beatnik parties didn't exactly begin. They developed kind of like the snowstorms, flurry after flurry. Shirley was supervising the cellar cleaning, and then the uncles plus a couple of their buddies dropped by to unload the food and liquor. Aunt Monika located the gallon bottles of burgundy, stored in the broom closet. A few stray oranges lay on the counter. A culinary genius, Monika stirred up some mulled Glühwein, and another party was under way. Shirley, Jack and I got into the Jolly Green Giant, a 1953 Chevy van, and collected stacks of old couch cushions from grandfather's upholstery shop, things that he hadn't gotten around to putting in the incinerator. We hauled the musty cushions down the rickety cellar stairs, and made groupings on the floor just like the descriptions of the Greenwich Village coffee houses. Then Shirley set up her long worktable with oilcloths on top. It was the same one she used for butchering rabbits and cleaning fish, activities that Ellie did not allow in the kitchen. We began hauling filthy old canning jars out of the fruit cellar and taking them upstairs to be washed. Gallo burgundy wine and martinis were to be served in canning jars. Mom was roasting a turkey, and the aroma filled the house. It was not on the menu for dinner. Bozo followed her around the kitchen, cleaned up the grease and scraps, then peed in the corner. This place was great!

On dark wintery afternoons, night falls early; on a party day, no one thought of supper. Instead, Mom got dressed. Nearly six feet tall, with a blonde ponytail to her waist, she didn't need to wear much, just tight black capris, her Capezios, and a low cut blouse with big earrings. Turtlenecks were not party clothes. Linda, the most wonderful mother in town, brought some party decorations – baby dolls painted blue with plastic bags over their heads.

Theatre people love to make a grand entrance. The front door was the place to see who was coming to the party, and what they were wearing to Ellie's events. Marsha was a pianist, and the piano in the entry foyer was clanging away. Jack and I were hiding quietly behind the spindles of the staircase, and we peered over the banister when Mom was out of the room. Somehow, Jack's hamster got loose, and it was very busy in a bowl of potato chips. Hamsters can sleep all day, and become very active in the evening. The hamster got frightened by the noise around the piano and ran through the creamy cheese dip, then across Marsha's ample belly, which was stuffed into a black velvet dress. Mom didn't want to yell at us in front of friends, so we were invited downstairs to say hello and retrieve the wild animal. Of course Jack's favorite song was selected next. His musical training was limited to Tom Lehrer songs and the *Bad Old King of England.*

*The minstrels sing of an English King of many long
years ago,
He ruled his land with an iron hand,
But his morals were weak and low.
His only undergarment was a dirty yellow shirt,
With which he tried to hide his hide,
But he couldn't hide the dirt.*

*He was dirty and lousy and full of fleas,
But he had his women in twos and threes
God Bless the bad old king of England!*

I slipped down the cellar stairs after his performance. It was very dark and there were lots of posts and small rooms to hide in, including my little playroom. People were drinking cheap red burgundy and martinis out of the canning jars. Inspired by the décor of cobwebs and raw bricks that they had all seen in Greenwich Village, nothing much had been cleaned up. Shirley and Ray sat on two of the old upholstery cushions, drinking. The young music teacher was snapping her fingers to the beat, and knew the words of many of the folk songs. She also had a genius for improvising lyrics on well known tunes.

*"Rapin' Hood, rapin' Hood, sneaking through the grass.
Rapin' Hood, rapin' Hood, looking for some ass.
With his shifty eyes, he takes one by surprise!
Oh Rapin' Hood . . .*

Uncle Bill came downstairs in his lederhosen and Alpine hat with the feather, carrying a platter of turkey parts. Ray grabbed a turkey leg. Shirley exclaimed, "what gorgeous legs," and pulled Bill close to her where she nuzzled his calf. Ray stood up. "We're leaving," pulled her up the cellar stairs and out the back door. He didn't leave. Instead, he was yelling. "You do not comment like that to a man, not ever. Why was that faggot wearing leather shorts anyway? What kind of outfit is that? Who are these people? They look and act like derelicts."

I ran up to mom's room, a little bit afraid of Ray. Maybe someone could get him to stop yelling at Shirley. But, then I heard the two of them in the hallway on the way up to her apartment. "Is this your idea of a career in the city? You need to come home to Pennsylvania." I decided to open the bathroom door. "If I ever, ever see you grab another man like that, we will be through."

Shirley stopped in the hall, then finally responded, "Maybe we already are."

"You're drunk. You need to get upstairs and sleep this off. This is worse than anything you ever did in college. You used to be really funny, but now you are out of control."

She stood in the hallway, with her hands clenched very tightly. Was this what they call "wringing your hands?" He reached for the light switch in the stairwell. She was rubbing her hands together. "Ray, get out!" and she pitched her diamond at him. He picked up the diamond from the corner where it had landed, and looked at her with a puzzled expression on his face. "We'll talk in a couple of days." Shirley then repaired her lipstick, and ran back down the stairs into the cellar. A sports car roared as he revved up the engine and sped out of the alley onto a slippery street.

By midnight the Beatnik Bash was in full swing, with more than 100 people in the house. The songs continued in the foyer, and dancing rocked the dining room. The little record player was appropriated for Cool Jazz, Harry Belafonte, and the Kingston Trio. Uncle John had brought in sound equipment from the radio station, bringing the decibel level up enough to shake paint chips off the dining room ceiling. His friend Doug began the Latin Dances with Mom, and a conga line writhed through the three stories of the main house, even into our bedrooms. In the cellar, another round of martinis were in the canning jars. No one knew where the olives were any more. Guitars and bongos appeared. The quieter "artists corner" was behind the furnace. John showed up in a clean beret with a pipe, and his newest poem. It was terrible but everybody clapped.

A strange buffet began to materialize on tables and counters as people brought their specialties – baked beans, onion dip, potato chips, pizzas and a lot of pickled things from the canning jars. Ellie's turkey came out of the oven, but she had made no plan as to how people might want to actually eat it. There were no utensils. She couldn't quite lift the bird out of the roaster and it broke into pieces. She set the pan down on the butcher's table down in the cellar. People began to tear at the extremities of the bird. Tonight Linda had a new specialty from the Bizarre Café in New York – chocolate covered ants. "Here, try one."

Upstairs in the foyer, Marcia didn't miss a beat. She played all night, even though she would be due at the Episcopal Church early the next morning to play the organ. God save us, every one.

# CHAPTER FOUR

## March Winds

Change came with the March winds.

> "*O Wandern, Wandern, meine Lust,*
> *O Wandern! Herr Meister und Frau Meisterin,*
> *Laßt mich in Frieden weiterziehn*
> *Und wandern.*"

> *Wandering, traveling is my desire*
> *Master and Mistress,*
> *Let me go abroad*
> *And wander.*

> *German Folk song*

Uncle Bill was banging on the piano again. We were singing
some folk tunes, anything to break the monotony of being trapped
under the wet snow. The restless promise of spring is part of the
upstate New York winter. Snowbound for weeks at a time, family
tensions build in the small bungalows with their sealed storm
windows and heavy front doors. By early March, snow and ice are no
longer beautiful, and the magic of winter is gone. Everyone wants

to get out into the light. Out of the house, out of classrooms where children's clothing has not been dry in weeks, out of town, out of the weather – it doesn't matter.

After work on Fridays, Louis would pick Mom up in his VW, and the two of them would take off downstate for Greenwich Village. They drove for hours through the muddy March slush, with promises of New York City lights beckoning them onward. Louis did not seem to have a home or apartment in New York; he "crashed" wherever and whenever he needed to. Mom said they mostly stayed up all night in the coffeehouses. So, apparently the idea was that Louis loved kids, but in his world, children were independent. They were free to do and learn what they wished. Babysitters were obsolete. Apparently after you are ten years old you shouldn't need one. I was in charge now. The first time that we were alone the smell of smoke came upstairs. Something was burning, and we couldn't find the fire so Ellie had to leave her party. A couple weeks later I was given another chance, but Jack fell down and got a really bloody nose and lip. Mom asked me to be more responsible. It wasn't enough to be in charge, I had to make sure we stayed safe.

I also found out that a Beatnik girl did not need dresses that matched the other girls' clothes. She just needed to be warm and dry. Little boys did not have to bathe or clean under their fingernails. Jack stank. I was frustrated. Bozo chewed up my glasses, and I had to wear them to school with teeth marks and scotch tape holding the bridge. The hamster chewed through the sleeve of my favorite yellow sweater. It was the only new thing in my closet and Mom could not know about the hole. She would throw it out, blaming me because the sweater somehow fell off the bed and onto the floor near Fuzzy's cage. Or was Fuzzy loose? Anyway, I had to clean the cage before anyone saw his bright yellow nest. Grandmother showed me how to darn the sweater on one of the endless laundry Sundays. Surprise! The five loads of weekly laundry had not magically disappeared.

On the weekends at Grandmother's I could have all the time I wanted to read. Grandmother's sofa was soft, and I stretched out with my box of tissues, sneezing, hacking and spitting while grandmother stalked around the house emptying ashtrays from six adult smokers. Children of Beatniks were not supposed to get snotty noses or cough up goo. This was not hip. Jack made a mural of boogers beside his bed. He didn't use tissues. Was that hip? But he didn't cough the way I did. My chest was always full of glop and grandmother put me under steamer tents. Then she would sit down to the piano to play American folk songs, Ragtime, and always Beethoven's "Moonlight Sonata."

Grandmother loved music and poetry, but she had spent her life raising the large family. Her favorites were something the grownups called "Romantic." I was not really sure what that was, because she was way to old to be in love. She knew lots of poems and could recite verses of Wordsworth, Shelley, or Milton from memory to illustrate her ideas, kind of like making word pictures. Sometimes she read from the newspaper. "President Eisenhower says that 'our nation is giddy with prosperity, infatuated with youth and glamour, and aiming increasingly for the easy life.' Luckily that doesn't fit our family." Her sons and daughter were too hard working to buy into Hollywood glamour, well, except maybe Ellie who had been in Vogue magazine, but they were romantic enough to seek their own destinies. When businesses and relationships failed, they could always come back home. Estelle's part of the bargain was to see that they had a pleasant house, meals on the table, and a forum for their discussions. It was to not see other things. Lovers invited to the table were called "friends." Alcohol was consumed on the porch or at other people's houses. In spite of the warm meals, minds and hearts began to wander far away from the comforts of her bungalow.

Grandma Estelle's wanderings took place in her armchair, where she read history and historical novels of the intrigues and peccadillos of the Plantagenets, a dynasty of French kings who ruled England for centuries. In her books were tales of conquest, corruption, and bastardy, contrasted with heroism of the crusades, as well as the development of the Magna Carta and representative government. Richard the Lionhearted's famed quote about his children "they come of the devil, and to the devil they will go" summed up some of the wild behaviors of her adult children. William, John,

Norman, Richard and Eleanor were all named after members of the Plantagenet dynasty, and somehow Estelle's tidy household was beginning to resemble the rowdy scenes in a twelfth century manor.

My favorite weekends were when Melanie invited me to stay over at her house. Linda would make a three-day chocolate cake and her dad played games with us.

I loved staying in Mel's cheery white room, with ruffled matching twin beds, and flowered quilts. Our friends Pam and Diane had just gotten new dolls for their birthdays, and all the girls were supposed to bring their best dolls and outfits for them to play fashion show. I had the best doll collection ever. I loved costumes and each year Uncle Bill brought me one or two dolls from his trips to Europe. When Mom went with him, they brought home eight dolls. My choice for the fashion weekend was La Poulet, a gorgeous French doll, all dressed in an orange satin ball gown and golden high heels. Her silk gauze face was brightly painted with red lips, shaded eyes, and eyelashes as long as whiskers. La Poulet stood nearly two feet tall. She had been a wedding gift to Bill and Monika, apparently because there is some German custom where they decorate the bed with a special kind of doll for a happy wedding night. Or did they give the special doll to make a baby? Maybe this didn't matter. La Poulet was the most beautiful doll I had ever seen. The doll always had a place of honor on a rocker in my bedroom, the one thing that was not covered with papers, books, or snacks. Even Bozo knew to not go near the chair.

Pam had received a new Ponytail Barbie. Diane had a Bubble Cut Barbie and a Ken doll. Mel had a Career Barbie with suits and briefcases, but no party dresses. Three Barbies, one Ken, and La Poulet. The girls began talking about all the outfits they could buy for their Barbies. They had ballgowns, swimsuits, Nighty Negligees, sheath dresses and little high heels with everything. Ken had shorts and a Hawaiian shirt. It was hard to make them kiss, even though Ken was Barbie's boyfriend. Her breasts were too big. The dolls had stiff arms and couldn't hug. As they undressed their dolls, Diane commented,

"Wow! Look how pretty she is. My mother has a big chest, but fat legs. I'm so fat. Should we put her in her ball gown next? Maybe they can go to a fancy party."

"My mom has long legs, but her chest is saggy. Dad says its like two eggs, fried. Barbie doesn't even need to wear a bra."

"Let's make her kiss Ken while she's naked!"

"Do you think they do it?"

"Do what?"

"Maybe she isn't really naked? How come she is all white everywhere? You know, like um, there . . ."

Mel got up and closed the doors to the den. "I saw my mom naked the other night." All the girls looked at her silently. "It was kind of odd. She had just had a bath because they were going out."

"Silly, everyone gets naked when they have a bath."

"But dad was getting dressed and she was just lying on the bed naked. Something was really weird. I don't know. I don't think there was anything wrong, it was just like I felt like I shouldn't have seen her there."

"Anyway, my mom isn't as pretty as Barbie either. But, let's get some chocolate cake!"

Instead, Diane began to undress Ken. He was not nearly as interesting as Barbie. Aren't guys supposed to have something in their pants? Nothing. I had a brother, and I was sure that something was very wrong with Ken. Pam volunteered,

"Maybe he's a homo!"

"What?"

"You know, a queer!"

"You're queer!"

"Am not."

"What's queer?"

"You know, like guys who are in love with other guys. There's something wrong with them, you know, down there."

"Your uncle is a queer."

"He is not. He works for the phone company."

"Why couldn't your mom get along with your dad? Is she queer?"

"Ladies can't be queer."

"Your mom's friends are queer."

"They are not. They're actors."

La Poulet sat in an armchair, watching the girls with her enormous blue eyes and her silken smile.

*   *   *

Grandmother said that nobody is queer. Some people just aren't married. Someday Uncle John would meet just the right lady. Maybe he would even get together with Shirley. Bill and Monika had been married for three years already, and everybody was waiting for them to have a baby. Maybe Louis would be right for Ellie. This was all very confusing. I didn't even have a picture of my father, but I had seen pictures of Mom in her wedding gown. She had gotten married because that's how you have kids. When Tommy Milnich and I had gotten married in first grade, we went under Tommy's forsythia bush to take off our clothes and kiss. But that was probably just some naughty mistake. People wouldn't be naked unless they were taking baths and someone came in to use the sink. Now Mom had changed the rules. Tommy could no longer play in in my room, even when we were working on projects. "Girls do not invite boys into their rooms." Where did she think we would play games without having Jack bother us? Also Mom said I couldn't get really married until I was 17, and that was a long way away. Anyway, marriage was a big "no" for me. Would that make me a queer? Is being queer catching?

So, what was wrong with men loving men? It's not like they were kissing or anything. How come Jack couldn't ever marry his best friend, when I could marry Tommy? Why was Ellie upset that Shirley had kissed me? Uncle John and Doug had been sharing John's boyhood room at Grandmother Estelle's for years, and she continued to call them "the boys" as if they were living some sort of extended pajama party. Doug was a permanent houseguest.

Mel's house was different. Unlike Grandmother Estelle, Linda not only was from New York City but she had been to coffeehouses. I liked to help her in the kitchen when she was making snacks for all of us. So, I asked Linda about New York City. What was it like? Could

45

I go sometime? She said that Mom and Louis were in Greenwich Village coffeehouses that stayed open all night, serving coffee with chocolate, candied pineapple and cherries, ginger, gooey caramel, whipped cream – or any combination that could be dreamed up. That part sounded good. They listened to folk singers at the Bitter End, and to poets everywhere. That might be a little boring, but you never know. After two nights in Greenwich Village, they would drive back to Elmira late Sunday night. Mom would arrive home in time to report to school on Monday, and then sleep afternoons for the rest of the week. Some days she even forgot her lipstick and earrings.

Louis did not have a home, but he liked ours fine. One of the ideals of the hepcats and kits on the beatnik scene was the ability to travel, to be free of a home. His plan was to keep rambling and roving. He liked selling cars because he could be outside a lot. We adored our three-story Victorian, and Mom was continuing to salvage its antique treasures. Secrets of the past appeared in every single room. There were brass gas jets long out of use, old wire rimmed eyeglasses, and tea sets with rust stained doilies. Ross Marvin's niece had sold it to us "as is," taken her personal effects, and left everything for us. But there were things we didn't have. Mom wouldn't have minded a washing machine of her very own. A dishwasher? Heaven. Flowers on a bare counter make a nice poem, but clean coffee cups would be even better.

Mom and Louis tried to explain to me that pursuit of possessions and pursuit of happiness are not the same thing. In other words, would I really be happier if I had a Barbie doll? Did I actually want one, or did I want one because the other girls had them? She said you have to understand what you really want. Being a Beatnik was a great lifestyle if you were paid $300 a month as a teacher. It meant that you didn't need to try and go shopping for new things, and you didn't need to buy stuff just because someone said so. Mom made fun of advertisements. Apparently most work for artists was "commercial art" and she had decided against it. She didn't like the messages.

Each week, my friends had more and more things including pretty dresses, music lessons, and the ever-growing collections of

Barbie dolls. I had an heirloom quilt that took grandmother Estelle 28 years to stitch by hand and an enviable collection of borrowed school art supplies. When I was invited to birthday parties, I took a box of art supplies wrapped up in newsprint that I drew designs on. Then, someone else would present the birthday girl with a Brownie camera in a brilliant black and gold box, or maybe some new Barbie outfits in a flowered package with a big bow. Everybody's mother drove a shiny station wagon, and my mom didn't even have a driver's license. Linda's cupboards were full of store bought cookies in bright packages filling the cupboards. Grandma Estelle and I baked 3 dozen cookies each weekend, to last one week for everyone.

All the girls talked about their "stuff."

"Let's go to Diana's house and play HORSE. She has a new basketball set up."

"Abe has new skis! Lois is going to get a pink Princess phone. Grant's dad bought a new boat, and it does, like 60 on the lake!"

"My mom may need to get a job." The girls looked at Pam.

"You mean like downtown? What can she do?"

"She might work in a store."

"Did you hear that the Andersons are building a bomb shelter?" The group went silent.

"Why?"

"For when the Commies come. Mr. Anderson was in the war, and he doesn't want the family to get bombed. They want to kill us all and take away our things."

Apparently adult life was about owning things like their own houses, their own cars, their own dishwashers. Louis said that if you didn't need things, you didn't need to work so hard to get them. He said we were afraid of communism because the communist threat was all about the right to own things. Mr. Diven had me start to read about communism. In communism, everyone shared, just like Grandma had said we should. Jesus even said we should share, and he shared wine and bread and fishes, unless of course the disciples and their wives made dinner for everyone. But our Jewish friends shared things. They shared a lot and they didn't even believe in Jesus. Sharing isn't a miracle, it's just common sense. But, communists did not believe that individuals had the right to own a lot of "stuff." It seemed that sharing was not our American way. We work hard for our things, and we have a right to them. Wasn't that in the Declaration of Independence?

"What about the poor people, someone like Mr. Holcomb who is sick?"

"He had a good job at the factory. He just had to retire early."

"How do they pay the doctor now?"

"I'm not too sure. But Mrs. H. always looks nice at church."

"Bonnie Griggs has five brothers. Lots of days she doesn't have a sandwich. I gave her my orange today."

"She can get school lunches for a quarter."

Mr. Diven said that in communism, everyone works and then the government gives out food and work uniforms, and assigns the places to live. Everyone shares the basic necessities. He wasn't a communist though. His family owned the candy store on Main Street, with dark Italian chocolates and the thickest milkshakes in town. But, we all heard that there were secret Nazis and Commies all over town; they would come one night when you were asleep and steal you for brainwashing, which apparently did not involve soap and water. Others said that Beatniks were Commies. Mom was not a Commie because no one would tell her where she should live or what she would wear. Then Mr. Diven started explaining about big businesses.

I didn't know what a big business was. The typewriter factory was big. It stretched for two blocks, but apparently it wasn't a big business. According to Time Magazine, "big businesses" in the US and government controls in the communist east were leading both societies to the brink of yet another war, with the nuclear weapons powerful enough to blow up all the "stuff" and the people who accompanied it. The Beatniks did not think that war was a good idea. Louis brought home copies of The Village Voice, a cool newspaper with Beatnik poetry and commentary. He and Uncle Bill talked about something called a Military Industrial Complex. Was that like a war factory? Or some sort of war amusement park, like the Fairplex? The Village Voice said that major corporations could have as much power and money as an entire country. A corporation was a group of people who didn't have to take any personal responsibility for their losses. If they gained a lot of money, they could use the money and power to sell more and more stuff to everyone. It was kind of like when you play Monopoly and even if you lose the game you don't really lose anything. Man, reading the Village Voice was hard work, even with adults to explain it. Anyway, the Beatniks said that big businesses were trying to own people, because they owned everything that people desired. Even I knew it was illegal to own people. We learned that in the fifth grade.

Mom explained that the Beatniks made it a point to be without possessions at a time when everyone needed a new house, a new car, and rooms full of powerful appliances that replaced long hours of housework. She wasn't sure that was true, but we were happy with an old house and no car. Louis didn't think we needed a washer and dryer and dishwasher. I wonder what he would have had for dinner if Mom didn't invite him to supper. But he was a person who shared. He often brought groceries or flowers or wine. The Beatnik writers might have traveled with what they could carry on their backs, but the questions they asked brought up some interesting dinner table topics. Mom and the uncles were talking a lot about the way things were in their ratrace and the way things should be if they were hep cats. The irony was not lost as Louis put on his beret and leather jacket on Friday nights, and then returned in tweed suits as a car salesman on Monday mornings. I knew better than to ask questions about that.

There was no question that the Wanderlust was biting hard. The details were not sorted out yet. Aunt Monika missed her mother and sisters in Germany. For three years she had been living with Uncle Bill in a tiny cellar apartment that he had converted from the old playrooms in grandmother's house. There was no natural sunlight, but he said the new fluorescent lamps were the same. A funny glare vibrated against the dark green concrete floor. Each evening, Monika sat upstairs on the wooly pink ottoman in Estelle's living room, while Estelle rocked in her matching pink chair, and they practiced English conversations about home life, friends, and cooking. There was exciting news. Uncle Bill had been awarded a Fulbright, and they would be moving to Europe for a year. He would teach English in an Austrian school, and the Austrian teacher would take his position in Elmira. My brother Jack was excited that they would see kangaroos, but I explained that Austria and Australia are not near each other.

Peter and Irene Moritz, the German/French uncle and aunt would be moving too. Peter had reenlisted in the US Army as a reserve, hoping to go to Japan. He was not concerned about the power of the immense military industrial complex. In his view, men with military experience had a shot at a job in big business, and big business was one way to attain the American Dream. There was opportunity and possibility in the U.S. He had left his home in Germany for that. Peter's military interests were a contrast at this dinner table. While the Osbornes were pacifists, mainly because three of the uncles were 4F, Peter believed that military preparedness was one way to keep peace. He came from a military tradition dating to when only landowners were allowed to ride horses and bear arms, and he lived his life by the chivalric code. Whether it was a pointed helmet of the Kaiser, or the modern helmet of an American lieutenant, the military was Peter's preferred career. He didn't get sent to Japan. As a bilingual soldier, he was assigned to Germany, the first line of defense against the looming Russian threats. Or at least it was the first line of defense until Russian missiles were spotted 90 miles away from Florida, in Cuba. Peter was being sent back to Germany, only this time in a US Army uniform.

Louis enjoyed his work at the Volkswagen dealership and wanted to make his way into the executive ranks, maybe even owning a dealership one day. Successful small town families were buying larger and larger station wagons, decorated with elaborate fins, cat-eye tail lights, and chrome trimmings that made them look something like rockets. The VW Beetle was the anti-car, but the funny little Beetle cars were beginning to appear on rural roads. One step of moving into VW management ranks, or before opening your own dealership, was to complete an internship at the factory in Wolfsburg, Germany. It was expected that a good salesman understood his product. Apparently this wasn't as difficult as it sounded. The back end of a Volkswagen looks pretty much like the inside of a sewing machine, only bigger. There is no radiator, very few hoses, and almost no electrical. Even I could understand how it worked.

Mom and Louis talked about his opportunity to move ahead in the Volkswagen company. She had a solid job and a nice house, so it would make no sense for her to pull up roots. He did mention that the US Department of Defense hired teachers to work on the military bases, and provide a US education to the dependent children of soldiers. Perhaps that would be an option if she did come to Germany with him.

Each of these grownups had a reason to move to Europe and had figured out a way to manage. They all spoke at least three languages. All the men had solid job offers. But somehow, it was obvious that the decisions to leave were not about careers. It was about wandering, traveling free and unencumbered of everything including family squabbles and Grandmother Estelle's rules of order.

Moving was not the plan for us. We were thriving at 112 Grove Street. The old rose bramble began to climb and cover the front porch, with heavy wood and thorns that were now part of the posts and beams, roots that were part of the foundation of the house. Like the rosebush, we were putting down roots. As the weather warmed, the Grove Street porch would fill up with people. Peter and Irene now had a little coach house on the river, right around the corner. They had named it Villa Virtue. The new American craze for folk music was under way. Peter strummed his guitar, and began playing folk songs from Germany, France and the US. Shirley's girlfriends came by on their shiny new Honda motorcycles. Shirley was now a biker. Honda was sponsoring a group of seven schoolteachers to travel across the US in the upcoming summer as an all female biker team. The official advertising motto was, "You meet the nicest people on a Honda." Their unofficial name was, "The Maidenhoods." Bill and Monika would come by with beer, and when the Italian restaurant finished its deliveries for the night, someone delivered pizzas to the front porch.

Each morning, two pieces of cold pizza were left in the box. Jack and I retrieved them for our breakfast and got ready for school. Life was good.

# CHAPTER FIVE

## Airlift

On the morning of Friday, May 5, 1961 all school classes stopped at 10:00 a.m. Mrs. Holloway had us put our pencils down while she began turning dials through the static of a portable radio. The radio broadcast of America's first manned ride into space began. Every kid knew about rockets, and we all wanted to go up in one some day. We even practiced countdowns when we jumped off walls on a dare. Now we listened to Mission Control as the radio broadcast the countdown and a description of the launch. Apparently you can't even see a launch. It goes so fast that first the rocket is there, and then it's not there. We heard the voices of astronaut Alan Shepard and President Kennedy. The United States was in outer space. The entire country was exploring.

In three weeks, Monika would be leaving to spend some time with her family in Berlin. Bill's Fulbright fellowship would make it possible for her to be nearer to her mother and sisters. She and Ellie were sharing a cup of coffee in the kitchen, while Jack was digging up worms and bugs outside and I was playing the piano. Suddenly, Mom asked me come into the kitchen. "How would you like to go to Berlin with Monika on May 24?" I stared at her, then at Monika. The women nodded, and I started to scream. Leaving coffee cups on the table, we piled into Bill and Moni's VW bug. Racing to the post office,

Mom completed my passport application and had instant pictures taken.

Then, Monika announced that my wardrobe would need to be replaced. At first I was unclear as to why this had to happen. Mom's new favorite color was royal purple, and she had just sewn my spring wardrobe of a purple skirt, lavender gingham dresses, and a favorite grown up girl dress with enormous cerise and purple roses. Ellie's wardrobe, besides her black leather art teacher outfit, held thrift store cocktail dresses: red satin, purple chiffon, embroidered cabbage roses, white Grecian with gold braid, and a collection of floral and lace shawls that Bill had brought back from his European trips. While other little girls wore tiny flowery prints, and pink dresses with white ruffles for parties, Mom and I had fiesta dresses, made with full skirts in turquoise fabric falling in tiers, and trimmed with more than 100 yards of rick-rack and ribbons.

Monika was in charge of the shopping. My brightly colored clothes would be unacceptable in a German school. Not one of the purple dresses was selected for the year in Germany. "We don't wear such things in Berlin. Mutti will just throw them out." I slowly nodded my head in agreement. I remembered Monika's sister who came from Berlin to attend our schools for a year. She wore sober blue and grey clothes. All of a sudden, the shopping became a very serious business. We drove to *Diskay*, the local discount house, because Ellie couldn't afford to fill a suitcase from the department stores downtown. But, some merchandise at the discount house was stylish and colorful. I began to look through cheery red plaid and blue gingham dresses. Monika took charge of the situation. "Here is a nice grey sweater." Bad idea. "Try on the beige skirt." Maybe. "The brown tweed jacket is good with your hair. You are so pale." I am? And brown tweed makes me look better? I have never in my life chosen anything brown, not even brown shoes. I wore red shoes with my brownie uniform. OK, that was brown, but it was a uniform. Monika also selected an olive green, tan, and mustard gold print blouse for a color accent. No turquoise; no purple; no fuchsia.

The bags were full, and we went to Grandmother's to announce the good news. Everyone looked forward to Grandmother's

53

Saturday night dinners of Boston baked beans and brown bread. Uncle Bill had been working on his apartment houses all day. Bill was stunned to see the living room full of shopping bags.

"Monika! Monika! My god, you must already have 20 dresses. You have more shoes than the rest of this family put together! I am wearing leather patches on my jacket sleeves! Now what have you done?"

"These are all Ellie's bags. The dresses are for Kate. I am going to take Kate with me to Berlin." Moni looked across at my mother for some sign of affirmation, or maybe an attempt to rescue her from a misunderstanding with her husband.

"Herzchen, I am going to Europe to work for the year. We want to start our own family. I don't even know where we will live." He sat down in a side chair, completely perplexed. Ellie could be impulsive, but Monika had never stepped out of bounds.

"Oh, she will stay with Mutti and Annike, it's all worked out."

His eyes widened. "And how does your mother know this?"

"We will give her a call tomorrow. Don't worry. She is lonely."

So over dinner, Bill began my instruction in German. "Bitte" means please, "Danke" means thank you. We would be using my real name, Katrine instead of Kate. Kate isn't a German name. Table manners were to be enforced at all times. As of that night, I was asked to move my fork to the left hand and place both wrists on the table. That was pretty funny. If Jack ate with his left hand or put his elbow on the table, he got smacked. Now, I had to eat that way, only not leaning on my elbows. The left hand fork business was awkward, but the dog enjoyed all the beans that fell in the efforts.

Each night, I updated my diary. Uncle Bill said that the diary was a great habit, and that I should make it a point to write every day now.

May 8, 1961

*"I told the kids that I was moving to Berlin for a year. Nearly everyone we know at school is from Europe. Tommy's parents are from Germany, and Danny's are from Poland. What kind of name is Szabotynskj? I guess I kind of fit in, because my father is from*

*Amsterdam. But I'm actually going there! Why don't the other families want to go there?"*

Tragedies and losses of the war were still too fresh for so many families. Children knew a few songs from their parents' countries. Mothers remembered some old recipes, and made them if they could find the ingredients. Caroljean Lugovskaya had a beautiful pair of red leather boots and an embroidered black dress. Nobody else had anything from Europe. The next two weeks were a constant run of family visits, surprise parties, and gifts from friends: a tiny stuffed skunk to snuggle at night, a mustard seed pendant, and a charm bracelet for luck. I even got attention from an eighth grade boy, a really handsome one. My suitcase continued to fill. Mom had an old canvas overseas bag with a big zipper. She said it was lightweight and that the airplane people weigh everything. I only hoped they wouldn't weigh me.

One evening a white haired lady walked down the street toward our house. It was Mrs. Doughton, my favorite teacher ever, who had come by to pay us a visit. Had I remembered my Spanish lessons from her fifth grade class? "Si, si!" You never know when you might need another language. She then pulled out a wrapped gift from her bag. It was the prettiest set of pink nylon pajamas ever, with white lace and blue embroidered flowers. They were as pretty as Barbie's Nighty Negligee! All I could think of was that so many, many kids loved Mrs. Doughton. I couldn't believe that she had done this for me. She was even better than the best teacher ever. She told me that what I was about to do was very important.

\*   \*   \*

Mr. Diven decided to change my lessons immediately. We had studies all around the world, but Europe and Germany in particular had not been part of those lessons. It was too close, and since I had an aunt from Berlin, why would we bother with lessons about Germany? As of this Monday, things were changed. The counselor opened the lesson with:

"So Kate, what happens after a war?"

55

"Ummm, someone wins and someone loses, and then they have peace?" I looked at him hopefully.

"Kate, have we ever had a war here, in New York State?"

"The American Revolution! It was over by Sullivan's monument."

"That is correct, but it is also a long time ago. We have school picnics on old battlefields, including the Newton Battlefield by the monument. But the world wars in Europe are recent. Everything changes after a war, and everything in Berlin changed more because it was such a big war. You need to know what happened to Berlin because you will meet people who had terrible things happen to them. You can't ask about the terrible things, but you need to know about them."

He took me to the library to read old newspapers and magazines about Berlin and how it had been the capital of Nazi Germany. It was still a big city but now it wasn't the capital of anything. World War II had been won by four Allies. The United States, Britain, France, and Russia were trying to come up with a plan to divide Germany and prevent it from ever being a national force again. They also divided Berlin into four pieces. But, for three years the four countries argued while the people of Germany were starving. The ones who suffered the most were little children who had never been Nazis. There was no money of any kind. There was no food, and there was no fuel. I read an interview:

>I remember the day when they told us our Reichmarks were no good. Every head of household was to be issued forty Deutschmarks, a small fortune, to begin again. West Germans, including West Berliners, were on their way to a new life. Meanwhile, the Russians decided to not give any of the new money to Germans who were living in their territory. Instead, they were trying to gather all German assets and send them to Russia. They collected farm equipment to melt down in Russian steel mills, and they even kidnapped German scientists to have them design nuclear weapons for Russia. Some of the scientists even committed suicide.

Meanwhile, the Russians put a blockade around Berlin, because the city lay in the Russian zone. The countryside around the city was rich, but the farmers were not allowed to sell food to Berliners. They could get shot if they tried to sell their food. Other supplies were stopped as well. Germany is very cold in the winter, and the Russians did not let any trains come through with coal or oil to heat homes and buildings. So, the American, English and French Allies had to figure out how to cross the blockades. There were no train tracks and no roads that they could use. Armed Russian soldiers threatened people who tried to pass through the countryside. They had to present identification that proved they belonged in East Germany. So much for peace.

The only remaining pathways were the three air corridors across Germany that had been left open for western planes on missions. American goodwill organizations and others decided to try to feed Berlin through the Berlin Airlift. An air cargo plane, a DC 47, could hold 3.5 tons of cargo. Hmmm, math time! What would it take to keep a city with two million people alive? And, how could you possibly get it there?

### AIRLIFT GROCERY LIST – DAILY SUPPLIES

| | |
|---:|---|
| 646 | tons of flour and wheat |
| 125 | tons of cereal |
| 64 | tons of fat |
| 109 | tons of meat and fish |
| 3 | tons of yeast to make bread |
| 144 | tons of dehydrated vegetables |
| 180 | tons of sugar |
| 11 | tons of coffee |
| 19 | tons of powdered milk |
| 5 | tons of whole milk for babies |
| 38 | tons of salt |
| 10 | tons of cheese |

The city would need 1534 tons of food to keep people alive, plus 1500 tons of coal and heating oil to run a power plant that still needed to be constructed in West Berlin.

I worked on the math. A hungry city would need 3475 tons of supplies each day, and each plane could only hold 3.5 tons. This meant that the Allies would need to send in 1,000 flights a day, and find trucks and workers to get the supplies to people. How did they solve that problem? Our local airport in Elmira ran about 6 flights a day for small planes. Apparently every US pilot who had returned from the war was drafted again to help out. Aircraft designers had a bigger plane built and in the air in weeks. So, for 24 hours a day, planes flew a continuous loop into Tempelhof Airport, where Berliners unloaded the supplies and got them moved into the city. Each plane needed to be unloaded and back in the air in 25 minutes so that the goal of 1,000 trips daily could be met. I understood what they did but not how they did it. Did they ever have traffic jams in the air?

\* \* \*

Saturday
May 27, 1961

Idyllwild Airport was the size of an entire city. Uncle Bill had driven all day to get us there. Half of the trip was just crossing New York City to the airport. Roads and streets wrapped around in all kinds of circles and tangles, with hundreds of signs. That was just for the cars, buses and trucks that were coming in and out. There were just as many roads on the airfields, runways for the planes to take off and land. We got there in time for our evening flight. Mom kissed me and hugged me really tight. I even hugged Jack. They were going to watch our plane take off. But when Monika and I showed the airline our tickets and passports, we learned that the airplane was not ready. Our flight was to be delayed overnight. Icelandic Air would let us stay in a hotel overnight, but there was no place for our family to stay. Uncle Bill decided to drive back to Elmira.

I had never stayed in a real hotel before. Elmira's Mark Twain hotel was too fancy for children even to go to a wedding or a special party. The Tom Sawyer motel outside of town had a swimming pool with a big plastic bubble over it where people could even swim in winter. We had never gotten to go there either. So now we were in a tall building, bigger than any in Elmira. Monika explained that we would be allowed to have anything we wanted from room service. I chose a hamburger. She picked shrimp cocktail and a steak, and turned on the color television. There was a scary movie on the TV. In the movie, a lady was staying in a hotel in New York, and someone wanted to kill her.

*Wait a minute, we are in a hotel in New York City.* After the villain's break in while the persecuted heroine wasn't at home, she had a chain put on her door. The villain returned to her apartment. He unlocked the door, but could not break through the chain. I was still watching the movie, and checked the door to our room. *OK, I can sleep, we have a chain.* The lady in the movie continued on her daily business, and went to bed the next evening. The villain returned with a bolt cutter, hacked through the chain, then continued on into the bedroom where the frightened lady slept. I lay wide awake the rest of the night, first worrying about the hotel, and then worrying about the plane ride. Planes could run out of fuel and drop from the sky; birds could fly into the propellers and cause engines to fail; a crazy passenger could open a door or window and cause everyone to be sucked outside. Plane crashes appeared regularly in World War II adventures, and maybe flying might not be a great idea. But, it was way too late to explain my problem to anyone. Besides, I had already been warned that I needed to act like an adult now.

Someone shook me in the dark.

"Get up!"

Panic struck. "What's wrong?"

"It's time to get dressed."

"What time is it?"

"Five o'clock. They will be taking us to the plane. Our suitcases need to be out in the hall by 6:00."

Monika had carefully selected the outfits for meeting her mother at the Berlin airport. Passengers on overseas flights dressed in their nicest business style clothes. Stewardess Barbie wore tailored suits with tight skirts and fitted jackets, hats and very neat bubble hairdos. Monika got me dressed first, in my new slip, the ivory colored skirt, and the gold and brown flowered blouse.

Unfortunately, I had to wear heavy black orthopedic shoes to try and correct my gait. We had gone to the foot doctor, and they were going to try to straighten out the bad foot. Monika said that I had to be careful not to toe out. Otherwise I would look and walk like a duck. I knew I should be wearing stockings and nice shoes, but Mom said I couldn't have stockings until my 12th birthday.

The wavy hair? Should it behave just because things would be different now? The cowlicks stuck out all over, and Monika spent some time trying to tame them with a little water and wave set. The hair would no longer be defiant. It had to stay in place for the 24 hour plane ride to Germany.

Then she got to work on herself. When Monika had arrived from Germany three years earlier, she was still a teenager, wearing her long skirts and sweaters, and bobby sox with sensible walking shoes. As a new bride, she finished high school during the months after her wedding. Now she wore stiletto heels with everything, all the time. Even in the cellar apartment, washing dishes, Moni was in high heels and graceful circular cut skirts. *Donald of the Ritz*, the Elmira hairdresser, had constructed a coiffure that was not supposed to break down in less than a week. This morning she repaired the edges of the coiffure, and sprayed it to hold for the long flight. After she put on her stockings, she opened a long plastic bag, and pulled out an elegant beige gabardine suit with a tight skirt and Chanel cut jacket. With the suit was a matching pillbox hat as well as a new pair of stiletto heels.

Finally, we were ready to approach the steps to the Icelandair DC3. Monika ascended the open metal stairs with her cosmetic case. I stumbled on the second step, then watched my footing on the open staircase. Like my mom, I was afraid of heights. The stewardesses at the door all greeted Monika like a movie star, "Elizabeth Taylor! Jackie Kennedy!" After they were seated, Monika abruptly ordered, "Stand up! Here, you have to do this." She had me grasp the sides of my skirt, and pull them taut underneath my bottom. That keeps the skirt from getting mussed on the long trip. What a great idea! It was clear that I was not to arrive rumpled and dirty. I looked out the window at the enormous wing with its shiny propellers. Mechanics on ladders were putting finishing touches on the plane.

The DC3 took 24 hours to travel from New York to Berlin. The Atlantic Ocean is not just a body of water. It is dotted with islands and peninsulas all the way across, sort of like chunks of fish in a bowl of chowder. The first stop was at Gander, Newfoundland, still in Canada and then on to Reykjavik, Iceland for refueling. A golden sun was visible in the graying blush of the evening sky. Curiosity and excitement began to wear into fatigue as the long trip continued.

We stopped for refueling, and the airline people gave us postcards. I decided to write my brother.

*Jack Schloss*
*112 Grove Street*
*Elmira, New York*

*Dear Jack,*
*It is 11:00 PM in Iceland, and the sun is out. They*
*fed us cold fish and peas on the airplane. It was slimy.*
*They have volcanoes here. Love, Kate*

Within an hour, the sun was bright again. Additional fuel was needed every few hours to keep the propellers in the air. At one point, a tanker plane arrived, and an enormous hose joined the tanker and the passenger plane as they refueled in mid-air, with both planes flying together, one just a few feet from the other, like a pair of geese bound together in a long journey. The plane stopped in Goteborg, Sweden and Hamburg Germany, with time for refueling and checking the mechanical components at each landing as they worked their way across the North Atlantic. I got an earache every time the altitude changed. There were airsick bags at every seat, and I did not want to use one. For one thing, I was afraid of what would come up. I really didn't want to see another herring in any form. The stormy North Atlantic Ocean kept us bumping along, taking off and landing in spring storms fed by cold and warm ocean currents. By the way, remember the red and blue arrows showing the Labrador current on your school maps? You can't actually see the current. How do they know if it's real? And how do they make up those maps?

But finally we were flying over the dark green forests that surround the city of Berlin. I could see the huge city, but not the airport. Berlin was not a glittering panorama of skyscrapers like New York, but a quiet gray landscape of streets and new buildings. Where was the airport? We had better find it before we end up landing on Main Street. Monika laughed. She pointed. There was a big hole in the city. The airfield was spot in the center of all the buildings.

Monika talked to me about the war in Germany. "The war ended when I was a little girl, about seven years old. Katrine, they think you have peace at the end of a war, but there was no peace for us. Our schools and homes were destroyed. The Russians wanted to punish us. Russian troops came through our streets, looking for any remaining men. If they couldn't find men they went to our houses and hurt the women as badly as they could. Sometimes they shot the women who disobeyed them. The farmlands were burnt into hard soil, and there were only the disabled men and a few women were left to take care of the land. Even little boys had been sent to war. My mother was smart. As soon as my mother understood that Berlin would be taken, she planted her "silver garden." Digging up the backyard, under sewers and behind sheds, she hid her jewelry and any pieces of silver that were in the house. We didn't have time to plant food and wait for it to grow, but sometimes Mutti would take a few pieces of silver out to a farm, and ask for potatoes, turnips or maybe even some sweet carrots. She would dress in rags and color her face with coal, so that soldiers would think she was an ugly dirty farmworker. Our people cut down trees in the parks for fuel, and we learned which kinds of grasses could be safely boiled into soups."

"Your Mutti was very, very brave wasn't she?" Monika stopped rummaging in her purse, as if she suddenly remembered something.

"Ja, ja . . . she was a widow, she had to care for us." She located her high heels underneath the seat, and pushed her feet into them.

"After my father's plane crashed, she kept his good pilot boots. When the Russians came through they searched our house for valuables . . . and they saw the boots. They grabbed her by the shoulders, made her kneel, and wanted her to tell them where the Nazi deserter was. She said there was no deserter. My sisters and I were hidden in the cellar. I heard the click of their rifles as they got ready to shoot her. Suddenly the door of the cellar opened, and our neighbor hurried us up the stairs. 'The man who owned those boots is dead. If you shoot this woman, they will not have a mother either.' The soldier lowered his gun. Even Russians could care about children."

Aunt Monika was very sorry about the airlift pilots who had died. Her father had died when she was four years old. She liked pilots a lot, and had her favorite. Uncle Wiggly was a special pilot. During the airlift he flew several missions to Berlin each day, and he noticed a lot kids watching the planes from the airfield. One time he had a little gum in his pocket, and walked over to the fence. "The kids used to watch the planes at the airfield, and he gave away his gum. The little kids had never tasted candy, ever. He promised to bring them some. "How will you do that?" "I will wiggle my wings." The next day at the airfield, a plane came in low, and tipped its wings from side to side. Then, out of the plane came small objects – candy bars tied to handkerchiefs, and flown down like tiny parachutes. More and more kids came to the airfields, and began writing letters to the US Air Force about the candy. Uncle Wiggly and his friends kept dropping candy bars in handkerchief parachutes."

In the fall of 1949, after 15 months of the airlift, the Soviets agreed to let the German people use the roads through East Germany. Now I understood Grandmother Estelle's admonitions. "Clean your plate, children in Europe are starving" had some meaning. If only the boiled onions and blue cheese could have been sent to those children. They were also welcome to any Jello they could catch in mid-air.

# CHAPTER SIX

## Postcards

*Miss Melanie Ryback*
*905 Hoffman Street*
*Elmira, New York*
*U.S.A.*

   *Dear Mel, How are you? I am fine. Everything in*
*Berlin is brand-new, even the buildings and the trees. I*
*got tired on the airplane. Kate*

   Finally we had descended the last set of airplane steps onto a
tarmac. Monika's mother Liddy was waiting behind the windows.
She was tall, as tall as my mother, with graying blonde hair and
piercing blue eyes. I have no idea how old she was. She looked old
like grandmother but she suddenly lifted two of the heavy suitcases
and took off through the busy airport with Monika. I startled, and
then followed her as quickly as I could. They didn't even look back
for me as they raced toward the shiny new Opel sedan, parked and
ready for takeoff.
   Suddenly I was in the back seat of a car with strangers. On the
long fast drive toward the green outskirts of the city, I couldn't
understand a word that was spoken in the car. Gardens and trees

appeared, along with unpronounceable names like "*Walporzheimer Straße.*" I couldn't read anything. When we arrived at the house, Liddy asked me if I would like a glass of milk. "Yes, please." A cold glass of milk sounded so good after all the strange foods, and Mutti Liddy brought a pretty flowered tray with milk and toast. I picked up the milk and took a long swallow. The milk was warm and sour. Apparently a glass of milk could be any beverage from a cold liquid fresh from the farm, to yogurt that had not yet been strained. Then Liddy set her beautiful table with a lace cloth, her elaborately decorated china, and five pieces of real silver at each place setting, plus a cloth napkin in a silver ring. This was a long way from Grandma Estelle's Pyrex plates and paper napkins for spills. Monika showed me how to place the napkin in my lap first, and then wait for Liddy. Each piece of silver had a special purpose and time to be used in the meal. Monika told me to just follow her, and use the same fork at the same time. When Liddy sat, I began to carefully pick up the correct fork. But then I forgot and put my hand in my lap, just like grandmother had taught me to do. The eyes all turned toward me. You are never, ever supposed to rest a hand in your lap. People who do that are too lazy to eat properly. Monika now took my left hand and placed the fork in it. The knife was to be held in my right hand, but always with an index finger resting on top. It wasn't like when you hold a knife to cook. I was instructed to cut everything into tiny morsels, moving the bites carefully onto the fork. Then, I was supposed to pick up the fork, turn it upside down, and carefully place the food in my mouth without letting it slip off the fork. It was clear that there could be consequences if anything fell between the fancy plate and my mouth. The first course was a special yellow asparagus that smelled faintly of gasoline. I practiced cutting it into morsels. The meat was another delicacy, white veal, from a butchered milk-fed baby calf. Queasy from the flight, I wasn't sure I could possibly cut or eat another bite. My big appetite was gone. The new language began to whirl around and the room began to spin. When I closed my eyes just to balance myself, Mutti Liddy took one look at my half eaten food. "*Bist du müde?* Are . . . you . . . tired?"

Then she turned to Monika to announce that I was very pale. "Katrine, where are your pajamas? My mother wants you to go to bed." I was a little puzzled. No one was angry, so I wasn't being sent to bed without my supper. All the events of the last two days were so exciting that sleep had not been an option. Their offer of a nap was a kind way to excuse the half eaten food, which might have gone to starving children in Europe, except now we were in Europe and the table was full. I was too nervous to understand anything. This was an easy set of directions to follow. In the suitcase were the lacy pink pajamas from Mrs. Doughton, and I couldn't wait to put them on and climb under clean sheets. Mutti Liddy had made up a daybed in the dining room, and it looked wonderful with a soft feather bed and enormous square pillows. Then Liddy and Monika started a quick conversation, a gentle combat in words. Finally Monika explains, "Mutti says those pajamas are not warm enough. She wants you to be much more covered up." Mutti went to the closets and pulled out a pair of long boy styled flannel pajamas, and an exhausted girl pulled them sadly over her head.

*   *   *

The sweetness of the stay in Berlin was a first clue that this was to be a special summer. In the morning, Mutti Liddy handed me an umbrella and a shopping bag for the daily trips to the open market. Once the vegetables and fresh milk were in her big leather bag, Liddy stopped at a candy stall and purchased a chocolate bar. I anxiously tried to communicate in German, "*Nein danke* – no thank you. I'm not supposed to eat sweets. Grandma Estelle does not allow us to have candy." Mutti Liddy responded that chocolate is good for you, and purchased a second bar. Then we sat down on a bench to enjoy the rich treat. *Schokolade* was my first German word after *danke* and *bitte*, thank you and please. In the neighboring shops, Liddy began to announce the names of common food items that you buy at the dairy, butcher, green grocer and baker. I tried to pronounce them as carefully as possible, but I couldn't say some parts of the hard words. There were some funny smeary vowels, sounds I had never heard before and couldn't say. Other words were just plain fun, like *kartoffel*, potato. It took the entire morning to shop and prepare the big midday meal. There were no cans to open, and there was no big refrigerator to store leftovers for reuse. Everything had to be made fresh. Liddy blanched a bag of fresh tomatoes, strained them through a colander and added cream and butter for fresh tomato soup. Campbells tomato soup had been in half of our daily recipes, and there was no such thing in Berlin. I also learned what happened if we didn't finish a meal. It would sit in a dish in the pantry until the next mealtime. Best to clean your plate on the first attempt.

On the first day Mutti Liddy went through the big canvas suitcase and dictated what I could or could not wear. Monika was not allowed to intervene, but she had to submit to an interrogation about my wardrobe. Yes, Monika had helped Ellie with the shopping, yes, this was the best quality that Ellie could afford, and yes, eleven year old girls in the US did wear pajamas made out of lingerie materials. The first items to be confiscated until later were the lacy pink pajamas, followed by training bras, a garter belt, and a pair of stockings. Mutti Liddy announced that such things were only appropriate after the sixteenth birthday, no matter how much the girl had developed. Monika's younger sister Annike agreed. She had returned from a student trip and asked me why my mother had sent these items with me. She was sixteen and was now allowed to wear them. The bras and stockings had been a rite of passage in New York, but apparently that rite of passage was not observed in Europe. I was now a little girl again and we were going shopping.

Modern Berlin was all glass and steel, with the burnt shell of an old church marking the effects of war for all to see. Everything had been designed and built in the fifteen years since the end of the war. KaDeWe was the nicest department store in downtown Berlin. Liddy and Monika marched me in to get properly outfitted. Their first selection was a pretty pastel pink dress with dainty white dots and a dark green sash. Monika had heard the fights about plaid shirt dresses for years, and I loved this dress with its narrow waist and long full skirt. Then, Liddy selected underwear for a little girl. The stockings and Queen Anne heels that had come to Berlin were a "no." She bought Strumpfhosen – knitted leggings – to wear with the dresses, and the leggings were purchased by my waist size. I may have only been eleven, but I was in a growth spurt and had just topped 5'6" a height not taken into consideration by the manufacturers of little girl's leggings. The Strumpfhosen were much too short. "They will stretch." Monika showed me how to pull them on gently, rolling them upward one piece at a time, but it wasn't enough. As we went walking along the fashionable Kufürstendamm, the tights began to roll and pull, down, and down, taking underwear with them. I tried to use my knees to control the twists of the fabric, and keep my underpants securely knotted up under a stiff cotton petticoat. I couldn't even imagine what would happen if I dropped my drawers right out in public. Meanwhile, Annike and Monika strode along at a rapid pace, moving like a team of prize horses in competition. Liddy was the coach driver, and instead of a fair princess following the troupe, an ugly duckling was in tow. The black orthopedic shoes were a nice touch with the pretty pink dress.

When we got home to hang up our city dresses, Annike started laughing. The mess of tangled tights, underwear, and a sticky cotton slip under the dress was enough information. She now had a mission. She had been following Liddy's directions for years with mixed results. From now on, Annike would take over as confidante, to assist with misunderstandings and help me understand what I needed to do. She sat down beside me at each meal, and instructed me in English which utensils I should use. The fish fork was most impressive one. Fresh trout was served on a beautiful spring day and Liddy had steamed it up in white wine. They were plated head and all. Lesson time. Moni jabbed the fish fork in right under the head of the trout, and removed the head and complete skeleton in a single piece. Then she tucked into her neatly fileted fish and buttered potatoes. I stared at my plate and fork, wondering how this was going to come out.

At supper, Annike showed me how to carefully build open-faced sandwiches, lifting slices of meat and cheese onto the bread, and then eating the late evening meal with knife and a fork. She reminded me to shake hands, and learn names of guests by looking at their faces. Annike modeled perfect behavior and then had me try it out. Mutti Liddy was amazed at her transformation as well as mine. As soon as guests left, we would get out the American Rock and Roll records that had been brought from the U.S. and practice our dancing. There were no boys or men visiting the Walporzheimer Strasse fortress. Annike did not have a boyfriend, and Monika was married. There were no old boyfriends, no boy acquaintances and no sons of friends. The war widows in the neighborhood all had daughters.

After the first week, I was issued a bicycle and a leather knapsack for school. I was to follow Annike daily to the Gymnasium, high school, and to be enrolled in 7th grade there. The big school break in Germany was a spring break in May, and the new school year was beginning. Annike was in the 11th grade, and introduced me to her teenaged friends. Then she made it a point to introduce herself to some 7th grade girls and explain that I might need some help in the classes. The day began. Mathematics was far above what had been taught in the states, but the illustrations of negative numbers and orders of operations made an interesting game. I carefully copied the examples in notebooks, and was able to solve some of the problems just by following the patterns and sequences of the symbols. Then came German Literature and History, a mish mash of sounds with no meaning at all. English was being taught by Mr. Hall, a Fulbright scholar like Uncle Bill. Mr. Hall had me do the beginning English lessons in reverse and helped out with some basic school survival German. Finally it was time for art class. A new set of Pelikan paints and a good brush were in my backpack, and I knew how to use them. I could show one teacher that I really could be an excellent student.

Homework was to be done immediately after school and the midday dinner. Every lesson was to be done perfectly, neatly inscribed into the notebooks. I was copying lessons one letter at time. Then came leisure time, a new event in my life. As the oldest girl in Elmira, I had worked in the kitchen and laundry since I was tall enough to reach the sinks while standing on a chair. Now, Mutti Liddy and Monika ran the household, and I was relieved of responsibilities. They worked terribly hard at tasks I had never seen before. There was no washer, and great kettles of boiling water on the stove kept everything immaculately white. We had used kettles at Grove Street. Mom dyed older underwear purple to avoid showing stains. Liddy and Monika instilled a new sense of pride. I now looked like a European schoolgirl, even when we walked in the forests.

Berlin's sandy soil seeds wild berries throughout the forests, all of which border upon East Germany. Often the berry bushes near the neatly trimmed paths have only a little fruit. Some is green and sour, and small berries appear here and there. But, Annike and I noticed that there were bigger and darker blueberries either at the fence line, or just on the other side of the fences. In some places the border was only marked with signs so we would run three feet across the invisible line, steal a few East German berries and then run out again. It was important to look out for VOPOs (*Volkspolizei,* East German Police) first and one afternoon we missed the young man in the black uniform. Annike shouted out, "Hey guys, don't shoot us! We'll make you a cake. Come on over to our house!" These officers, near our age, carried real guns, and would never be allowed to cross the fence. But they would not get in trouble if they shot playful girls.

In the late afternoons, when we returned with fresh fruit in pails, we helped Liddy make a simple tart with a buttery crust, berries, and a little sugar. When it was slightly warm from the oven, tea was served. The tea parties were real, not just a game for dolls any more. Lovely tables were set with silver, pastries, real whipped cream, roses on the table and small talk, all in German, followed by card games. Conversations often went far into the evening over games of canasta and pinochle. First Annike explained the rules in English, and then Monika enforced them in German. But, there was always a second game in the first game – the anti-rules, a gray area with banter about cheating, and made up rules. The tricky jesting and accusations were always lighthearted, and hopelessly confusing. If tempers began to flare, a badminton net was stretched across the street for a different game, one with clearer outcomes. The long June days often stretched until late at night when the sun finally went down for a few hours.

The idyllic spring woods around Berlin concealed a growing menace. Our lovely neighborhood of Frohnau bordered the East German countryside, and there were restrictions as to who could go to which parks. In some places the border was open, and West Berliners could travel into the Russian sector of the city. East Berliners might be able to go to work or visit friends and family in Western sections of the city if they had the correct paperwork. In the immediate neighborhood was a small brown house that sat directly on the border. A wire fence marked the split in the house, which was surrounded by police on both sides. The residents, who couldn't live in two worlds any more, eventually dug a tunnel out underneath the foundation.

*Mrs. Estelle Osborne*
*537 Mac Dowell Place*
*Elmira, New York*

*Dear Grandmother, How are you? I am fine. Remember how you taught us that we are all free to speak our minds? Annike says that in East Berlin people can't argue or say whatever they want. People don't necessarily like the Russians even if they live in East Berlin. Are they still Commies if they don't agree with the Russians?*

*Love, Kate*

After supper on June 17, Annike had steered two bicycles out to the front of the house. It was getting dark and nearly my bedtime. I gave Mutti and Monika a puzzled look, and they said, "Yes, you are going somewhere with Annike." Mounting the bicycles, the two of us went for several minutes along familiar streets, but then turned along a winding road, with dense bushes and trees on both sides. We began a very long climb uphill in the dark. The trees cleared, and we arrived high above a new section of the city, where smaller houses wound around dark streets. A large group of young people was already in the clearing, and had collected sticks, branches and logs for an enormous bonfire. As it started to blaze, we all looked across at other hilltops and saw other fires lighting an arc across the city. In 1953, eight years ago, there had been an uprising in East Berlin and people had tried to defect. Now, on June 17th each year, West Berliners lit the fires to let their friends and relatives know that they were not forgotten. Fire surrounded the barriers in the city. Hearts were warm, but we couldn't touch, even if our families were separated.

The idea of these barriers was new to me. In Elmira neighborhoods children ran in a pack, from one house to another, through open backyards and along the river.

I had never lived with fences or gates. Keys were a new mystery. I honestly don't know if Mom used keys in Elmira. I never had one. Then again, who would come to steal a bunch of purple painted antiques?

*Miss Shirley Ostrander*
*112 Grove Street*
*Elmira, New York*

*Dear Shirley,*
*You know how I am not allowed to have a key because I might lose it? Now I have keys just to come home from school. People have to lock up everything, even their garden gates. I don't think it's dangerous. There aren't even any guys, let alone bad guys.*
*I miss you.*

*Love, Kate*

Suddenly I had to learn to manipulate double doors on the outside, a gate, and keys to each room, even keys to the clothes closets. Why do we lock up our dresses in those closets?

One Friday afternoon Annike and I were bathed. Our hair was done. Annike had put on her cream colored tricot slip with the lace edging. I was in my immaculate white starched petticoat.

"Katrine, go get the closet key."

I skipped down the hall to get the key off the hook. It wasn't there.

"Anni, I can't find it!"

"Did you use it today?"

"I don't know. I don't think so. How will we get our dresses out?"

Monika came in. "Aren't you two ready yet?"

"We can't find the keys to the closet."

Monika's wide hazel eyes lit directly on Annike. She paused, and then stated, "Well, you can't go like that, and Mutti is waiting."

"Could we just wear our school clothes today?"

She shook her head, "Oh, I don't think so. I guess you and your lovely dresses will miss out on our trip downtown to a nice café."

Mutti came into the small room to investigate the delay. "They have lost the closet key."

Annika looked at her mother's stern face, and gently asked, "Couldn't we please just wear our school skirts? At least they are clean and neat." Mutti and Monika looked at each other and left the room. The car started up, and then Annika said, "Let's go play some badminton."

As we set up the nets in the street, Susanni came out of her house. She was Monika's age, 21 and very beautiful. She liked to play cards with us with even though she was far more sophisticated.

"So, Annike, do you have a boyfriend yet?" Susanni questioned and Annike demurred.

"Let me show you my new tea set this afternoon. It is fine china from England, and has all matching plates and pots."

"Why English? Isn't German china good enough?"

Susi laughed, "Because, silly, it is a gift! From Charles, an English officer. If I play my cards right, I might be introduced to the queen someday. I had better know about English china. Why do you think I practice badminton with you? I can already speak English as well as you can, but I need to practice. Come inside."

The three young ladies washed their hands and faces, and then Susi suggested they try out her French perfumes. Ooh la la! She brought out her silver tray with several small bottles, sniffed at each of the girls and made suggestions. Annike tried a deep floral scent, and I preferred citrus. Susi put on a bit of her Chanel #5. They were now ready for coffee. Suddenly they were both speaking French. Susi, or Suzette now, could talk of romance and films. Annike could follow her conversation, but didn't talk a lot. I had only memorized "*je ferme—nous fermons – vous fermez*" or how to close the window. That wasn't really helpful on such a lovely day.

Suzette now pulled out a set of cornichons, hollow pastry shells shaped like trumpets. The three of us were busily whipping cream and stuffing the shells before they dipping them in chocolate sprinkles. Suzette admonished me to not push the cream out of the end of the shells, and she laughed and looked at Annike, who blushed. I carefully prepared my shell. Actually, I wanted to lick the bowl, but it was clear that mademoiselles did not do such things.

Over coffee, Susan brought out the American cigarettes, still another gift from an officer, but not the Englishman. These were from Al, a guy from Chicago. She pulled out three cigarettes and a Zippo lighter. Gracefully, she lifted her cigarette between two fingers and lit it, taking a deep drag. She handed one to Annike. Annike also knew how to take the cigarette, and Susan tried to light it. But Annike didn't inhale deeply enough, and the cigarette went out a couple times before she got the hang of it. Now it was my turn. I hated cigarettes, but I wasn't going to admit it. I grasped the paper stick with my fist, and placed it squarely between two pairs of fingers, just like Ellie did when she was talking with Linda. My whole hand was in front of my face, and I was ready to light up. Sue lit the cigarette, and I showed off by taking a huge drag off of it. I immediately began coughing and gagging, dropping the cigarette on the table. Susanni cleaned off the ash, and put my cigarette back into the packet.

Annike thought that perhaps it would be a good idea to be home before Mutti Liddy arrived. But she was curious about all the fine things at Susanni's house. Had she ever known any Russians?

"Russki? I would tell them, 'Thanks for Shit!' I would never take a gift from a Russian. They are pigs who pissed on mama's Persian carpets."

*   *   *

74

At last Annike and I were allowed to travel alone through the city to visit the art museum. I desperately wanted to see Nefertiti because they all said she looked like my mother. Ellie had pictures of Nefertiti in her classroom, and sometimes dressed up as the Egyptian Queen with her long straight nose and graceful neck. I was going to see her. We rode through neighborhoods of block houses, and then through the shiny downtown. Then our subway car left an immaculate tiled station and began driving through black tunnels of fallen concrete and steel, gnarled into grotesque lines and forms. Anni said we were under East Berlin now. In a few more minutes the train pulled into a clean tunnel and a modern station. Apparently either the train lines or the borders zig-zagged a bit.

I had wanted to see this museum since Mom had made her first trip to Berlin three years before. Antiquities fascinated me and the Egyptian collection in Berlin is one of the finest in the world. The best part of antiquities is that people are dead but not gone. That's different from the religious paintings, where death is presented as some sort of monster movie. "You will suffer and die. Then you will go to hell." Yikes. The Berlin Museum had long galleries of religious paintings from a cross section of the centuries. Tired and a feeling a bit peckish, Annike pulled a candy bar out of her purse, while we talked about what they saw in a diptych of heaven and hell. The panel depicting Heaven was all in the sky, but the angels didn't have anything to do. Do angels live on air? Can dogs be angels? The side with hell had lusty lovers kissing and fondling, all sorts of animals playing and gluttony with its feasts of bread, cheese, fruit and wines. Hell depicted some of our favorite sins. Greed worked, money could buy comforts, and we had personally stolen East German blueberries. So we quietly peeled back the foil and furtively nipped at our chocolate. A guard yelled at us – "Empty your hands. There is no eating in the gallery." I looked at Anni standing in front of the images of hell and commented in English, "I guess we'll get to go there if we eat any more chocolate in museums."

Sad times were coming. Mutti Liddy became ill for much of the summer. A first shingles attack was followed by one even worse. Her doctors could not get her immune system under control. A visit to a gypsy herbalist was not any more helpful. An additional houseguest was quite a strain. She and Monika were speaking of boarding school in the fall. We were supposed to have a special tea party for my birthday and it was cancelled due to Liddy's illness, which eventually laid her up the rest of the summer. So July 10 was going to be like any other day, except that in Berlin, it was a school day. School days started very early. Maybe we could go swimming in the afternoon.

*Mrs. Eleanor Schloss*
*112 Grove Street*
*Elmira, New York*
*U.S.A.*

*Dear Mom,*
*When I got up this morning, the dining room doors were closed. Suddenly Aunt Monika opened the door and there in the room was a beautiful table, laid out with flowers, gifts, and sweet rolls for breakfast. Mutti Liddy gave me a grown up watch. The girls at school wear real watches and real jewelry. Now I really do need to learn how to tell time. Do you know they use a different clock here? School lets out a 13:00. Anyway, I had a great day. I have never been to school on my birthday before. I like being twelve. Did you go to the lake without me?*

*Love, Katrine*

Mutti Liddy and Monika did have a big surprise. They told me that they now trusted me to act like proper young lady. Arrangements had been made to attend summer camp in Holland. Finally this Dutch girl was going to see her father's homeland. The camp was sponsored by a SDP – Socialist Demokratische Partei. It was the further left of the German political parties, and this was to be an exercise in communal living and the sharing of responsibilities. Preparations for this trip involved several visits into East Berlin to get the right visas for an American child. Visiting the Russian sector in East Berlin was a shock, especially coming from a French sector neighborhood with lush parks and elegant new shops.

*Mrs. Eleanor Schloss*
*112 Grove Street*
*Elmira, New York U.S.A.*

*Dear Mom,*
   *Today Annike took me on the subway, across the big gate with the horses on top. The street is covered in dirt and rocks. Annike says those are bomb ruins, rubble. It is supposed to have gardens and beautiful trees, but there are weeds growing up between cobblestones. The people of East Berlin are very poor, with broken houses and walls everywhere. It looks even worse than when we worked in the cellar at home.*
                                                              *Love, Kate*

Fifteen years after the German surrender, East Berlin was still a war zone. The Russians had left the city in ruins, and prevented the people from rebuilding. The result was that Berliners depended on each other. There was very little work in East Berlin. Many people who had jobs worked for families and businesses in West Berlin. Frau Hoffman, our housekeeper, was from East Berlin, and had been taking the train to the garden neighborhood daily for years. She was part of our Frohnau families. Frau Hoffman kept the homes tidy, and she was able to use her income to buy necessities for her family. Simple gifts of used sweaters and maybe a can or two of a treat like condensed milk were bonuses. Even basic products like soaps and canned goods came from West Berlin shops. Behind the Iron Curtain, the government took charge of all manufacturing, and told people what they could or could not buy. All coats were gray and in the same factory style, there was only one kind of mustard, and all pickles were one brand. Popular American brands, like Coca Cola and Hersheys did not exist.

Our first views of East Germany did not really counter this idea. The SDP camp was a 30 hour train ride into Holland, aboard old steam trains. There were no sleeping arrangements on the train, so some 2,000 kids bundled on top of the bed rolls for a few hours of rest here and there. Finally we arrived at a tent city outside of Callantsoog, by the sand dunes of the North Sea. In the middle of a giant soggy field, huge sleeping tents accommodated about 20 teenagers each, and there was absolutely no privacy. Girls just stripped out of their traveling clothes. I had not seen bathrooms and couldn't figure out how to find one. I was also too shy to ask the girls in our tent as they rattled away in long conversations. They laughed hysterically when they figured out what I needed, and taught me a lot of new words for evacuating my bladder and bowels. A big dark ditch full of water and mud separated the sleeping tents from the outhouses and the beer tent. It rained almost nightly and the girls and boys were covered with mud, slipping in mud, or stuck in mud most of the time. A second muddy ditch separated the bathing tents, one for boys, and one for girls. A hermaphrodite was assigned to the girl's side.

*Mr. Tommy Milunich*
*548 Mt. Zoar Street*
*Elmira, New York U.S.A.*

*Hey Tommy,*
*I am at camp now with my 2000 best friends.*
*Guess what. I met a hermaphrodite. He—she—it has*
*to sponge bathe and shower with the rest of us, but*
*she has little boy's equipment and little breasts. Pretty*
*strange huh? I haven't asked her if she is queer. It is*
*muddy here. Love, Kate*

It was just a short walk to the beach, but the North Sea is not exactly a swimming hole. It is very windy, with sand dunes that rise several feet, and then change places day after day. In order to play in the water, you wear a large wool sweater over your bathing suit, walk into the waves, scream and then toss the sweater back on the sand before diving under a wave. The frigid salty excitement lasts a few minutes, and then you race out to find your sweater. Shacks along the beach sell paper cones of hot French fries, with rich yellow mayonnaise for dipping. The beach excursions were much more about the French fries than the swimming.

I began to wonder about my early childhood, and my father's stories about Amsterdam and Holland. The only image I had was a photograph of a little blonde girl in a Dutch bonnet.

*Mr. William Osborne*
*537 McDowell Place*
*Elmira, New York U.S.A.*

*Dear Uncle Bill,*
*Remember how you told me that I have an aunt in Amsterdam? I wish I knew how to find her. We had a field trip to Amsterdam. Anne Frank's house was sad. They say the Germans murdered six million Jews. Even little girls like Mel and Bethie. My German friends were sad. Do you know which house was my father's? I didn't have his address. I'm glad you are coming to Berlin soon. Love, Kate*

The obligatory canal city tour went right by the houses on the Herengracht, Gentleman's canal, when they talk about the Patrician Houses. It was around the corner from the Anne Frank house. It turned out that father's home was Herengracht 94, and it still sits overlooking the boatloads of tourists. They lost the home in the war, when all Jewish property was confiscated. My father was a Dutch Jew, like the people who had been taken away and murdered.

Uncle Bill had told me that my father was Jewish when I asked if Susan Roth could come over to play. There were Jewish kids in elementary school. They did not believe in Jesus, and I wondered if it was OK to be friends.

"Oh sweetie, of course it is. You are probably partly Jewish yourself."

"What does that mean?"

"Well, your aunt was in a special place where they put the Jews. She told me that they were Jewish, but your father warned her that she should never, ever let us know. So we kept it a secret. Otherwise she would have gotten into trouble." Uncle Bill had kept my aunt's secret for a long time, until that afternoon, when a little girl was simply wondering if she could invite a Jewish friend over for cookies and dolls. But now I wanted to know so much more.

Anne Frank was my age, twelve years old when she went into hiding. At her house I didn't know whether to quietly focus on the exhibits and the German-speaking guide, or to watch the German teenagers take in the horrors of the Holocaust, and try to understand why it had happened, and what, if anything, it had to do with them. As the kids were trying to grasp the ideas of ultimate hatred and destruction of innocent people, I was looking at photographs of the grandparents I never knew. I was standing with the children of German murderers, and was seeing the first time the way in which my own family was murdered. We were all learning to bear witness from the same experience, and it was shocking and awful. None of us would ever be the same. New friends were learning that their parents and grandparents had been part of the single most heinous event in human history. Kids who had been born into the shadows of war were being asked to bear consequences for something that they had never done. How could any of that be their fault? Was it OK to be friends with Germans? It must be. That day I was the lucky one. I knew that American kids, even Jewish ones whose families were from Europe, looked forward toward bright futures.

\* \* \*

North Sea camping with 2,000 people required that new skills were learned almost daily to keep the tent city functional. I learned how to peel potatoes and vegetables with a knife. One reason that most daily food was glop over potatoes was that the kids prepared all the meals. Very few of us had prior experience in home kitchens, let alone an enormous tent kitchen. The food also had to be cheap. Each tent took turns doing the preparation for hundreds of young people. The twelve and thirteen year old girls were assigned to prepare Hungarian Goulasch, made with horsemeat and paprikas, and served over potatoes.

> *Mr. John Osborne*
> *537 Mac Dowell Place*
> *Elmira, New York U.S.A.*
>
> *Dear Uncle John,*
> *I learned to use a paring knife, and personally*
> *peeled 200 potatoes in one afternoon plus most of my*
> *left hand. Human blood as a condiment. Interesting.*
> *Love, Kate*

The student camp did have a large beer tent, serving beer, wine and pickled herrings. American soft drinks were too expensive. After a couple of beers the teens all got out on the dirt floor gyrating and twisting to scratchy loudspeakers. It did not look like American Bandstand; it looked more like a tub full of eels. There were no words and hardly a melody could be understood, but the bass line kept the teens moving like schools of fish. The evening ended as kids tried to cross the muddy ditch to their tent villages. Tipsy boys would end up trying to jump across the little canals, which by August were covered with green slime and stank. The more adept gymnastic types would turn cartwheels across the ditch to see who would not fall into the brackish water. It was impossible to just walk across, and I didn't have a pair of the wooden soled clogs that the German girls wore everywhere. Everyone ended just rolling across in the mud.

On rainy nights, boys would invade the girls tents, looking for underwear and personal items—panty raids! Success was measured by how many boys were wearing bras around the next day.

*Miss Mel Ryback*
*905 Hoffman Street*
*Elmira, New York U.S.A.*

*Dear Mel,*
*I'm going to be in big trouble now. Mutti Liddy*
*loaned me a blanket to use for my bedroll, and I slept*
*in mud and straw for three weeks. Last night the boys*
*came to our tent and during a wrestling match the*
*blanket got ripped. I only had 8 marks available to buy*
*the replacement. I guess that everyone will pitch in to*
*replace the blanket. I'm still afraid of what Mutti Liddy*
*will say. Wonder if I'll get sent back to Elmira?*

*Stay tuned,*
*Kate*

Mom's old canvas suitcase had not survived being stacked with 2,000 sturdy leather German bags. The zipper was broken, and the whole bag was tied up with tent ropes. Everything inside the bag was muddy. The large muddy parcel and a new yellow blanket were pushed off the train onto the platform before I jumped down. I was back in one piece and the evidence of Dutch coeducational mud wrestling was no longer visible. Mutti, Monika, and Annike wanted to know why I had not brought them anything from Holland. They were hoping for good strong Dutch coffee and buttery chocolates. Instead, I had learned how young people could work together to make things right for everyone in a community of 12-18 year olds. How do you share that gift?

*Mrs. Eleanor Schloss*
*112 Grove Street*
*Elmira, New York U.S.A.*

*Dear Mom,*
*I broke my suitcase. I'm sorry.*

*Kate*

On Saturday, August 13 the world changed again. Mutti Liddy picked up the paper, opened it, and fell into the chair with a fainting spell. Moni and Anni ran to her side and conversation was very rapid and anxious. I understood parts of it . . . something about how Frau Hoffman, the housekeeper, couldn't come across any more. The public transportation system that linked the entire city was compromised. VOPOs were all over the place, and looking very hostile. East Berlin was being walled off and West Berlin would be enclosed completely. Everyone was paralyzed with fear. We all went to a nice garden restaurant to meet with friends and calm down the escalating fears. Somehow I doubted that our East Berlin friends and their families could just open up a bottle of wine and hope that this would go away.

Uncle Bill arrived in Berlin two days later with smiles and big hugs for all. He was delighted that I could speak some German, and said I looked good to him. In spite of the pastries and chocolates, my waist had dropped by nearly six inches over the summer, and the asthma was gone. He brought me a Swiss Army Knife. Then the adults briefly discussed changes in the city, and Bill and Moni left to see a play at a famous East Berlin theatre. When they tried to return home, they didn't have the correct documentation. Bill's American passport was locked up at the house, and Moni had an International driver's license but no proof of citizenship or current Berlin residency. All the rules had changed in two days, and they were detained for hours.

On Wednesday Bill had to go into East Berlin again. This time I was going with Uncle Bill. American citizens were being evacuated from Berlin. He needed to get a visa saying that he was married to a German and entitled to stay in Berlin. He also hoped that he could visit some famous old cities in East Germany, but he could not get the permission. His guest privileges were only for the West. I could not get any kind of permission to stay in Berlin and I would need to be evacuated. Bill kept speaking rapid German with the men in the offices, but we were told to return the following day. The people in the offices didn't quite know how to do this. They wanted to have a parent accompany me. My mother had been called in New York, and she was on her way to Europe with Jack. This wasn't going to solve the problem, because she would not be allowed to come to Berlin to get me.

Then Bill announced, "We are going to do something very special. It is important that you remember this for the rest of your life." We went to a rally at the Brandenburg gate because he wanted me to see Konrad Adenauer and Willy Brandt, and understand what they were saying. There were more than 200,000 people in the crowd. He grabbed my waist and began to lift. "No! I'm way too heavy." He lifted me onto his shoulders for a view of the great leaders, who were speaking very rapidly into huge microphones. Uncle Bill made it clear that the fate of Europe, America and the East lay on the shoulders of Adenauer, Brandt and Kennedy. Compared to that, a 110 lb. girl on his was nothing."

# CHAPTER SEVEN

## Borders

August 18, 1961

*"Your name?*

*When were you born?*

*Where do you live?*

*Where was your father on September 1, 1939?"*

My student visa was cancelled. The tense officer addressed us directly, and the bare lights in the room threw a menacing glow on everything. Uncle Bill and I were now at the East Berlin Reiseburo, an official government transport office, negotiating the steps to get me to West Germany within the next three days.

*"What is your relationship to this American girl?"*

*"Where are her parents?"*

*"Your wife is a Berliner? You understand that if you leave to escort the child, you may not return to Berlin?"*

Bill smiled and explained that he was a U.S. teacher, with a work permit for the year.

*"I will ask my superior."* The official turned away from us and went to a desk in the back.

*"No, there are no family visas, transit visas, or work permits. All Americans are to exit Berlin via GDR transports. No one will be allowed*

*to enter Berlin. You may stay with your wife and her family, or you may escort your niece."*

The dilapidated government offices had not been rebuilt since the war. Pale paint was peeling off the walls, and patches of brick and rock showed through the plaster. Lines of Germans and international visitors were everywhere, requesting assistance from an anonymous authority. East Berlin was a new Iron Curtain country that had only had physical borders for a couple days. Clerks were improvising procedures as they revoked visas, separated families and negated people's rights. Suddenly no West Berliners were allowed on the subway through East Berlin, even though one of the main arteries of the subway had gone under East Berlin before coming up at the West Berlin Zoo, museums, and parks. Public transport was divided into a series of legs by bus and train that circumvented East Berlin. Everyone carried full ID everywhere – passports and proof of citizenship were needed even to go to work at jobs people had held for years.

The West German government requested evacuation of all non-Berliners by the end of the week – Sunday, August 20th. The Cold War was on the verge of erupting into a hot war. Border incidents were being logged at the rate of several a day. Daring escapes and attempted escapes were reported in Western media, as Berliners tried to bring their families together across the divided landscape of the city. East Berliners dug, ran, and shot their way out. A young VOPO jumped the wire fences, machine gun and all, leaving his East German life behind. Now that my visa was cancelled I was supposed to leave immediately, but it turned out I would be going alone. Uncle Bill had not found a way to take me across the border and then return to his family in Berlin. The country was no longer safe. Back at Mutti Liddy's house another string of directions followed as Monika packed my things.

Germans like to have precise systems in place. The trains run on time, everyone is accounted for, and papers are checked and cross-checked. Although the West German government requested evacuation, only the East German government could issue the transportation visas. The two German governments were not in agreement as to how this was to be accomplished. For three days in a row we traveled back and forth to complete stacks of forms that no one understood. On the first day, it was an excursion, but the sober people in the streets and empty cafes were a jarring sight. People walked with heads down and faces concealed. Some disappeared into the uniform rows of gray block buildings. On the second visit the officials tried to ask me questions by myself. I just stared at them, and I couldn't answer them or read the papers. Cold sweat was everywhere in the room even though it was a hot afternoon. Uncle Bill calmly began translating words and ideas that I did not understand, not even in English. His blue eyes moved constantly as he looked into the unblinking stares of the officers. I knew this was scary but I wasn't sure what I was supposed to be afraid of.

The stomachaches started in the car. My passport was stamped and Bill had the ticket to West Germany. Safely back at Mutti Liddy's, the adults tried compresses on my tummy, and mixed up potions to drink. Thermometers were unreliable in the hot August weather – a fever may not be a fever. A doctor came by. Finally the illness was diagnosed as "nerves" and the day had arrived. It was time to leave. There was just one more hitch in the plans. Train travel across Germany had been halted as "escape fever" had spread through the countryside. This afternoon Berlin passengers were put into a series of buses with government escorts, unloaded at borders, walked across, and reboarded. Just a week earlier, these buses had traveled back and forth along the corridor without interruption.

On the ride to the train station and the buses, Uncle Bill repeated the complicated instructions for the trip. He tried to cheer me up. *"A worker comes to the office to join the Communist Party. The clerk asks him, "Which do you prefer, Pravda (Russian state newspaper) or Radio Free Europe? Oh, Pravda, of course. And why is that? Because you can't wrap herring in a radio."* Bill did his best to convince me that everything would be fine, but he kept his eyes on the road. As they loaded suitcases, he talked to the bus driver and introduced me. I was to sit behind the driver. Then he waited, waving as the bus pulled away from the stop. My mother and I were to call as soon as the bus arrived in Braunschweig in West Germany.

The first stop was for documentation at a Brandenburg checkpoint. We were now entering East Germany. Suddenly, a few seats back, a loud argument erupted. The VOPOs escorted two passengers off the bus at gunpoint. The big guns with heavy stocks and long barrels were raised to waist level, or eye level for a child in a front seat. Still and silent, the tears came, obscuring the pages of a new book. No instructions were needed about keeping my head down. The Iron Curtain was real, with block walls and barbed wire, anti-vehicle ditches and booby traps. Red and white signs indicated that the area was full of land mines. Finally the bus pulled away as a light rain began to spray across the gray countryside. Not daring to look out of the obscured window, I kept my head down for a few silent hours until the second checkpoint was reached.

The bus arrived at the train station in Braunschweig, Federal Republic of Germany. Where was Mom? Two polo shirts, one yellow and one blue, came running and shouting down the platform. Jack and Louis had their arms around me with mom's long arms around everyone.

"Mom, we have to call Berlin. Uncle Bill said that we needed to call the minute I arrived."

Mom squeezed me. "We'll look for a pay phone. There's probably one here in the train station." Then she collected Jack from a kiosk with interesting signs.

"I really need to call. He's waiting. Please can we find one right now?" Just four hours ago, Uncle Bill made it very clear that he was expecting this call. He didn't say he was scared but his message was one of caution, even as he told his silly jokes. Ellie and Louis, free spirits now, had no idea of what the past week in Berlin was like, and didn't understand the urgency, or why Bill would be so worried. There was no phone in the train station. Phones were only available at the Post Office, and it was impossible to get a line through to Berlin. In fact, when Louis and Mom had called to make final arrangements for meeting the transport, their attempt to phone Berlin had taken two days to get through. Louis said they would try again in a day or two after the mandatory evacuations were lifted.

Years later, Uncle Bill talked about how he had waited up that night for the phone call, worried sick. He had realized that the border trip was very dangerous. The VOPOs were shooting at anyone who looked suspicious. He was sorry that I had to travel by myself. It was so scary with all those armed men, the barbed wire, and the very aggressive treatment at the border. Actually, in some way, the situation didn't seem so real to me until we visited a concentration camp months later, with the photographs of people being shot and piled into the graves. After that I became terrified of the VOPOs.

But that night, an immediate celebration was in order. There was a carnival near the Braunschweig train station. The fairgrounds were tented and canopied. Each tent featured a variety of beer and sausages, with live bands and folk dancers in each tent. Accordion music was everywhere. There were rides, and sweets for children. The family tested beers – nine year old Jack rambling down the fairway with "So this is what it's like to be drunk? This is wuuuunderrful!" The entire crowd was inebriated. The funniest sight was of two young men, obviously drinking buddies, who had tied their neckties together to keep from getting lost. They kept staggering in opposite directions – pulling each other along, sliding around in the rain.

Everywhere, children and adults were dancing to the bands. I knew about beer tents from Holland, but now I fell down the steps of a beer tent in my good ivory travel skirt. It was covered in mud and straw. "Hey Latrine, watch your steps!" Jack was already annoying. Mom ran behind the three of us as we jumped onto the last train back to Wolfsburg. For the first time, it felt like family again, laughing, hugging, and talking as fast as we could.

*   *   *

Jack's first impressions of Europe were quite different from mine. In Amsterdam they had taken the boat tour, which included the "patrician houses of the Herengracht" and Ellie had pointed out 94 Herengracht where our father had been raised. Then, the history lesson was over. Louis walked them off the tour boat through the adjoining Red Light District. I had not been to the Red Light

District on our tour of Amsterdam, but it sounded like it must be pretty. It seemed that Louis had some friends there. He was quite interested in seeing that Jack had a liberal education. As he entered the "hotels" looking for a cheap place to stay, the ladies of the night would begin screaming at him. "We don't mind the wife, if that pleases you. Get the child out of here, now! You filthy derelict!" At a neighborhood bar, one of the ladies was quite taken with Jack. "Here's my card. I want you to come back for a free night on the house when you grow up to be a GI." Jack showed me the card. Mom explained that the houses were for women who sleep with men, and that this was illegal in the US. Jack added his own insight. "Gee, I don't know why this is illegal. It shouldn't be against the law just to sleep in a hotel." After seeing the sights, the three of them had settled into one of the special hotels for the night, where Louis was friends with the owner.

Their stories were silly, but their naughtiness was refreshing. They were so easy to be with. This was all so confusing. I liked pleasing Mutti Liddy in Berlin, and learning the manners of a cosmopolitan young woman. Mutti Liddy was like many of my favorite teachers. Now, I had all the advantages of girls who wore pastel dresses and real jewelry. I was taller, thinner and had been to a French hairdresser. Ooh la la.

So Mom figured that I was all grown up now. She decided to treat me like a girlfriend. She had had so many good friends in Elmira. Now who could she talk to? We went to take baths, and she shared intimate secrets about the family and friends. Some of the secrets were a little nasty. Bill had been worried about rejoining Monika in Berlin. Mom suspected that Monika was terribly disappointed with her life in the United States, and that she would leave Bill, except that he had taken her virginity. That meant that she couldn't start over and marry someone else. Just exactly how do you share your secrets when your friends and family are somewhere else? Who knows what Monika really thought about any of us? Now that I had been to Berlin and also knew the cozy cellar apartment, I could see how Monika might be disappointed. We sure were not rich Americans. She had a nicer home with Mutti Liddy.

"What is your virginity?"

"A piece of skin."

"Where is it?"

"You can't see it."

"If you can't see it, how could it possibly be important?"

But, apparently, virginity is valuable, and without it, a young woman is worthless. This made absolutely no sense. "Kate, you need to really soap and rinse under your arms. Women smell bad if they don't do that. Also, wash between your legs. You need to keep that part as clean as your face. As we bathed together, Mom commented on my changes and started talking about some movie called, "Lolita." She took me shopping for underwear. It was clear that Ellie and Mutti Liddy did not see eye to eye on lingerie. Thank God I would never again have to worry about children's size stockings rolling down in public.

Mom washed and set my hair to keep up the new French style, and lent me her prettiest new sandals. More confidences were shared. "Louis and I might get married. Isn't that exciting?" Ellie was like a teenager, crazy in love with a wonderful man who actually liked her two children. To Louis, we were still kids, all three of us. He loved pointing out interesting sights, telling jokes, taking us on walks, and buying pastries – especially the chocolate and rum confections. Jack, with a chocolate in his mouth, chortled,

"This is life!"

"What is Life?"

"It's a magazine: costs 25cents. That's life."

"What's Life?" "It's a magazine; costs 25 cents."

A Time Magazine cover about the Berlin Wall was featured at the local newsstand. I stopped to look at it. Louis turned around and bought the magazine for me to read. Finally there was some real information, a real picture of what was going on in Berlin and why it was important. The political perspective was the thousand piece jigsaw puzzle, and the personal experience was just a few fuzzy green pieces of a tree in the corner. It's one thing to be in a city where people cannot cross streets or speak with friends, and it's quite different when you read all the insights, and everyone's discussion of the consequences. People were afraid of Russians, but not of their own neighborhoods. The magazine writers talked about "The most dangerous place on earth" as Russian and American tanks lined up on each side of the fences and gates of my adopted city.

Wolfsburg was to be our new home. It was a small industrial town, built after 1945. The focal point was the Volkswagen factory, a mile long block building that ran along the outside of the city like a medieval fortress. Its parking lots were full of shiny new Beetles, and some VW trucks and Microbuses. It was hard to tell the difference between employee lots and the manufacturing lot, but at the edge of the factory lot stood loading equipment to send the little cars to German cities and European seaports. After that came rows of apartment blocks, gray and white rectangular buildings, with hundreds of identical apartments inside. This wasn't a bit like the broad tree lined avenues and homes of Berlin.

Louis started work at the VW Factory. Mom, Jack and I began walking through the town looking for a place to live. Beyond city hall, the town outskirts were far nicer than the concrete city centre. Just a little way in any direction, land was set aside into little gardens. Most people didn't have yards at their houses. They went to the garden area on long summer evenings and weekends to grow a few vegetables and flowers. On one parcel of land as many as twenty or thirty families would grow their vegetables and some showy flowers to decorate their homes.

Louis had helped Mom read the advertisements for lodging and we found a single room not too far from the center of town. Frau Bauer's house was built of a funny grey pebbly mortar that looked like ground up rubble. Mom guessed that rubble could be a great building material if you knew how to make it back into bricks. You could make bricks out of nearly anything. Concrete is just ground up rock, so why not ground up rubble? By the time we arrived after walking two kilometers in the brilliant sun, I fainted in the cool darkened living room. The new landlady accepted mom's cash and then offered us salted peanuts and a glass of water before we undertook the long walk back to get our belongings out of the hotel.

Frau Bauer had a teenaged niece and the High School was nearby. Things were going to be all right.

Frau Bauer was renting out rooms to help with her expenses. Most families did not own their own homes. In a rebuilding country, houses are expensive to own and maintain. First, there is a shortage of available housing for residents of the town who have jobs at the local factories. There is nearly nothing available for others. People lived in apartment blocks or shared their residences with renters. Frau Bauer had a nice home, but she needed to share it. The upstairs room was very comfortable, bright and sunny with large windows, three beds and a bath down the hall. Hot water cost extra, so we enjoyed cold baths on the warm September days.

The practice of actually living in another country presented challenges for every little chore. Mom was helpless. There were no Laundromats but I already knew how to do laundry by boiling it in a kettle on top of the stove. Items in stores were unrecognizable. There were no similar American products. Ellie had been opening cans for years, but now she limited her culinary skills to cheese, bread and sausage. Sometimes a fresh tomato or red currants could be added for a feast. I was pretty sure I could cook, but the room did not include cooking privileges. We bought a bread knife and Mom and I learned how to slice bread.

The family of six lived downstairs, and included Frau Bauer's sisters and brothers, as well as a friendly 17 year-old niece, Brigitte. Brigitte and I enrolled in a machine sewing class. Night after night, girls whirled the buttons on the machines and learned how to change colors and thread up the fancy stitches correctly. The first project was to learn to sew a variety of stitches in straight lines, create a seam and produce a flat machine embroidered case for pressed handkerchiefs. The process was a lot like constructing an old-fashioned embroidery sampler to learn all sorts of fancy stitches. German girls learned to embroider household items, from tablecloths, placemats and napkins to hems of dresses and aprons. Ellie, who had begun making dresses at the age of 10, was astonished at the impracticality of it all. I learned to sew in a straight line and loved watching the variegated yellow and green strands form bands and patterns across the fabric.

The three of us were cozy in the big room, with occasional roughhousing or squabbling breaking evening quiet. But when Louis came over, it became raucous and fun. Birgitte's grandmother complained about the noise. *"Können sie nicht ruhiger sein?"* (Can't you be quieter?) Mom didn't understand her. Was it the children's incessant fighting? The laughter from still another of Louis' pranks? Or was it the time that Louis and Ellie spent alone in the little room with just the twin beds and a table, drinking wine while the children played downstairs? Mom never complained about these visits, but Jack was very concerned about the bruises on her neck. Louis said it was from kissing, and that mommy wasn't hurt, and so Jack practiced kissing and biting on the soft part of his arms to make the purple bruises. Apparently a man was supposed to be able to kiss really, really hard. You need to suck to make your arm turn purple. This was really, really creepy. When I asked Brigitte about kissing bruises, she just stared at me.

After a week in the new room, Ellie came home from the shops with cheese, bread and salami. She and Louis were going away for the weekend. She paid for a hot bath and washed her long blonde hair. Louis had told her that they would only take what she could fit into her large purse, so black underwear and a new lipstick went into the side pockets. She put on her black clothes, kissed us goodbye, and asked us to please not get into a fight or make any noise. I was to take care of Jack.

By Sunday morning, Frau Bauer realized that we were alone, so on the day of rest, Brigitte invited me to help prepare the main meal while the other women went to church. The kitchen work began at mid-morning, cleaning vegetables from the gardens, trimming meat, and preparing buttery sauces. At 1:00 a full meal was in place for eight people, schnitzels, tiny spaetzle dumplings, broccoli and a salad fresh from the garden. It took two hours to wash the dishes before serving coffee and an apple cake. By the time that was cleared out, the men were asking for fried eggs and potatoes plus cold meats for an evening supper. When did the girls have rest and time for card games? Brigitte explained that the entire woman's day is spent in the kitchen, and it would be so when she married. She did not have a boyfriend yet, but at 17 she was a good enough cook to get married if she met someone.

At first the rented room in Wolfsburg seemed cheap compared to what housing cost in the US at the time, but families didn't earn much. A factory job paid about $100 per month and that could easily support a couple. Mom's U.S. teaching job had paid $400 per month, and we were receiving child support of $70 per month, so long as Hermann did not find out that we were in Europe. Shirley took care of the Elmira house and deposited checks each month before she forwarded mom's money from the U.S. It could take up to two weeks to arrive. Hermann, who was happily remarried with a new family, never missed a payment. Ellie was expecting to get a job that would use some of her qualifications as a teacher or a seamstress. But, as a new resident of Germany, Ellie did not have enough language to even read and write on a job application. She had all kinds of work experience in sales and teaching, but no way to use her experiences without the language. After a few weeks, it appeared that Mom could not get a good job without better command of the German language. Somehow the unencumbered life was not going to work without employment. You don't have much freedom when you are broke with two kids to take care of.

*   *   *

One night after work at the VW factory, Louis announced that we would make a little family trip to Munich for the weekend. This was to be the first of many weekly journeys. First, there was Jack's German Language lesson: "Mein Vater ist tod und meine Mutter ist verrückt." (My father is dead and my mother is crazy.) Louis told Jack that if he got lost he was to say that to strangers and they would help him. Ellie laughed hysterically. I was not sure that the statement was false. But I looked under the bed for my white train case and began to pack it with underwear, soap, a clean blouse and a little stuffed skunk, Tinky. Jack continued to get all sorts of attention, because he said his sentence over and over with the adults burbling on about how cute he was.

Suddenly, Ellie and Louis looked over at me.

"What are you doing?"

"I'm all packed."

"Oh honey, you're not taking that."

"Where do I put my things?"

"Everything goes in my purse."

"We can't carry everything for a trip in your purse!"

"You will need two pairs of underpants and a toothbrush. Everything else stays. No toys, no books, no games."

"I am going to take Tinky."

"Actually you are not . . . ."

"Then I am staying home with Brigitte."

Louis intervened and found a corner of his bag for Tinky. He had also packed a mini-chess set and two new magazines.

Louis had asked Mom to purchase Eurailpasses in the US, good for unlimited European first class travel. He than entered the start dates in pencil, since European conductors were not familiar with the one month pass. Every month, he erased the date, and changed it to the following month. This wasn't exactly legal, but Louis was not a stickler for the law. The idea was that each Friday after work, we could board an overnight train, sleep on the train, and then go sightseeing for two days. First class compartments had nice bunks, and we could save on hotels. A new brown canvas rucksack held bread, cheese, salami and apples for the weekend. I loathed salami and fatty meats. I liked vegetables, and there weren't any.

"I'm sorry sir, we, don't have a first class car on this train. The brakes were faulty. We will need to find you seats in the main coach," the conductor responded when Louis presented the new passes. Instead of resting in the bunks, we arrived in Munich at 5:00 a.m. with no sleep. Louis announced that the proper breakfast would be Weissbier and Weisswurst – beer and veal sausage. Beer for breakfast at 5:30 a.m. was a novel idea. So is the idea of floating lemon seeds up and down in the tall glasses. Unfortunately, I was still nauseous from the train ride. "Oh, lemon will cure that. She has too much bitter in her system. The lemon will straighten her right out." Ellie looked at Louis helplessly —my constant stomachaches were getting on her nerves. "Here, take this lemon and suck all the juice from it. It will taste sour, then sweet, and you'll feel much better." It didn't work. We ran frantically for the bathrooms.

Lesson time. Ellie excitedly spoke about an "old peanut" the Alte Pinakothek, a very famous art museum. She had a list of the artworks that she wanted to see. Louis suggested that everyone needed to learn about German cars and engineering. Somehow, Louis and Jack end up leading the way to the Deutsches Museum to investigate machinery for the day and we trudged dutifully behind them.

On the Sunday night train back to Wolfsburg, the two adults placed Jack and me in one car, and then found another compartment for their trip back. Jack had no idea what to do. Forget "don't talk to strangers." Strangers were the only people who were curious about the two kids traveling without adults. The brown canvas rucksack was empty and there was no money. Maybe we could get a drink from the lavatory, but the sign said "Eau non potable/ Kein Trinkwasser." We were not supposed to drink the water from the faucets. Could it be any worse than the breakfast beers? Jack drank some. I held the little skunk tightly under my neck as the train rocked back and forth.

# CHAPTER EIGHT

## The Fairy Tale

Are there holes in the Harz mountains where children can be taken, never to be heard from again? Do pagan spirits still live and bring a force of evil into the world? The Harz mountains are the settings for many of the fairytales of the Grimm Brothers—warnings to children that step parents may wish them dead, that strangers may not be kind, to beware of old ladies, and to watch out for wolves or attractive men on the road.

Mom was taking us to Goslar. On the train we read from Grimm's fairy tales, the scary German ones, not the Disney princess versions. Real witches live in the forests of the Harz mountains. In fact any older woman without a man may be one. The old ladies believe in the power of herbs, and in the transformations of love and loss. Dwarfism exists, and some children and adults have stunted and bent bones. Long ago the bent children were sent out to live in the mountains until they died from exposure or found a community of others like them. The little towns in these mountains each have their own powers, and the pagan spirits of the mountains emerge even during Christian holidays. By the time we arrived, Mom had us wondering about what had really happened to the children of nearby Hameln. Had a piper really taken them away, or was this a tale of tragedy from the days of the Black Plague? First the rats, then the children . . . what was this about? Would Goslar be dark and creepy, or would it be fun?

We stepped off the train, and walked through the town. Tiny doorways looked as if they led into the ground. They were just right for elves, fairies, and dwarves, but not nearly high enough for Mom and me to stand up in.

"People used to be much smaller."

Eight year old Jack was playing with the child sized door. "Why?"

"Maybe we eat more now."

"But then we would just be fat, wouldn't we?" Mom wasn't sure. If babies and children do not have enough to eat, they may not grow to full height. Or maybe the people here were really shorter. The streets were so close that the sun couldn't reach us. Suddenly we stood in a large open plaza with a thousand year old cathedral shading one entire side. The doors of the cathedral were the height of several men. Maybe dwarves and giants had really lived side by side.

Jack ran around the cathedral, then came squealing back. On one side of the cathedral is the local patron "saint" – Goslar, a dwarf who shits gold. A little man clings to a column, with gilded turds coming out of his ass. The quiet prosperity of the town with its evidence of guilds and respect for hard work is largely attributed to Goslar, but Christian prayers are chanted inside the cathedral, just to make sure. The mountains hide all sorts of secrets. Maybe the townspeople have shared a supernatural secret there for generations. It is said that a hunter tied his horse up more than a thousand years ago, and that as the horse pawed at the earth, a vein of pure silver appeared. A visit to the nearby mines brought images of seven little men digging into the earth, then returning to their cottage for dinner with Snow White. If the ground beneath the town were silver, then wouldn't everyone be rich?

Things in Goslar were older than we could imagine. The Germany that we lived in was less than fifteen years old. Suddenly every house in town was 500 years old, and the major buildings were even older. Mom explained how the quaint black-brown and white houses were built of timber, framed in timber, and filled in with rocks and mud so that the whitewashed front of each house was a design of dark timbers and bright plastered and painted surfaces. The intricate designs continued in the mullioned windows with their patterns of leaded panes. Grapevines grew along the walls, and boxes of red geraniums hung from the windows. It was enchanting.

"I have an idea for a game." Mom was teaching again. "Let's guess what these signs are. Before people could read and write, craftsmen had to make a picture sign so that kids and adults could buy or trade for the things they needed. Look, there is a tailor, with a spool of thread and a needle." The guild signs provided our vocabulary lessons during the weekend. Jack found a bakery. I noticed a shoemaker's sign with funny pointed boots. No French high heels in there. "Why is there a rope maker? Couldn't people just buy the rope?" Mom twisted her ponytail tightly, let it fall loose, and then explained, "They had to be able to make everything they needed. People traded what they had." She twisted the ponytail again. "It's a lot of work to twist fibers into a strong rope." She pinned the knot of hair securely to the back of her head, and went on. "People make things. In fact, our family built ships. Grandfather has a big leather and copper book with family and business records back to 1452. Funny enough, grandmother's family made masts for ships a hundred years before they ever met each other." "So grandmother's friend Mrs. Schumacher came from a family of cobblers?" "Maybe, and how about Carpenter, Smith and Taylor? Those are all trades too. Some of the guild signs and trades don't seem to fit in this day and age, but then neither does Goslar." Jack was lost in thought. Then he offered his observation. "I need to go to the bathroom. If it comes out gold, then I never ever have to do any work." I slugged him.

Late in the evening we settled into a small room in a hotel that was actually part of the city gates. Long after dark, voices of children singing and shouting got louder and louder. Every child in Goslar was dressed in white and carrying a torch, marching through the town and through the gate. "Mom, please can we go? We want to see where they are going!" Thinking of what happened to children in nearby Hamelin, Mom said, "You will see so much more of their celebration right here from this upstairs window. Look, you can see the entire procession, and they can't." We watched until the last child had left the town. The singing and lights continued into the distance.

I pulled out my deck of cards and began teaching Jack the numbers and the German names of the face cards. American cards have a Jack, but the Jack in a German deck is called "Bube" or boy. Jack was fascinated with his new name, "Bube." My dumb brother was "the booboo." But, he was the only one in the family who was named with a face card. Mom made a pretty good queen of diamonds with her wild earrings and rings, but she didn't actually have any diamonds. She didn't care for them. In the room that night there was a tiny white moth, and Jack named him Bube. He chased the moth around the room until he fell asleep. In the morning the moth was found dead. But when the white moths returned each spring, well, who knew? Maybe Bube would start out again as a worm and come back.

On Sunday morning we walked through the streets, cleansed of the pagan spirits from the night before. Either that or we had joined the fairy tale ourselves. Jack now wore a single pair of lederhosen all the time and everywhere. It was a cheaper way to deal with his ever lengthening legs and our lack of a proper laundry. He blended right into the groups of other boys. I was in some motley mess of gold plaid slacks from an outfit that I had not been allowed to wear in Berlin, mixed with a gold floral top that had once been acceptable. I didn't blend with anything. Mom was in black, from her cap and sweater to her pointy toed boots. All we needed was a cat.

In the dirt ahead of us lay a ten Mark bill. Often the budget for an entire weekend trip was ten Marks, so Mom suggested that we each pick out a gift to celebrate our good fortune. At the cigarette shop, I chose a little red headed witch, the kind that people hang in their kitchens, and Jack picked out a picture postcard and a pin of Goslar, the little man who shits gold.

# CHAPTER NINE

## Independence

Every child dreams of a world without adults and their rules. My storybook heroine was Pippi Longstocking, or *Pippi Langenstrumpf* as she is known in Germany. *Handarbeit* is what we call fancywork and on Tuesdays the girls would sit for two hours and embroider or knit, while readers took turns reading aloud from the adventures of Pippi Longstocking. Pippi was a little girl who lived entirely alone, and whose resourcefulness was the envy of all little girls. Louis and Ellie decided that I was ready to have a go at independence and could take care of Jack for a weekend.

On Friday, Louis arrived at the rented room soon after work. Ellie had packed the rucksack with sandwiches, hardboiled eggs, and some fruit for the weekend, and they walked to the train station. All trains to larger cities connected through Hanover, a much larger town in the region. The Wolfsburg-Hanover train left at 7:00 p.m., or 19:00, arriving in Hanover around 21:00. The big continental overnight trains left close to midnight. They were off on their adult adventure.

In the Wolfsburg room, I got everything ready for the weekend. The camembert cheese was not ripe yet, so I hung it outside the window of the room. That way it would ripen in the sun and not stink the place up. Jack and I decided to play games and tell secrets. "Do you think Louis will ask Mom to marry him? I think she wants him to."

I dealt the cards. Jack looked at his, and tried to put them in order. He kept dropping them. Then he sniffled. "I miss Bozo a lot. Do you think he likes living with Mel and Linda?"

"Jack, you need to draw a card and throw one away. If you have three of the same kind, that's good. Keep them together. And don't show them."

"What do you mean by kind? The pictures or the numbers?"

"Either one. Three numbers in a row with a matching picture, or the same number three times with different pictures."

"I don't understand how this goes. Do you think they will give us more brothers and sisters?"

"Who will?"

"Mom and Louis."

"Good Grief Jack, they don't even want to take care of us! And I'm not going to take care of any babies unless I get paid. I don't even know if they do . . . . that."

"Do what?"

"Oh never mind. Gin."

We added up Mom's plusses and minuses. She was pretty and knew how to fix a house. She was not a good cook. She was really tired in the mornings, but Louis was bouncy and happy enough for both of them. Louis was perfect – the first person Ellie had dated who would be a cool dad.

There were no kitchen privileges in our room. By Saturday evening the wheel of Camembert cheese still hung in a bag outside the sunny window. The cheese went runny and stinky. The stale brown bread was stored in a dresser, along with a large serrated knife. I knew how to use a paring knife with adult supervision, but I had not used the bread knife by myself. The heavy bread was like a lump of partially dried clay, a baking project gone bad. I placed it on the table, and began to saw through it. Suddenly the knife slipped off the hard crust and two fingers were cut to the bone. I started to cry, and Jack ran outside screaming for help. Neighbors came and tried to stop the bleeding. They packed dirty cobwebs all over the fingers. Then the hand was tied up with a splint and a bandage. Clearly we would not be eating our three day old bread and cheese. Someone must have mentioned the predicament to the grandmother downstairs. As tired as she was of children's noise, she invited us to her kitchen for Hungarian Goulasch with fresh dumplings. It was our first hot meal in three days and it was wonderful.

That Sunday night we could stay up as late as we wanted. Monday school was far, far away. I might not even go. There was no parent to tuck us in. Hours after midnight, the door opened. Louis was kissing Ellie. Jack sat up, "Mommy!"

"Oh baby – I missed you so much." Ellie sat down on his bed, and stroked his hair.

"You're lying."

"Hi honey . . . how was your weekend?"

I did not respond. A freezing silence followed Ellie's question.

"Kate?"

"I'm not talking to you."

Louis then intervened. "Hey Kate, I brought you something." He had a little doll with him, a cute blonde plastic figure, chubby, with a Bier Stein in each hand. He set it beside me in the bed. I looked at it closely, then broke off its hand with the Bier Stein.

"My god, Kate! What is wrong with you?" Mom grabbed at my arm and then noticed the filthy bloody bandage and the homemade splint.

"What happened?"

"Kate cut her hand when she was making me a sandwich. The bread knife is different, and the bread was hard. It slipped and she got hurt." Jack spoke sadly of the accident.

"Who wrapped up her hand?"

"Brigitte helped her, but Kate needs to go to the doctor, but we don't have any money, do we? The grandmother gave her cobwebs for the bleeding."

I was so quiet that I could hear my own breathing. There were no words and there were no tears. Mom looked at Louis. This situation clearly needed an adult to tell Louis and Ellie what to do. Finally some words came. "I found Hermann's address in your papers when I was looking for some money to buy food. He lives in Salt Lake City. If you ever take off like this again, I will write him and ask him to send for Jack and me." Then I rolled over on my stomach and covered the tears in my pillow.

Mom really got everything wrong. In a popular book called *Lolita*, a man dated a woman, but he really wanted her teenaged daughter for his lover. Obviously he hadn't spent a lot of time talking to the girl about this. Anyway, Mom was retelling *Lolita* over and over in her head. She thought that I was attracted to Louis, because it didn't seem logical that a capable young girl would want attention from a mother. After all I had a young woman's body. In the old days, I would have been ready to be married and on my own at twelve. Her confused interpretations of the people around us made things worse. She was certainly reading the wrong books. Maybe she needed to reread "Heidi" and send us back to our grandparents. If we were orphans we could get on with normal lives.

As far as Mom was concerned, things had to get straightened out in a hurry. The Frankfurt Auto Show was the following weekend, and the VW marketing staff was invited to bring their families along. We were going as Louis' family. This was important because a salesman should not be single. Men with families deserve promotions. He might get a promotion if his family was nice. So, Mom bought me a very pretty white satin garter belt and stockings, a wonderful, indulgent gift. We were supposed to look our very best and make a nice impression on the VW executives. A clean bandage was wrapped around the cuts, and they were beginning to close up. I was instructed to act the part of an adult, and that in turn, I would be treated like one.

That Friday, we boarded the train in our best clothes, Louis in a business suit, Mom in a proper black dress, and me in the pink polka dotted Berlin dress with the green sash. I don't know why we couldn't take a suitcase of clean clothes, just for this one trip. Maybe it was not all about clean clothes. For Jack, the main issue was to keep his hands and face clean. His fingernails had gotten so dirty that Louis told him to hide his hands when train conductors and immigration officials came through. There was no money for hotels, and we had to look nice for an entire weekend, even without bathrooms to wash up in, or beds to get enough sleep. Louis' idea was to teach us to sleep on command. Astronauts do that, and we could be as smart as astronauts if we tried. We were ordered to sleep from 7:00 – 9:00 on the Wolfsburg train, then to sleep from 11:00 PM to 3:30 AM on the Frankfurt train. Louis never wore a watch, but he always knew the time within 10 minutes. He could sleep and wake up on cue. Sure enough, we were awakened and ready to move when the train pulled into Frankfurt at 3:57 a.m. The concept was that six hours of sleep time had been available. With time out for fighting and complaining, Jack and I had each had about three hours sleep. Louis would treat us to a hotel room on Saturday night so that we could all take baths and sleep in beds.

We arrived on the showroom floor at 08:00 and Louis was proudly manning a display of 1961 Volkswagens. The VW Beetle behind him was number five million, and had just rolled off the assembly line. For two days we looked at displays of cars, never leaving the convention hall or straying out of sight of the adults. Mom's task was to keep walking the hall, with Jack and me in tow. Jack was fascinated with all the cars. He found the largest, the smallest and the fastest moving land vehicles. Mom was trying to point out design features and ask questions. I was laughing at Mom's sudden interest in cars. We didn't even have a car in Elmira.

\*   \*   \*

Between our improvised weekend trips, Jack and I went to our respective schools. The Gymnasium is a type of high school for students who show the potential to have a university education. An educator at heart, Louis often brought books and magazines over, engaged me in academic conversations, and helped me understand my German schoolwork. Algebra explanations had to be filtered from German to English, which only worked if I had taken clear notes in the German. I was developing excellent work habits, but with no comprehension of the content. Explaining symbols and abstract ideas is difficult enough in any language. Louis did everything possible to make study both recreational and relevant. Because Berlin was such a hot worldwide issue, he used it as a study topic. I was assigned reading from Time (in English) and Der Spiegel (in German). Then we would sit on the long train rides, discuss the study topics and compare perspectives in the two publications on world issues.

Trying to learn a complex language like German without a solid foundation in English grammar was a perplexing and pretty much exasperating affair. Jack picked up basic playground language rapidly. I didn't want to communicate in baby talk. I was an advanced reader and writer in English and really struggled with expressing my genuine thoughts in German. German classmates were learning French, and the plan was, "I can make a chart of the French verb and its forms, write the German next to that, and the English next to that. That way, I will pass French, and learn proper German quickly." But, often the rules were not the same for the three languages, so there was a complete breakdown of the meanings. It was like playing telephone, where the meaning changed with each repetition of the words.

On long train rides, Louis drilled us in conjugating verbs. Mom really tried hard to get her lessons right. Apparently a lot of German verbs are irregular. She didn't really like regular things, so this should be right up her alley but she couldn't remember them from one week to the next. Louis explained the process in English before we began our German recitations. "Conjugate? Mom, isn't that what planaria (microscopic worms) do to make even littler planaria. Didn't you show us that when you took biology last summer? Does that work with words too?"

Louis explained that fluent sentences were all a result of our ability to conjugate verbs. The vocabulary was difficult enough, but changing it every time you open your mouth? He tried to make sense out of this process.

"It is how we choose the verbs that will help us put the sentence together. In English, the verb drives the sentence, and it is close to the beginning so that we know what we are talking about, who or what is taking the action, and how. Neat little phrases follow along, like the cars on a freight train. In German, the verb can be stuck on the back end of the sentence like a caboose. Even more interesting is the case of a split verb, one where the beginning part is in one piece of the sentence, and the ending is somewhere else."

Okay, now I was lost. Not only do we not know who is driving the train, we don't even know if the train is being driven. Is there an engineer on board? Do we have a destination?"

Maybe conjugating has something to do with the endless *compoundcompoundcompound* words, sort of linguistic freight cars. Who ever thought of jamming eight and ten syllables together into something that cannot be pronounced or identified once it has been decoded? Apparently the verbs are tied to people and things, time, and moods, and each time you use one you have to speak and write it differently. Brilliant. *"He goes now away running. I go now away from my studies in frustration screaming."*

The rules of grammar seemed to refute the concept of the orderly German mind. A long sentence can easily be 50-75 words and seem to have no sense of direction until the last word is read or spoken. I had been thrown under the train long before that point or as the German statement goes, *"I am under the train beaten."* Is the English image messy enough? In English a word is a subject of something, or an object, indicated by its placement in the phrase. Every noun, pronoun, and adjective in German has a multiple guess game attached to it, with a trail of suffixes revealing the role of the word in this grammatical train wreck. Then, in case you memorized all of these, there are three choices of masculine, feminine and neuter that attaches to nouns, pronouns and adjectives. Each of the nouns has an assigned gender and its attached pronouns and adjectives share the gender assignation. This means that as a young girl, a Mädchen, is a neuter. A Junge, or boy, is masculine. So is his dog, even if it is a bitch. A Frau, like mother is feminine, but I didn't even have the status of a housecat, unless it has been spayed, (in English of course.) Louis laughed. "Gender is overrated anyway."

There was one good part to using German in school. I could fake reading and writing really easily. The vowels and consonants all had consistent sounds. For instance, in English, there were at least five sounds just for the letter "o" and a little kid had to learn them in order to read a story about "Once there was a brown doggie who went bow-wow for a bone on a hot day." In German, an "o" was an "o" and I could read anything aloud, and sound just great. I have no idea what we studied, except that "Prinz Eugenius was an edle Ritter." Oh, well. Sure hope he had a nice dog."

# CHAPTER TEN

## New Wine/Life Song

The harvest ritual had changed very little over the centuries. The late September days were busy ones. School was out for a couple weeks, because the kids who lived on farms needed to help get the crops in. With the shortage of labor in Germany, every family member had work to do. Grasses were cut by hand and bound into little conical bundles to dry. Sometimes enormous cylinders of hay lay on the ground, baled by horse drawn machinery. The cutting and drying had to happen quickly, before the rains came. These grasses were winter food and bedding for the animals. Grain was to be milled for breads or brewed into beer. Local carnivals with homemade brews and fresh sausages were set up everywhere.

Uncle Bill had written us to say that Mutti Liddy and Annike were coming to visit Vienna during the fall holiday. Bill and Monika were now living in Eisenstadt, out in the wine country east of the city. So, when the last paragraph of the letter included an invitation for us to join the group in Vienna, I was thrilled and ready to start packing. There was no way that we were going to live out of mom's purse when we were going for a holiday in Vienna. The packing project was not very successful. Nice new clothes were now stained and worn, and it had been weeks since any of us had had a hot bath or shampoo. Even worse, my filthy little brother could now drink, gamble and swear in German. Once Liddy took a close look at Mom and Louis in their black leathers, the jig would be up. I would not be able to convince anyone that I was a young lady waiting to bloom.

On the up side, it would be a lot of fun to see them again. By now I really missed the Berlin family, the walks and bike rides, and breakfasts on the sunny porch. I even missed the school and the polite girls in my classes. Would Liddy believe me if I said my real family had been killed in a train wreck, and poor Jack and I had been left to these gypsies? Since Jack was scheduled to spend his two-week school vacation at Uncle Bill's, I wasn't sure how that story would fly. Looking out the window after a few hours of rolling sleep, I pondered this scenario and other ideas.

Just after a gray dawn the train was crossing southern Germany into Austria. The hay-ricks began to stack up like tents across the fields. Behind them floated silver rivers and golden mountains, with the onion towers of churches and town halls. Mom explained that as we grew closer and closer to Eastern Europe, we would see changes in the architecture, because two great empires had fought along this river for hundreds of years, leaving their marks in the way they built their castles. We fell in love with the fancies of the Baroque, especially an enormous golden palace that straddled the mountaintops, floating above the Danube. Louis said it was a monastery but how could that be true? Monks live simply and make everything they need. He had shown me that.

Arriving in Vienna after twelve hours on the train, the extended family of various in-laws and out-laws all met up for the first time since the Berlin Wall had been built. "I know this wonderful Weinstube," announced Bill, and he and Monika were under way with six others in tow. At the café the waiters began to pour Neuwein, a two week old crush, very cloudy with a lot of fizz. It tasted like grape soda, a little earthier, and very sweet. The adults warned that it had a very high alcohol content and that the kids would have to drink soda pop instead. Annike then explained that new wine makes people drunk because the grape juice is full of sugar. Logically, then, if we added sugar to the adults' wine, we could watch them get really silly and then do whatever we pleased for the day. So, Annike, Jack and I emptied packets of sugar into the jugs of wine, just to see how the adults would behave. Jack of course had a purely scientific interest. I wanted to see Mutti Liddy out of control, just once, and Annike thought my mother would be funny no matter what. After two hours of glass tipping and snacking, it was time to go and see the city.

High above the city, on top of St. Stephan's cathedral with its zig-zagged roof, Mutti Liddy suddenly panicked, too dizzy to continue the climb across the top. Ellie and Louis considered flying. Jack leaned over the edge, and I began to feel guilty about the sugar. What if these silly adults did something really dangerous? What if someone fell off the steep roof because they were drunk? Drunk people fall and don't even know they are hurt. But the cobblestones below didn't look like a very good place to land.

Bill turned to us, "How would you kids like to ride the largest Ferris wheel in the world?" He piled the group onto the trams and followed in the VW. This Prater Ferris wheel stands more than 200 feet tall, the size of a 20 story office tower. Instead of open seats, cars the size of small train cars enclose passengers in windowed compartments. At the top of the ride, Annike, Jack and I looked out over the entire city of Vienna. Then Jack got the idea of running and jumping from side to side, just to make the car swing a little more. Mom and Liddy were convinced that the world was turning beneath them.

Uncle Bill decided to take them both to Eisenstadt and put them to bed.

*   *   *

Going to bed and actually sleeping are not the same thing. Bill's generosity meant that six people were sharing a single bedroom/living room for the weekend. Some of the air mattresses from his camping years worked. Others were leaky. I had one of the leaky ones. But once we were all up and about for a day of fun together, the sleep didn't matter so much.

We left Eisenstadt on Sunday afternoon, full of hugs and happiness. For once our conversations would not be monopolized by

Jack's antics. He was going to remain in Eisenstadt for a while, and it was expected that Uncle Bill would straighten out his manners and his language. Mom and I returned to Wolfsburg with Louis. Mom had a plan for the break as well. Her new job would not begin until the following Monday. She was going to take me to Paris for the week, just the two of us. I couldn't wait for my long promised visit to Paris, and to see the Mona Lisa herself. Mom said that the Louvre is so big that it would take days just to see it all. So on Tuesday I washed the floor of our room, shopped, and packed the rucksack with everything we would need.

The plan was to take the commuter train to Hanover, and then go to Freiburg to surprise Uncle Pete and Aunt Irene. They had moved back to Germany from Elmira, and from Freiburg they could either stay with Peter's family or visit Irene's family in France. They also had a brand new baby.

"Mom, will they be meeting us at the train? How do we know where they live?" She shrugged her shoulders. Obviously communicating with Uncle Pete had not been a part of her planning. It was pretty clear that she had not written. Then she straightened herself up and announced:

"When we get to Freiburg, we will look up the address in the phone book there."

The unanswered question was, "How big is Freiburg and can we walk to Uncle Pete's from the train station?" Another query in this line of thinking was, "If they are living with his family, will they have the same names?" Instead, I reminded Mom of her own rules.

"Shouldn't we call them? You always tell me to call my friends in case they are too busy to play."

"Honey, we don't have a telephone, and I can't understand the operators on the long distance lines."

Ellie had a lot of difficulty using a pay phone. Every call from the railroad station was long distance and needed the assistance of an operator. The operator spoke too quickly, in a voice that was sometimes covered by distortion from the speakers . . . . ccchhhhc . . . name? . . . chhhhhc . . . . hh wahwahwah . . . nummer . . . . The static on phone lines was bad enough, but

operators were very frustrated when they could not understand
a foreign accent. Ellie's funny long American "RRRs" were an
incomprehensible sound to the German ladies. She got almost every
single vowel wrong on names – "Peter" in German should actually
sound like "Pae—t-ʋ –hhh" so they had no idea whom she was trying
to reach. "Dieter? We have no listing."

Once the commuter train arrived in Hannover, Louis decided to
sneak the three of us into the opera. Louis was an artist at sneaking
into theatres. By wearing black performance attire, he could walk
right past a house manager and toward the orchestra pit. If the
house was crowded, "I'm so sorry, I left my stub in my jacket. May
I get it and show it to you?" The TEE (Trans European Express)
wouldn't be leaving until nearly midnight.

The modern Hannover opera house was a favorite stop, and its
colors reminded me a little of home. The main hall was a soft blue
gray with white marble columns and rich violet carpeting. Velvet
curtains and brass fixtures complemented the simply designed
modern interior. But, the opera tonight was incomprehensible.
Antigonae, written by Carl Orff, did not have wonderful singing,
memorable melodies, or meaningful acting. The tragic story was
difficult to understand and uncomfortable listening. I knew enough
to sit quietly through the howling and began to watch what was
happening in the orchestra pit. This seemed to be by far the most
intriguing part of the program, because the orchestra did not look
at all like a symphony orchestra. There were a good dozen pianos,
six funny looking xylophones, three harps, piles of drums, several
violins and some horns. Musicians plucked piano strings, pounded on
the harps, played the xylophones with their fingers and no mallets,
and banged the drums with the cymbals. Obviously Antigonae was
all about percussion, but I couldn't connect the dots very well. It all
sounded like an eggbeater with some screaming on top.

The TEE was full that night. The plan for this night was to travel
to Freiburg, in the Black Forest. Uncle Pete had been reassigned
by the US Army, and was now living in there at his family's country
estate. We were on board ten minutes before departure, but ended
up crowding in with four other people. Each compartment had six

seats that could unfold into three couchettes, so this meant the couchettes could not be pulled down for the night.

"Louis, we don't have any place to sleep." Mom hated it when I complained about uncomfortable train rides. This was going to be a long night. She gave me "the look," and then spoke through her teeth.

"Yes, I know you had to get up at 5:30 this morning to get to school before it was even light. Yes, you walked all the way back, cleaned the room, packed, and walked into town again. Thank you for the nice job."

"I'm tired! It is almost midnight. Can't we just find another car?"

"Kate, there is no solution to this problem."

Since our train trips were planned for eight-hour overnight accommodations in sleeping cars, a full train was a lost night of sleep that could not be made up. By this time, Mom knew that having to sit up all night would affect the entire weekend. She would miss her beauty sleep and get moody. Louis would not be feeling very romantic, which would make her mood worse. My discomfort would get everyone angry, but the problem wouldn't get solved. It was a kind of post-nuclear chain reaction, and no matter what, I was going to be at fault. I was an uncooperative hobo. But, we were going to see Uncle Pete. There would probably even be guest beds with feather pillows at his house. I hadn't slept in a feather bed in two months and would like that very much on these chilly nights.

There was reason to hope for a feather bed. The Moritz family owned one of the finest riding schools in Europe. They took in summer boarders but it was October now and the riding school would be closed for the school year. These were the horses of kings, or at least the kings of horses. Peter showed me a picture of himself riding a horse before he was two years old. He said one day his 92 year-old grandfather drove a horse drawn plough from dawn to dusk, rode home, and just toppled from his mount. The old man had spent his entire life in the saddle. The family had occupied these lands since the 1300s, and during the 18th and 19th centuries, they kept horses for the Kaisers. After the world wars of the 20th century, they decided not to give up the country estate and instead began to board horses and to teach riding to newer generations. Students came from all over Europe, including several from Berlin. Because Berlin was enclosed, children from the city could not get out to the countryside for short visits, so a month at riding school was a real privilege. Teenagers from wealthy homes, luxury city condominiums and other country estates would pay tuition for the summer privileges of grooming horses, mucking stables and learning to ride.

Nearly forty horses were stabled there, lined up in their stalls. We walked down the aisle greeting every horse. There were short and tall, dark horses and light, and a different personality for each animal. Some were for riding, some for shows, and there were ponies for little kids.

Peter stopped at one stall, "Bonjour Roland! And how is the prince of all horses this morning?" Roland was a prize winning thoroughbred jumper; he had even won a high jump award at the Grand Prix, leaping nearly seven feet over barriers. "Roland can turn, see an obstacle coming, and plan just how he will leap over it. He is one of the great animals. Would you like to give him a carrot?" As I placed the carrot in the palm of my hand and looked up at Peter, he continued, "Many horses will be afraid of the barriers in a jumping contest, but Roland is bold." His dark forehead was soft and velvety, and he nuzzled me silently – the strongest and the bravest of all the animals.

We walked on. Entire rooms were full of riding tack, saddles and leather bridles. Some very plain leather harnesses were used for farm work, and some elaborately decorated saddles trimmed with silver were used in shows and parades. There was a collection of more than 50 pairs of different kinds of stirrups. These hundreds of pieces of leather and metal equipment had a single use, which was to help a rider hold onto a horse. The smaller carriages and buggies were right out of storybooks. You could imagine your favorite characters being transported by a coachman, maybe to secret meeting places. Peter explained that in order to drive just two horses, the driver would have to handle several leather traces in his hand, and know which ones to pull to get the horses to move, speed up, slow down, or turn. In the next barn were the large

coaches like the illustrations in fairy tale books – fancy enough
to carry Cinderella. Some of these were more than 200 years old.
Peter explained that the family had been professional cavaliers for
centuries until the mid twentieth century when horses had become a
luxury item instead of a necessity.

The light in the Black Forest is a puzzle. We stepped outside
the dark barns into the bright October sunlight, and then within
a few steps we would be cast into the forests that surrounded the
property. The Black Forest was so thick that you could not see the
sky. It actually was black as night, from the soft pine needles on the
ground, up through the green-black branches of trees, and toward
an imagined space beyond the forest. Darkness and light alternated
as we walked along.

Uncle Pete was a favorite of all children, very stern, but always
with an interesting story or something to do. In Elmira he had taken
us on hikes, told jokes, played guitar and sang silly songs. A favorite
was, "*Meine Oma hat Toilettenpapier mit Blumen – My grandmother
has flowered toilet paper.*" The song was even funnier now, because
the soft white tissues used in the U.S. were a fantasy from the past.
It had been months since we had seen commercials of cute babies
cuddled up next to toilet paper. Coarse scratchy pieces of paper
toweling, and even pieces of newspaper were laid out in public
bathrooms for people to clean their butts. Sometimes a girl could
only wish for an Oma with soft flowered paper and maybe even
some sweet smelling soaps.

While Peter took me to the stables, Mom and Louis learned that
they had arrived in Freiburg unannounced on the busiest day of the
year. There would be no meals or tea at the house on this day, and
all beds were going to be occupied by paying guests. The Harvest
weekend was an exhibition day, when young riders from all over
the countryside would be demonstrating what they had learned.
All forty of the Moritz horses were bathed, brushed and groomed
until they were shining. The leather tack, saddles, and braces
were smooth and supple from all the buffing. Every piece of metal
had been polished. But, Peter had to run the entire show himself,
organizing and timing one routine after another. The students and

horses had learned their paces, but Moritz horsemen still needed to observe every step of the day to keep the students and animals safe. It had been a difficult week already. Peter's cousin and partner in the riding academy had broken his leg in a fall from a horse. Then a new racehorse had tried to break out of its fetters, and had cut its knee to the bone. Just a month ago, another horse had reared up with a rider on its back and fallen over backwards, sustaining a fatal head injury.

But this was a new day. Always energetic and enthusiastic, Peter led me over to the barn to watch dressage, horses that learn to dance. The beautiful animals and their young riders coordinated each movement in time to music, dancing a four footed ballet. Sometimes pairs and teams of four moved together, each foot pacing at the same time, each head bowing or lifting simultaneously. The open viewing stand at the end of the arena faced both inside and outside, so that viewers could watch exhibitions in the barn and then turn outside to see riders who were galloping, jumping hurdles and leaping over high gates. Horses and riders jumped higher and higher, faster and faster as if they were flying. The horses understood all types of commands that I could not begin to comprehend.

After seeing several routines, I walked down to the apartment where Irene and Ellie were talking, thinking that maybe I could join in with the women. Irene had a new baby, and it would have been fun except it was too little to play. All you could do was hold it, and after a while babies get heavy and sometimes a little soggy. Mom and Aunt Irene were talking about some pills, and Ellie was very excited about the information. The new pills were supposed to keep women from having babies. This conversation made no sense, because clearly Irene loved her new baby, and since she had a baby, she would not want to take pills to keep babies away. Ellie was not married to Louis, so she couldn't have a baby, so she didn't need pills either. It was a mystery as to why she would want some. Boring.

I headed back toward the barns. The most exciting part of the tournament, high jumping, was beginning. Each horse and rider had to jump hurdles, walls, or objects. Suddenly, there was screaming and whinnying outside the arena. Roland was coming forward with

Peter and two other men. The king of all horses was limping on three feet, and the right forefoot was horribly injured. Loud applause and shouting came from the big barn, as animals and students each made their runs on the obstacle course.

Several pools of blood and clumps of tissue on the cobblestone pathway indicated that another accident had occurred. Uncle Pete had led the horse to a place between the stables and the hay barn, where he couldn't escape. Apparently the animal had kicked his forefoot with his hindfoot when he was going over a tight pair of hurdles. Half of his foot was broken off, with just the hard portion of the hoof remaining. Horses' legs are very delicate, and a thousand pound horse cannot survive without full use of his legs and hooves. The animal is on its feet for its entire life. He stands almost immediately after birth; his first meal is taken standing up next to the mare. He sleeps standing up, and when he is not standing, he is walking or running, or even towing heavy farm equipment. Like our own feet and hands, the hoof area is extremely sensitive, and once it is injured the animal is in agony.

The screams continued. A veterinarian had been called to put the horse down, but since it was Saturday, he suggested that they just try to comfort the animal for a while. Hoses were dragged across the yard, and a spray of cold water was used to counteract the pain. After two hours, the doctor arrived and examined the animal. He opened his black leather bag and removed a syringe and a vial. Very carefully he poured the liquid into the syringe. Peter held the horse's head and looked into the eyes of the poor animal. The flood of its thoughts drowned us as we shared its agony.

"What is happening to me?
What have you done to me?
What did I do wrong?
Why does my chest hurt?
Who are you?
Where am I?" The flanks began to drop toward the cobblestones, and the other men tried to direct the fall. The knees buckled, and Roland slipped to the ground. Finally Peter put the head down and placed his hand over the horse's chest. The animal had been beaten,

and he had been beaten. Peter hoped that the horse had gone on to a better place.

This was not going to be the night for a little carefree Bohemian laughter and some drinking songs. We quietly left Irene and walked away from the courtyard. Louis gathered us up and we headed back to the train station, where they discussed a revision of plans. Ellie kissed Louis goodbye. Louis was going to return to Wolfsburg for his work. Mom's new job was not going to start for another week. My school holiday had just begun and we intended to use it well. A long line of people waiting for the Paris train signaled us that the cars would be too crowded, and accommodations would be full. There was a train headed back northward to Hamburg. This train was very crowded also, and for the second night, there was no sleep to be had. By morning the sun wasn't up, and neither were we.

# CHAPTER ELEVEN

## Mermaids

Hamburg was all gray: the skies, the buildings and peoples' clothes. Even Sunday best was dull, gloomy gray and black. Women didn't even wear colored scarves. We exited the train station and strolled down a narrow alleyway to find a little café. Instead we found an old church with a new metal steeple, put up after the war. Suddenly the morning chimes began to ring and echo down the little street – tone upon tone, color on color, no particular melodies, but each bell seemed to pick up the harmonies of the others. I begged mother to stay in the alley, and just listen. Then we walked very slowly back to the train station, with the music ringing in our ears.

In 1961 the Hamburg train station was completely black, black iron framing, black soot, black trains. Mom commented, "Of all the things that were destroyed in the war, how in hell did they miss this train station?" Good question. But the train to Copenhagen was pulling onto the track.

This time, after two nights with no sleep, we had an entire compartment to ourselves. The beautiful blue Scandinavian car was nicer than any hostel we had ever stayed in. Mom fell over onto the soft couch, put her sweater under her head and was asleep before we began to roll. Our naps were interrupted at the end of land in Germany, where the train tracks end and all train cars were loaded onto ferry boats to go to Denmark. Passenger cars, trucks, freight trains and people filled up the enormous boats. Once on the boat, people left their compartments, and went upstairs to the main dining salon. Most of the trip was to be over water, and the smorgasbord on the ferry was the main entertainment. More than 500 elaborately plated dishes were served: soups, cold meats and fishes, displays of herring and eel, cheeses, salads, carved vegetables, meats, pastries and puddings, little swans made out of creampuffs and filled with custard, and giant swans carved from ice. We only tried things that we had never seen before, and after three trips to the buffet there wasn't even room for a second cream puff swan. The shores of Denmark were in sight.

One of my proudest childhood possessions was a magnificent edition of the stories of Hans Christian Andersen. Mom had given it to me for Christmas when I was nine. All the illustrations had been drawn by children from around the world. How could an art teacher not buy this book? Even the very youngest artists had captured the joy and sadness of the stories. A hopelessly clumsy duck was painted by a four year old. A startling image of the little match girl and her glorious vision of heaven was painted by an Egyptian child who had never known the cold of a Scandinavian Christmas. So, a decision was made to follow the trail of this favorite author around Copenhagen. The Little Mermaid was seated silently in the harbor, having given up her voice in hopes of being with her lover for all time.

Ellie stood silently, retelling the famous story in her mind. *"Can I not do anything to win an immortal soul?" "No!" answered the grandmother. "Only if a man were to love you so that you should be more to him than father or mother; if he should cling to you with his every thought and with all his love, and let the priest lay his right hand in yours with a promise of faithfulness here and in all eternity, then his soul would be imparted to your body, and you would receive a share of the happiness of mankind."* (H.C. Andersen)

Why wasn't the mermaid wearing a bra, or at least something to cover her teenage breasts? Couldn't the sculptor have at least put a bathing suit on her? It was embarrassing.

"Mom, I'm hungry."

Mom turned and looked at me, "I have been hearing about Danish pastry my entire life. Let's go get some." So, we walked to the nearby bakery, whose smells had been wafting through the air, and selected a fluffy, buttery almond filled treat.

"Mom, what were you thinking about at the statue?"

Ellie was still lost in thought. "*Day by day, the Prince grew more fond of her. He loved her as one loves a dear, good child, but it never came into his head to make her his wife; and yet she must become his wife . . .*"

"What are we doing here? Don't you miss home? I thought you and Louis might get married, but he sure doesn't act like a dad. We don't even really have a place to live together."

"He hasn't said anything – it's just complicated right now."

"Have you asked him?"

"You know Kate, the Little Mermaid gave up her voice to be with the prince. Louis needs to travel right now, and we are with him."

"But Mom, she threw herself into the sea because she couldn't change things. Now she's a cold piece of bronze in the harbor, it's raining, and a bird just shit on her head."

"Enjoy your pastry honey and let's talk about something else."

I took a Berlin lady-like bite of the pastry and thought about Mom and Louis.

"Okay. What about the steadfast tin soldier? He gave everything he had for love and ended up in a puddle of lead and tin."

"Kate, Kate, Kate. Love is not a fairy tale." Mom took a strong gulp of coffee and lit up a cigarette. "All of these stories, the movies, the songs – are for a little girl . . ."

"I'm not a little girl, Mom."

"For a young lady, and that's what you are turning into right before my eyes like the swan."

"I know, from an ugly duckling."

"You were *never* ugly, you were just a duck that's all. But anyway, these confections that everyone shoves off on us as love are just more fairy tales. How do we know if anyone lived happily ever after? It seems simple, but love isn't that easy." Ellie took a wolf bite out of her pastry. "Shall we get another pastry? Apricot or berry?" "I know your grandmother tells you that love is like a garden, you have to till it and water it and keep working at it. But let me tell you what I think. I think love is more like a casino. You go in with some idea of what you want. At first it certainly seems like there is everything there you could possibly want and so you take the risks. You lay your heart on the table and sometimes you win a little and sometimes you lose a lot. And you're right honey, at this moment it looks like we're losing. I also think we can win this one if we invest some time in it."

"But you don't go to casinos. You didn't even want to go to Atlantic City."

Ellie stamped out her cigarette and ordered another two pastries, only this time with double scoops of *schlag*, stiff whipped cream, made with real cream, real sugar and real abandon.

There was not enough money to go to the famous amusement park, Tivoli Gardens, but museum admissions were nearly free. So, that day, Ellie began to teach again. I was learning to look at sculpture and to find the stories carved into stones and metal. Because mom had worked in metal, she could explain how bronze is cast to make a Rodin. Apparently freshly quarried marble can be cut with the metals in a knife blade. She studied Rodin's "The Kiss", with the bodies entwined, oblivious to the sightseers, the teachers, and the museum visitors. I didn't want to think about that story.

Hostel stays were an added expense. Mom had planned an overnight train to Oslo and I was in charge of the schedules. With a photographic memory for numbers, I had become expert in deciphering international train schedules, complete with the 24 hour clock, train, car, platform and track numbers, and my watch precisely set to each train station clock. This obsession with minutiae annoyed Ellie, who had hated that trait in my father. However, the ability to retrieve information precisely was helpful for getting to the right place at the right time. But, tonight there was some confusion —were we supposed to be on platform 2, track 1 or was it platform 1, track 2? We waited on the platform, knapsacks ready to load into the train. Then, we looked at each other, and at the train on the next platform. For nearly an hour, we had been standing on the wrong platform, as the overnight train was loading and preparing to pull out. "Oh no! Wait! Halte!" The only way to make the train was to run back down two flights of stairs, select the correct tunnels, and run up two more flights of stairs, in less than a minute. As we arrived on the correct platform the train was beginning to move, so one conductor pushed Ellie into the car, and the other pulled up our knapsacks. When he let go, the pair of us ended up flying straight across the aisles, landing on our bottoms, laughing hysterically.

Too late, Mom realized that an overnight hostel in Copenhagen would have been a better choice. The holiday week had filled this train too. Again, much of this trip would be over water, so the train ride was first a short trip through Denmark, then boarding a boat across the sea, and a third train up the coast of Sweden. The way trains work is that the cars can be detached and moved. A long train will have several cars of people and goods going to multiple destinations. But at various towns along the line, a car can be switched out to join up with another group of cars. This makes it possible for cars to be distributed to various towns along a route. Special cars, such as sleepers or dining cars, can be added to the train or removed from the lineup at any time. The ferry boats actually have train tracks in the boat, so to travel over water the car is switched off the main track and then rolls onto the boat. After leaving Copenhagen and trying to find a late night place to rest, Mom enthusiastically woke me to see Elsinore Castle in the dark, as she babbled entire speeches from Hamlet. *"What art thou then, that usurpts this time of night, together with that fair and warlike form in which the majesty of buried Denmark did sometimes march? By Heaven, I charge thee, speak!"* (Hamlet, Act I, Sc. 1.) Somehow, at 1:00 a.m. I was not thrilled about having my sleep usurped. The excitement of King Hamlet's ghost at the ramparts of Elsinore was not contagious. "Geez Mom, who cares? There's no such thing as ghosts anyway." A third night was passing with no sleep. Finally, as the car approached the coast of Sweden, cars were switched back on to the train. The conductor and passport control came by, and noticed that the Eurailpasses were valid for first class travel. "Please follow me." Had we finally been caught using outdated passes? Instead, he unlocked the doors to a first class car that had been added on at the coast of Sweden. We were finally able to go and sleep for a few hours on the beautiful blue couchettes.

Oslo is surrounded by water. "Kate, look, everything here is light blue, your favorite color." Uh, oh. It was a school day. Ellie's project for today was, "Let's make a list of all the things that show the influence of sea life on the people." Hmm . . . this was going to be trickier than counting and naming graham cracker animals in German, which was Jack's favorite travel game. I got out my journal and a pencil. People were eating fish for breakfast, everything was painted blue, even the street cars. Woodcarvings were in the shape of sea monsters, and people were working on boats. The second lesson that emerged that morning was the idea of craftsmanship – how people use materials at hand to make the things they need, and how even the most utilitarian objects can be made beautifully. In previous trips to museums, Mom would point out everything that people made with their hands, graphically flashing her hands through the air to show us precisely how things were made. She showed us how people used the materials around them. Those lessons had been taught to little kids learning about Native Americans, but in Oslo, these lessons suddenly became very clear to me.

I found a new passion. The Viking ships were the most spectacular hand made objects I had ever seen. The Viking ships are made of wood, but their gorgeous curved forms are stronger than rectangles, float better, and can be maneuvered in the rolling waves of the open sea. How did people curve the wood into these shapes? Why did they carve monsters onto their boats? And why did they set their ships on fire, with the bodies of dead rulers aboard? What made these people want to leave their land to spend months in an open boat with no food or drinking water? Did they drink beer all the time? Why do we think they got across the Atlantic more than 500 years before Christopher Columbus? The intricately knotted metal work in the Viking hoards did not really answer these questions. Because I had been reading about explorers for nearly two years, we also went to see the KonTiki, Thor Hyerdahl's raft. Hyerdahl's idea was that people could have migrated thousands of years ago and from many places. Not everyone on the planet was from Europe, and the migration theory could be established and accepted because people have the vision and courage to replicate dangerous experiences. And of course, Norway's attempt at reaching the North Pole had to be examined, since I had already had studied the successful Peary expedition. It was suddenly clear that Mom was a gifted teacher. Why was she staying in Europe with Louis?

For the third day in a row, it rained again. We gave up on being warm and dry and decided to embrace the elements. The amusement du jour was a day at the outdoor sculpture park. An enormous monolith by Gustav Vigeland was supposed to reveal the entire human story. At first it looked like one writhing mass of human anatomy, a massive stacked wrestling match. Then it began to tell a story. Every sculpture in the park was a nude, and the nudes were not the beautiful young men and women of the Greeks. At first it was jarring to see everyone, from babies to grandfathers, sculpted in the nude, but it made us realize that everyone is nude, whether or not they have clothes. These figures were man in his truest form. So we went on to observe lovers joined at the hip for eternity, families cradling each other, and a figure of death crushing a young couple. A naked man was wrestling four little babies—or was he throwing them? Was this a family game like wrestling with the uncles, or was it a comment about judgment, and evil having power over even the most innocent of us? A furious little boy in the throes of a tantrum came to life with tears of rain dripping onto his face and body. Gradually, we began to slow down at each of these stories in stone or iron, and to learn to see parts of life.

Meanwhile, nature had caught up with the two mermaids. Statues could be naked in the rain, but after three days outside in the rain, we were soaked to the point where we could not go on. We would have to catch a train just to get some shelter and a place to dry our clothes. Ellie led the run back to the train station. In the ladies room, we undressed completely, just to try and dry off with some paper towels. My cotton knit clothes had turned into a dishrag. The only warm piece of clothing between the two of us was Mom's black lace slip, which she gave me to wear. Then Mom took off her old red coat, and put that over me, even though it hung nearly to my ankles. She put her wet black leather clothes on again. I was not allowed to leave her side, not even to look at snacks, because a train station is no place for a naked twelve year old girl in a red coat and a black lace slip.

# CHAPTER TWELVE

## Jack's Eier

Mom's job offer fell through. After two months she still had not found work, and the room in Frau Bauer's cozy house was more than we could afford. We had to move. Louis helped us find a furnished rental room on a farm outside of town. The enterprising farmer had constructed three rooms above his barn to house day laborers. The shortage of labor in Germany meant that workers had to be imported from Spain, southeastern Europe and Turkey. The other roomers above the barn included two couples from Spain who shared a room with two twin beds, and a Bulgarian man who played the accordion. Down the hall was a large open room with a sink, a toilet and a shower. It had never been cleaned. To the people from Spain, the shower was a luxury. They had spent their lives in huts with no indoor plumbing. The ladies used the shower to hang laundry, and to dump waste. Why would you need a toilet too? Their staccato speech was mingled with sounds in the farmyard – ki-kiri-ki! chickens, and the farmwife screaming at the animals as she ran around the yard with grain and pails of water. The Bauernfrau, farmwife, was in charge. She was enormous, quick on her feet and knew how to handle an axe. Everything stank from the animals who shared the house and yards. Pig manure, cow manure, horse manure, and chicken guano wafted through the air, into clothing, and clung to bodies.

The room was intended for one person and had one twin bed, one table, and no cooking facilities. The farmworkers ate in the large serving kitchens during the work day. We were on our own to figure out how to eat. By now our family possessions had grown and included the coil heater for hot water, the bread knife, an army blanket, a simple cot like the kind people carry to the beach for sunbathing, and Louis' old air mattress with a few patches on it. I did not appreciate the poetry of Beatnik life any more. The cot with the army blanket was cold and saggy under my backside. Jack had the air mattress with mom's old coat. The air mattress leaked.

The days were getting dark and cold. Mom and I were beginning to fight a lot because I was no longer fun to take along on her great outings. I wanted her to get a job and a nice warm apartment. I wanted a simple pair of slacks and a pullover sweater to wear to school. I wanted some socks that didn't slip down into my shoes, rubbing the backs of my heels. I wanted an umbrella.

Louis and Ellie wanted some adult time. They decided to go south to Würzburg one weekend to meet up with Jeff Hoffman, a young friend from Elmira who now was a GI stationed in Germany. Jeff had been acquiring possessions too. On a recent trip to Spain he and some other GIs drank and gambled in bodegas until their sense of responsibility left them. Somehow, they returned to Germany with a matador cape and a gorgeous "*traje de luces*" matador jacket, velvet brocade covered in gilt, sequins, beads and embroidery. Louis said they had stolen the items from the wall in a bar. Mom said the items had been a gift from a friend. The jacket fit me, but I wasn't allowed to put it on. It was an art object. Purchase? Gambling? Theft? The details were unclear, but there seemed to be some secret guilt involved. The red and gold cape was lightweight wool, and since Jack had no blanket other than Mom's red coat, he was thrilled to be given the cape to use as a wrap. The bloodstains and the dirt were not a problem for him. Jack was living the life.

This great adventure was neither fun nor exciting. I hated the farm with its cold rooms and the filth. No friends could come visit me any more. I couldn't keep myself clean and neat enough to keep the friends that I already had. I was ashamed to go to their houses. It was no longer an issue of Berlin manners. Of course I knew how to act. It was a matter of total disgrace, the embarrassment of being hungry and cold most of the time.

Mom solved our clothing problem a different way. There were no laundry facilities in the farmhouse. Clothes could be washed in cold water in the sink, and then hung in the unheated bathroom or outside on the line, where they froze. The freeze-dried clothes would be removed from the line, but when they heated to room temperature they were, well, damp. Everything we had ever learned about "you'll catch your death . . ." We weren't dead yet. Ellie's solution was the same solution used by Levi Strauss for cowboys on the trail. Levi Strauss took canvas, dyed it indigo blue, and made it into pants that wore like iron and never needed to be washed. Ellie took every outer garment we owned to a laundry in town. Everything was dyed deep navy blue – no more ivory skirt, no more coral red coat. The ugly gold blouse was gone. Now the whole group looked like Beatniks, or the photos of displaced persons from 15 years earlier. But, the deep blue-black would not need to be washed.

*   *   *

Another set of problems surfaced. Jack and I had always attended the same schools, and we had learned from the same teachers. From year to year I would tell him what to expect and how to behave. Neighborhood children would play school using names everybody knew, and game rules that we all understood. Now Jack would be attending a local *Volksschule*, an elementary school for all lower grade children. He was a third grader. I would be going to secondary school. In Germany all children took an examination in the fifth grade that determined their secondary school choices. My New York records indicated that I belonged in the Gymnasium, a type of high school for university bound students. The Wolfsburg high school was now three kilometers away and the days were getting short.

Our school days started at 7:00 am and ended at 1:00 in time for a midday meal at home. We got up in the dark and I tried to cut off pieces of hard dark rye bread and cheese for our sandwiches. Mom needed to sleep later because she and Louis kept late evenings. Cutting bread and cheese was a skill yet to be mastered. The scars on my fingers were beginning to fade, and I intended to be in absolute control of the knife. My efforts to slice bread exactly straight produced results that were in need of improvement. The task was more difficult in the dark mornings of the shortening days. My school was all the way across Wolfsburg, so I often left at 5:30 in the morning to walk the three kilometers. The dark country roads turned into a stream of lights from VW Beetles entering and exiting the factory at the shift change. After walking the length of the factory, the gray sky daylight over Wolfsburg would lighten as I walked across town to the city center and my Gymnasium.

Mother was spending her days looking for work. Instead of making new friends and playing in the afternoons, I needed to return to the farm immediately and take care of my silly brother. The early schedule gave children on nearby farms time to help in the fields each afternoon. Older sisters could take care of younger children. Teenagers could cook and clean. There were no card games and there were no tea parties. Country life was not quite like the walks in the forests that had characterized outdoor life in Berlin. The air was not fresh. The farms stank and so did the children who lived on them.

Jack may have been everyone's favorite but he had his faults. *Escargot*, also known as *Snail*, was a wanderer. He dawdled and he forgot things. He often forgot what he was supposed to do. He was not a star student. When Jack left the house on his first day of school, he heard his last English words. I went to the left, toward my school in town, and he turned right toward the little *Volksschule*. He was advised not to introduce himself to the school Director with "Mein Vater ist tod, und . . . ." even if his mother was crazy. All he needed to do was keep quiet and follow as many directions as he understood.

I arrived home to my babysitting duty, and there was no Jack. I called for him down in the barnyard, but no one had seen him that day. His school was just across the common fields. In a farming village, houses are clustered together in the center and fields are parceled out all around the homes. The stench from harvested sugar beets surrounded us. From any of the fields you can see where the village was. How could he have possibly gotten lost? I started walking and calling across the short distances. At the side of a path, sitting in the dirt, was my little brother. His tear streaked face and torn plaid shirt let me know it had been a bad day. He had not eaten his snack, but the paper was torn up. He was playing with some grasses that he had tied into little stick figures.

"Jack, what happened?"

He sniffled, then wiped his nose with his shirt. "I don't know." The tears came again, leaking here and there.

After being shown a seat by the school Director, he had sat quietly at a desk and fiddled with his paper and pencils. Around him the classroom was bedlam. Third grade students were shouting, tossing books and keeping a lookout for adults. Suddenly, the kids started to stand up by the sides of their chairs, and the room went silent. He didn't understand why were they doing this.

"Oh, everyone is super well behaved when the teacher is in the room, and we can talk while the teachers are changing classes. But no one was mean to you, were they?"

"And everyone was at attention all of a sudden." I could picture this. He had remained in his seat staring blankly at the wall, and hopelessly confused.

Silence had not helped Jack fit into his new school. Obviously he was dumb. Jack learned his first new word at the mid-morning recess. A much larger boy came up to him on the playground, and began to taunt him. A circle gathered, making fun of everything – his clothes, his inability to communicate, and his crooked lumpy sandwich. Finally the larger boy grabbed him by the collar to punch him out, and kicked him in the "*eier*." As Jack screamed and started to cry, some of the other boys helped him up, and tried to explain everything what had happened, in German. The only word Jack remembered was "*eier*".

"Oh for Gosh sakes, those boys are mean! Do you know what they were saying?"

Jack shook his head, but looked at his lap. He clearly remembered the site of his injury.

"That's the general idea. Jack, the word also means eggs. But either way they shouldn't have done that. What did the teacher do?" He shook his head.

We walked toward the village with its little bakery, dairy and butcher shops. There was no greengrocer because farmers grew their own vegetables. I was supposed to buy sausages for dinner. Instead I chose a big bar of chocolate and decided on hardboiled eggs instead of sausage for dinner. I was angry that he had been hurt, but he would need to return to classes the next day. I was not going to solve the problem by teaching him to punch someone out because I was no good at that. We shared the chocolate.

"Jack, there must have been some class you liked. Did they do sports?"

Who knows why I asked that. Neither of us liked sports. Athletics are a part of the German school experience, and in the winter, gymnastics is an important part of physical education. Jack had never liked or trusted the group of male actors and dancers that our mother partied with. He had refused to have anything to do with their dance school, even though it was free. He had balked at the family outings on ice skates, and wouldn't step into a pair of the stiff unstable boots on blades. Suddenly he was faced with gymnastics classes, and was unable to perform the simplest movement. Left handed, he could not throw or catch a ball correctly. With a nickname like Escargot, he was not about to run around a track. And forget anything that involved combat.

The athletics teacher had him line up with all the boys. He did not know how to kick a soccer ball. Now his peers selected him for punishment for two reasons, his lack of skills and his lack of aggressive behavior. Jack was a wimp.

Couldn't he do anything right? I sure didn't want to take him anywhere with me, because he would make mistakes. Jack was so stupid that he didn't even know which bathroom he should use. He was always walking into the wrong restroom, not knowing that Damen and Herren were opposites, thinking that Herren had "her" in it, he chose the wrong one. Clearly, he needed some guidance.

Uncle Bill and Monika came to the rescue. After his disastrous start in the Volkschule, he would return to Eisenstadt for an extended stay. It was time to straighten him out. His legs were growing long, but his head was still full of, well, what animals leave all over the barnyard. Uncle Bill and Louis had provided a few details about becoming a man, most of which made no sense for a nine year old. I no longer had a clue as to what a lady might be. The examples from Mom, Grandmother Estelle and Mutti Liddy did not add up. They couldn't even agree on where to set spoons on a table or how to eat. Luckily with a diet of sandwiches and hardboiled eggs, table settings no longer mattered. For the time being, Ellie's ideas prevailed.

All German children know a storybook, *Der Struwwelpeter* which translates to *Pete the Slob.* Uncle Bill was the teacher, and Jack was his pupil. *Der Struwwelpeter* is a humorous black comedy about little boys. The character in the illustrations displays long hair that has perhaps never been combed. Crud is crusted all over his face and filthy fingernails extend across the cover of the book. His manners are even worse than his appearance. The idea is that dirty children with bad manners are monstrous. *Der Struwwelpeter* is reviled because of his poor grooming. Many of the bad children in the verses die as a result of their errors in judgment. This book has been purchased by households for more than 100 years because parents think it is hilarious.

*Der Struwwelpeter* would serve nicely as a textbook. Jack's first decision after thumbing through the cartoons was that yes, he would like a bath. He had not been in a warm soapy tub for nearly three months, and because he was a boy, no one had been supervising his baths. There was a bathtub outside Bill and Monika's apartment, and water was heated for him to soak. New sponges and soaps were added to the mix, and rub a dub, dub. He washed his arms, legs and tummy. Bill came in for an inspection.

"You have to wash all the inside parts too, the stuff that other people don't see, and don't touch on a big boy. Pretend you are cleaning up a baby for a new diaper and wash all that."

"Haven't you ever washed your hair? Big boys don't get all upset over soap in their eyes. Here's more soap – scrub, scrub, scrub all the way down to the scalp, dig in behind those ears."

"NO – your hands are not clean yet. We'll cut your nails when you dry off – Take this little brush and scrub the ends of your fingers until your claws are white – completely white."

"OK – here is a towel; use it everywhere. Don't drop it! You need to fold it and hang it up. No, you don't wipe dirty stuff with a towel – it is to dry you off after you are clean."

"Good God! Your feet – get between those toes, and scrub the talons. I'll help you cut them."

After his bath, Jack was not allowed to put on the clothes he had worn to Eisenstadt. Bill looked through his things.

"What do you mean, you only travel with underwear and a toothbrush? And you can't use the toothbrush because the water in trains should not be consumed!

Let's see your teeth. Yechh! Man, you won't be able to kiss any girls like that – not even your mother."

Bill found a man's undershirt in a drawer, and located Jack's clean underwear in his backpack. The rest of the backpack was stuffed with little toys and some used tissues. At a simple shop in town they located a pair of brown slacks, clean undershirts and a green sweater, suitable for school. With a trip to the barber, Jack was presentable.

But, before he could go to school, he would need to be able to read and write a little in German, because third graders can read and write. It would not do for a professor's visiting child to be illiterate. From the "Hans Guck in die Luft" (airhead) book he learned about what happens to boys who walk around with their faces turned toward the sky – they can fall into a river and have all their possessions swept away. It was time to learn to look people in the eye and shake hands. If the person was older than you, you bowed at the waist and clicked your heels. Whoops! That doesn't work in ratty old sneakers – Jack would need some leather shoes for school.

Bill had his own challenges. For the time being they were a team of bachelors while Monika went to spend time with her sisters. Unfortunately Bill did not know how to cook. He decided to make pea soup from a mix, and even though he stressed the importance of reading to his students, he did not read the directions. He put an iron skillet on the stove, and then scattered in the mix. Oops, you had to add water. By now, the burnt globs of soup mix were starting to smell, and the water just sat on top. Bill grabbed a spoon, and tried to mix it. Something like paste formed in part of the skillet, then burned on like cement. Jack was now reading aloud the story of Kaspar, the healthy boy who starves to death because he will not eat his soup.

"Uncle Bill, the Struwwelpeter lessons were important, but do we really have to eat this?"

Bill was tall and very thin. He actually didn't care whether he ate or not. The soup was unappetizing, but the principle is that you eat what you must when it is put in front of you. The short answer then was "Yes."

"Can't we eat the sausage?" Jack was always hungry but the burned soup was not something he thought he could stomach. He wanted to be helpful and was hoping for some collaboration on the soup debacle.

"No, it needs to be cooked and the pan is a mess."

"I can eat it raw. We eat cold food all the time."

"No, you will get a tapeworm."

"What's that?"

Jack was told that a tapeworm is a huge parasite that will eat you from the inside out. It's very difficult to get rid of, and you would be very, very sick. To underscore the lesson Uncle Bill told Jack the story of this man who had a terrible huge tapeworm, and he was so sick to his stomach he thought he was going to die. He went to the doctor, and the doctor said, "Hmm, This is a tough one to cure, but I want you to come back tomorrow." The man went back, and the doctor said, "Drop your pants, and get up on this table. The table had stirrups for his feet. The doctor reached into the pocket of his lab coat, pulled out an egg and a cookie. He shoved the egg up the man's ass, and then the scratchy cookie. "Come back next Tuesday." "Is that all you are going to do?" "Yes, until Tuesday, then." The man came back the next Tuesday. He got up on the table, and they repeated the actions with the egg and the cookie. "I want you to come back in a week." "But Dr., I'm not feeling any better" "You will." The man came back the following week and noticed the doctor had an egg and a hammer. The man groaned in pain as he got up on the table and spread his legs. The doctor shoved in the egg. Then, a great rumbling went through the man's guts, and the tapeworm poked his head out. "Where's my cookie?!" BAM!

By late afternoon both their stomachs were rumbling. As a final exam on his storybook, Uncle Bill took little Jack out to the pastry shop. There, they had gooey pastries, "Watch out for the crumbs, don't let them fall off your plate," and an Eiskaffee – a cold coffee topped with ice cream and whipped cream – "don't slurp it." As the family of a student came into the café, Jack stood, clicked his heels, put out his hand, and said, "Grüss Gott," a greeting for friends."

*   *   *

After three weeks apart, even a helpless and annoying little brother can be missed. Bill and Ellie had planned that Jack would arrive in Munich on the train. Bill would place him on the train in Vienna, and he would get off the train in Munich. By now he had been traveling on trains with adults several times, and he would know the Munich stop. He would not need to be able to read a schedule or to tell time. On that cloudy Saturday afternoon Mom, Louis and I arrived in the Munich train station and found a bench on the platform. Holding hands, they talked about some problems that were emerging. She had had no luck in getting a job that was anywhere close to her qualifications as a college educated woman. Louis was at work all week, and the weekend trips basically involved sleeping on a train, or not, looking at some wonderful things, and not even being able to sit down in a sidewalk café and drink a cup of good coffee. In fact, for weeks now Ellie had faced her mornings with some instant brew that tasted like burned grain. I wandered back and forth looking at kiosks and sitting down with them from time to time. Big News. Mom had to figure out what to do with herself. It was clear that we were not thriving in our life on the tracks.

The train from Vienna came in, and one by one passengers climbed down the steps, lugging their parcels and suitcases. Louis took charge. "Ellie, I'm going to go to the next bench down this platform, so that no matter which car he is on, he sees one of us right away." The cars kept on emptying, but there were no unattended children coming off the train. Mom began to panic, and then cry.

As the sky darkened, and rain threatened, a second train came in from Vienna. Louis and I took our places on the platform again. Sure enough, a bewildered little boy clambered down the steps, looked around, and then came running toward me like a lost puppy. When he threw his arms around me we both almost tipped onto the tracks.

Jack set down his rucksack. "Mommy! Kate! Louis! I'm here."

"My God Jack! It's so late. We were afraid you had missed the stop."

"Uncle Bill put me on this train. We missed the other one. He said I was supposed to get out at Munich where Mommy and Louis would meet me. The train started to move, and I sat in this car with adults reading newspapers without comics. I'm so happy to see you. I didn't really understand what the train people were saying, or where we were, or what I was supposed to do. I figured out how to work all the levers and switches, you know Louis, like you showed me. But I knew not to pull on anything marked in red."

We celebrated with a late dinner at Lowenbrau, our favorite beer hall, brightly lit with lots of other families around. Jack was a different boy. He knew how to order his own meal. He knew how to say please and thank you. He asked to wash his hands. He tried to pay attention to his surroundings. Jack had been developing other new skills for eating in restaurants, thanks to Uncle Bill. At the table he built forts out of beer coasters, and he also had learned several tricks that involved rolling coasters around each other in a sequence, juggling coasters, and making beer glasses sing by running your finger around the rim. We celebrated with our platters of sauerkraut and meat.

Louis did not order a pitcher of beer. Ellie had not lost her taste for red rotgut wine. Louis had acquired a bota, a goatskin, so that jug wine could be poured and carried on trips. Anything out of a bota smells and tastes like tar and dead goat. But, Jack took it up as another way to entertain people.

"You've got to remember that the trick with the bota is to keep your mouth open, all the time." I took a try. It was just too nasty to swallow and I dribbled the red wine all over the place. Jack started laughing. "Look, she's like the guys on the TV. Blood comes out when they get socked in the kisser." Was it even possible for these people, just once, to not make a spectacle of themselves? "Oh, right, like I'm going to smell that thing and open my mouth at the same time?" Louis was more patient. "Here, keep the bota at arm's length, and keep swallowing. You have to swallow with your mouth open, it's a little skill you have to learn, and you'll make some little slobbery mistakes." The wine filled my sinuses, and I sneezed wine all over the long beer hall table. Vesuvius had nothing on this exploding girl.

"You might want to practice with water so that you can stay sober enough to learn how to work this thing." The water was rank, but sometimes the wine would leave a vile taste for hours.

Now Louis added a third gentleman's skill to Jack's repertoire. Jack learned to smoke a pipe. There was a lot to this one. He had to learn how to clean the pipe, tamp the tobacco, and light the pipe properly. Louis even provided him with his own tools and a pouch, things that go with this male ritual. Jack even learned how to smoke like Popeye the sailor. In high winds you turn the pipe upside down so that it won't go out.

Good idea. Rough seas were ahead.

# CHAPTER THIRTEEN

## Schlacht Und Tod

When Jack returned to the farm school, he was able to start making friends. Fritz Becker, a boy at the farm village school, invited him several times to help out with chores on the farm – cooking and mashing sugar beets for the pigs, piling hay, and sweeping the cobblestone courtyard. He and two other classmates enjoyed the work and the hot meals that went with it. Jack just loved the baby piglets. The nine tiny babies ran all over their enclosure, squealing and rolling. The farm boys told Jack that the mother pigs were dangerous, and to stay out of the pigpens. If one of the children got bit, no one inside would come out to help. Still they spent hours by the side of the pigpen, watching the babies chase the mother, and watching her nuzzle and nurse them.

Fritz had a big sister Heidi. She was thirteen, but she went to a local school for the farm kids. Heidi already knew how to cook big hot farm meals. One day squealing could be heard throughout the village. As my brother and I entered the farmyard, there was not a piglet to be seen. What had happened to them? In Elmira, Mom had always spoken of hosting a feast with a roasted suckling pig, complete with an apple in its mouth. Now it seemed like the worst idea ever. We knew that harvest time was also the time to butcher, but the thought of one of the babies on a platter with an apple in its mouth was really upsetting. We hurried across the courtyard to the back of the barns, not stopping at the sty. Suddenly the squeals stopped. A few minutes later, the mother pig started down the ramp proudly, with nine freshly bathed baby piglets behind her."

\*   \*   \*

We obviously didn't understand why the pigs had been bathed. On Tuesday afternoon, Fritz, his older brother, and Jack were ordered to go around the side of the barn. I was told to immediately report to the kitchen. Ahead of us, four men were struggling with the largest and meanest of the Becker's pigs. The pig was pulled around the corner, out of the children's sight, where one of the men hit it between the eyes with the back of an axe. With a horrible squeal, the pig fell over, semi-conscious.

Then we listened to the men struggling to lift the animal by its hind legs to pin it into an upside down position, place a basin under its head to catch the blood for blutwurst (a rich dark sausage,) and then slit its main artery. At this point they boys were asked to come in close, and observe the precise preparation procedures. I was frozen against the corner of the barn. Huge vats of steaming water were used to sterilize every part of the dead animal. The men were already busy shaving and cleaning the animal with a large round knife.

They gutted this warm beast, first hanging it upside down, then slitting it down the middle. The guts fell out of this thing, in one piece, into a wheelbarrow. There was no blood, just a huge shining mass, composed of all these odd forms, and this funny kind of a rounded knife. The whole process of butchering was immaculate, a tidy assemblage of parts and a whole.

One man separated the glistening intestines that came out of the animal, and then they started taking the small intestine and pushing out the stuff that was inside. For some reason the intestine turned itself inside out as they cleaned it, and then it rolled along the clean paved area behind the barn. It just kind of continued to unravel as they were cleaning it out. Basically they were squeezing it like a tube and running their fingers down it. As they squeezed it, the only glop was at the very end of it. The clean intestine is used to make sausage. In the kitchen the women were taking the blood for the blutwurst, and making it curdle, adding fat and salt to their brew, and processing this stuff by squirting it into the casing, and then tying the sausages up. Then they cooked the head and the feet for other sausages. Meanwhile the men continued to dismember and clean the animal.

As Heidi and the others worked, the entire process looked like something out of one of the worst fairytales ever. They talked like witches, heaving blood, fat and body parts around into huge bowls and steaming pots on every surface of the kitchen. I cut onions and herbs into fine bits, taking my time so that I would not need to touch death. Its meat was still warm. The next day Jack couldn't wait to go over to the farmhouse for the midday meal. Heidi and her mother had made *saumagen*, fresh pig stomach washed and stuffed with meats and spices, then boiled for hours until it is edible. They also had fresh liver. Jack said it was a sweet, big, wonderful meal.

A few days later they butchered the sow.

\*   \*   \*

Some events will haunt people for multiple lifetimes. Jack and I were somehow hoping for a real family of any kind, farm life, city life, beatnik life . . . we really didn't care which. Mom's marriage to Hermann had ended when I was six and Jack was three. Little Kate had sat mute in her first grade class, refusing to read or to pick up a pencil. Jack had cried for weeks. Our one possession from before the divorce days was a studio photograph that had been taken with daddy. It was his final gift to us. The photo disappeared shortly after we moved to Elmira. We ransacked grandmother's house looking for it, even tearing out the drywall in the attic where we thought there was a secret hiding place under the eaves.

Now we were in Europe, where our dad had been raised. Tour guides in Amsterdam had explained that the Herengracht homes had been among the most elegant residences in the world for centuries. It was hard to imagine that Daddy had ever come from a wealthy family. Neither of us had any idea what that really meant. Is wealth a shiny new bicycle? Maybe some new shoes? Mom told us that Hermann liked to act like a rich guy, but he was broke when they met. He had concealed that fact until after he had his bride. Their hopes and dreams lay in the idea that things would be fine once the house in Amsterdam was sold. No one understood what this was about, but the house did eventually get sold for about ten percent of its value and dad was furious. And then things were not fine after all.

Louis bought me "The Diary of Anne Frank." He thought I would like it because Anne Frank was also 12 years old, and kept journals just as I did. He and Bill had a long conversation about Hermann, Ellie's husband, and it was decided that the family group should make a trip to Bergen Belsen, to bear witness to how Hermann's family had been imprisoned and died. Bill mentioned that our aunt Sophia had been in Bergen Belsen for three years, and survived. She was very much alive, but he did not know where she lived any more. He said she was pretty and smart. When Sophia was captured and taken to Bergen Belsen, an SS officer looked at her in a line up. She looked right back at him and smiling. "You are so pretty. Why don't you have yourself declared Aryan?" She laughed, "It's a little late for that, don't you think?" He took her as a servant for the duration of the war. After the war, he suggested they move to Argentina and get married. But, she could never bring herself to marry a captor, even one who saved her life. Bill did not know what had happened to the rest of their large family. He only knew that they did not survive.

The hills at Bergen Belsen are mass graves. The soil is composed of thousands of bodies. No flowers rest on tidy granite stones to tell us that life is all around us. Instead there is a kind of bleak silence, a nothingness. The exhibits continued with all the pictures of tortured and dead people, gas ovens, and barbed wire fences. Jack became hysterical at the sights of the skeletons, some walking and some thrown into the ground. The savagery of this was beyond our comprehension. I silently gazed at the photos, and at the thought that my grandparents, uncles, and aunts were lying in those pits or others like them. It was an immense grief for those I had never known. I did not cry, I did not blink in the silence of those surroundings.

Mom walked with Louis, tears in her eyes. A few days later Mom talked to me about my dad and his family, about how unprepared she had been for dealing with Hermann's paranoia, his puzzling anger, and of her sorrow at not having understood him better. I looked at her and wondered, "What was there to understand?"

# CHAPTER FOURTEEN

## Pschitt! A Weekend in Paris

There was lots more to not understand.

After a year of wearing their berets, Ellie and Louis had finally made it to Paris for a taste of the real thing – *la vie Boheme*, the Bohemian life. Mon Dieu! Jack went wild. The first thing he saw at the train station was a cart of soft drinks, with a brand of lemonade called Pschitt! The English cognate for this comes from a German root; the French name is intended to mimic the sound of taking the cap off a refreshing carbonated beverage. A new word was added to the lexicon – and we were allowed to say Pschitt! for the entire weekend.

Mom and Louis were putting a lot of thought into our education, a "liberal education" whatever that was. Some subjects were totally ignored. It was assumed that Jack would be able to learn multiplication in short order when he returned to the United States. Instead and in the meantime, our merry little band took off for the day's lesson in engineering, the Eiffel Tower. The little models and photos don't really prepare a child for the immense steel structure, which gets bigger and bigger as you walk toward it. It's not like approaching a building; the experience is more like entering the largest sculpture in the world. Mom began to explain how the look of modern cities was a result of people figuring out how to use steel in construction. Steel frames made buildings bigger and taller than ever before. The Eiffel Tower was a model of how this could be done. At the observation deck Louis offered some science tidbits. "If you spit off the top, the spit would evaporate before it hit the ground. NO! I didn't say to do it!" "OK Jack, listen very carefully. If you throw a penny, it would gather the momentum of a speeding bullet, and become a lethal weapon. You <u>are not</u> allowed to throw a penny and see if this is true." Then Louis spent quite a lot of time explaining more about the structures and building materials that made this tower a possibility. He said it would have been impossible to build from wood, and that the use of steel changed how city buildings would be constructed for the foreseeable future. That afternoon we tumbled on the grass and learned about structural forms. If two kids stand straight up with a stick across both their shoulders, the stick will fall if one of them wiggles, even a little bit. The structure fails. People have been building in rectangles for millennia, but the rectangle is not the strongest shape. If a 90 degree angle slips just a little bit, something slides off or tips over. But, if two kids lean into each other back to back, in sort of an "A" formation, they exert pressure and support that keeps them from falling down. The concept works unless, of course, one kid is a lot taller and heavier than the other. Then the big kid gets to push the little kid down and make him eat grass. So, Jack and I learned why the Tower is shaped as it is, and how the intersecting triangles in the ironwork all combined to make an extremely strong structure.

I was thrilled to be on the Champs Elysees. We had had countless shopping lessons in our French classes in Berlin. Since Frohnau was in the French sector of the city, French was a second language and culture under the Berlin occupation. The Parisian shop windows were full of extravagant displays, sleek dresses, purses and fanciful high heeled shoes. "Je vousdrai un . . ." except of course I couldn't actually buy anything. But at 5'7" and with evidence of some curves—OK, the fat tummy was now turning into hips—I could imagine what I would look like in the dresses, maybe with a pair of high heels and a pretty hat. I attempted to revive some Kufurstendamm manners by staying as far away from the antics of these people as possible.

I even knew how to order and eat at the cafés, except there was no money to stop at one. Pschitt!, yogurt, and pastries were the diet for this trip.

Staying far away from Louis and Jack was imperative. Louis was showing Jack *les pissoirs* – public urinals for men. If a woman needed to use a toilet in Paris she was out of luck, but the men could stop on every corner to use *le pissoir*. Jack wanted to stop at every single one of them. Suddenly Jack asked where he could use a flush toilet. Louis kept offering to buy him another bottle of Pschitt! Jack lost his sense of humor and started to cry. It was decided that they had better get to an inexpensive café for sandwiches and plumbing. Once we were seated and busily deciphering menus written in French, Jack ran desperately for the stairs to the bathrooms. Another family problem was solved. But, a few moments later, Jack appeared back at the table, still with a pained expression on his face. He tugged at Mom's sleeve, "Mother, which is which, Adam or Eve?" She looked across at me, and I ran back downstairs with him. Jack was missing another significant area of his education – somehow he had escaped Bible School.

Louis descended into a tunnel beneath the street, taking all of us with him. A ride on the Paris Metro took the ended up near Montmartre, at Sacre Coeur, a gorgeous almost Byzantine white church. The church is an image straight from 1001 Arabian Nights, white stones carved into lace with a spectacular dome at the top. Terraced hills, formerly grape vineyards that served the nobility, extend from the riverbank up several flights of stairs to the carved stone church. Ellie patiently began explaining the reasons for the unusual architecture. The *vie Boheme* extended from the riverbank all the way up to the church, and then down a series of alleys into the nearby neighborhoods. The area is called Montmartre, and for more than a hundred years, it had been home to artists. Some of them were French painters who lived and died in poverty, and whose paintings now sold for millions of dollars. Others had traveled to Paris from other countries to experience the life of an artist. On the terraces and steps of the churchyard lounged group after group of young adults. Some were playing guitars and singing. Others seemed to be drinking and listening. Occasional speakers would be ranting their concerns in loud French. Discontents were mingled with peaceful protestors, poets, and musicians. Louis would have easily disappeared into the crowd, with his leather jacket and dark clothing, except that he turned to Mom and me. "Let's stay close together. Not everybody here wants to make friends." "Hey, *escargot*, hurry up!" Jack was gazing blankly into the crowds instead of listening. As we turned to grab each other's hands, Jack was already missing in the crowd.

> *Plantons la vigne*
> *La voilà la jolie vigne*
> *Vigni, vigna, vignons le vin,*
> *La voilà la jolie vigne au vin*
> *La voilà la jolie vigne*
>
> *De Feuille en grappe . . .*
> *De grappe en cueille . . .*
> *De presse en cuvee . . .*
> *De cuvee en tonne . . .*
> *De tonne en cave . . .*
> *De cave en cruche . . .*
> *De cruche en verre . . .*
> *De verre en gueule . . .*
> *De guile en pane . . .*
> *De panse en pisse . . .*
> *De pisse en terre . . .*
> *De terre en vigne . . .*

Jack was standing in the middle of a group of young adults with his bota. They were singing an endless drinking song about the life cycle of wine. *First you plant the vine, then the fruit grows, you pick the fruit, put in in the tub and crush it. Pour the juice into a barrel, and let it ripen. Drink it, and piss it into the ground, plant a new vine.* He was gulping wine with every verse. Louis stepped into the group, and retrieved the nine-year old derelict.

Mom and I had been left near the steps of the church. Unfortunately, Ellie was carrying her large handbag, which in Paris can also signify that the woman is a prostitute. At first we were talking about the scenes all around us. As it went dark, some of the adults had built bonfires. Others were rolling out sleeping bags. Then two men approached us. Ellie glanced at them, and continued her comments on the scene. She was living in a Toulouse Lautrec painting at the moment. The men came closer. With a cigarette hanging out of his mouth, the elder of the two asked, "Are you lost?" He looked at Mom, and at her worn coat and dirty hair. The circles under her eyes were a record of many uncomfortable nights. "Non parle Francais." "Do you have a place to stay?" He took a swig of his beer and continued to speak to Ellie, who was saying that her friend would be back. Suddenly he turned to me, pulled off my glasses, and ran his dirty hand down my cheek.

"La petite poulette, est belle,—a pretty young chick." "Combien? How much for this one?"

Ellie stepped forward, glaring at the man, and growled, "She does not smoke." Ellie took the cigarette out of his mouth. "And she does not drink." Ellie dropped his cigarette into his beer. Pschitt! It sizzled as it hit the beverage.

Louis and Jack returned to the steps, giggling as they pretended to stagger. Jack was wearing a new beret of his very own, a gift from one of the singers. In front of the church, they found Ellie furious and me confused and a little shaken. Ellie announced that we would not be camping out in the park nor would we be staying at the residences of any of his "friends." She demanded that we get to an all night café immediately, one that would be safe for children. They found a place and then Ellie announced to Louis that the pair of them would be taking turns sitting up all night to watch over us. Louis stopped laughing and walked ahead silently. At a café he pulled together two chairs for Jack, and announced that it was time to go to sleep. I decided to sit up with mother but we fell asleep on each other's shoulders.

Louis stood the first watch, a bottle of Pschitt! in his hand.

# CHAPTER FIFTEEN

## Rejection

At last Mom had a job. It was not a great job, but there was nothing else available for a college-educated woman who was not fluent in German. She also did not have the correct type of visa. As far as the German civil service was concerned, we were illegal guests. Ellie was now a seamstress in a sweatshop. Day after day she sat at her sewing machine, unable to carry on a conversation in German. The other ladies laughed and chatted about their clever children and lazy husbands while they pushed their machines at top speed. The work was tedious, manufacturing durable jackets for some type of heavy labor. Everything was the same shade of olive brown, and the pieces were identical. Ellie's task was to fit a patch inside the elbow of each sleeve, stitch it into place, and then close up the sleeve. She got paid for each bundle of twelve sleeves that she completed, but she was not terribly fast.

Now that Mom was working, she had us spend some time with the Spanish neighbors in the afternoons. Maria and Carla kept something cooking on their hot plate nearly all day. Their husbands worked on the assembly lines at the VW factory. Because World War II had all but annihilated the male population of Germany, thousands of Turkish and Spanish men were invited to take manufacturing jobs. They weren't exactly migrants but they weren't immigrants either.

Work permits for factory jobs were given to men of any nationality. This helped the Germans become a manufacturing power again. Their wages helped feed the large families that they had left behind.

The Spanish people were peasants from Badajoz, somewhere in the mountains next to Portugal. The ladies didn't speak a word of English or German, but my fifth grade Spanish was a start at conversation. At home, Maria had ten children and Carla had six. The ladies missed their children terribly but they couldn't even read or write in Spanish so they had very few letters. They were very kind, and my brother and I were now speaking more Spanish than German at home. "*Como se dice . . . . ?* What do you call this?" Maria was a mimic who could tell any story with her hands. It was a good thing because even the names of the animal sounds were pronounced differently. Cock-a-doodle-do is Kiri-kiri-ki in Spanish. We loved making all the animal sounds using different people sounds. Carla and her husband showed Jack how to use his toreador cape for real, taking it down to the barnyard and practicing. "*Venga, toro, toro!*" The cow didn't care.

We loved the ladies and they loved to cook for us. I learned how to make a wonderful chicken soup. Mom would pay Frau Schreinecke to butcher a chicken. The fat, pregnant farmwife would chase a chicken around the pig yard. I would look away just as the woman picked up the ax. Jack watched in fascination. He said that the ducks weren't so bad, and that if he had to butcher something, he would just kill a duck. The chickens would run, squawk, and then twitch when it was supposed to be over. The warm body would then be delivered to clean and pluck in the bathroom sink. I always felt queasy when I started the task. You have to plunge your hands in to gut the warm bird. Pulling the feathers off was a real chore. It took a long time to clean the skin and the insides of all the glop.

Maria and Carla added the vegetables: carrots, tomatoes, beans and potatoes. It was then that I learned a really important cooking lesson; drop an entire head of garlic into the broth. If you leave the paper on, you will get a rich flavor, but not one that is too sharp. The ladies made a delicious soup of the chicken and root vegetables steaming on their hot plate. Lesson two was café de leche. You can grind coffee beans with a beer bottle, and steam them up with milk for a hot drink to help you do your homework.

The good news in these days was that Mom now had a little income. The weekend trips continued. The winter holidays were approaching, and she was beginning to sing in the mornings as the three of us got up together for our treks to school and work. Mom and I walked toward town, and Jack skipped off down the lane through the fields to meet his friends at school. In the United States, Thanksgiving was coming. This was Grandmother Estelle's favorite holiday, and one that we all enjoyed together year after year. Mom had a plan. She had invited Jeff Hoffman and four of his friends from Wurzburg to join us. They had said they would definitely take the train north for their leave. They had even hatched out the plan to finance their trip by bringing extra booze and cigarettes from the Post Exchange to sell. It wasn't particularly legal, but it was one way to pay for a few off base privileges.

We were excited about our visitors. Jack was practicing his toreador moves in the barnyard. The cows were still not interested, but there was a little terrier puppy that loved the game. Jack wanted to show Jeff that he could now twirl the cape. Mom and I began to plan a dinner for our guests. Our farm only had chickens and ducks. No one had seen turkey except in pictures. Frau Schreineke had us visit a neighbor who had geese.

"Mom, what does goose taste like? Is it the same as turkey?" The geese were mean. They followed me around the barnyard, biting my legs. We were supposed to pick one out. This time I did not care if we wrung its neck. These birds deserved it. Apparently roast goose is delicious, and that was enough for me. A price was agreed upon and the farmer then hooked our bird and set it into a little cage. They would even roast it for us, along with some potatoes. Louis would be bringing the beer.

"You would like this for your Sunday dinner, yes?"

Mom didn't know the days of the week. "Mom, I don't think you want this on Sunday."

Ellie was digging around in her handbag, counting out the bills and change. "Oh dear no, it is for an American holiday. Thanksgiving Day is next Thursday.

I talked to the farmwife again and asked for the goose to be ready on Thursday.

"There is no holiday on Thursday. Do you want it on Saturday?"

"No, Thursday is American Thanksgiving. We will come by at 14:00 on Thursday to pick up the goose and the potatoes. We will be having many guests."

With the transactions completed, we waited all afternoon on Wednesday for our guests. Louis brought the beers over. There was a way to leave messages at the bachelor home, and he had given them the phone number. "You know, they may have some duties. We won't know for sure what time they will come. The country is still on alert and these young men may not be able to get away."

"Then how will they let us know?"

"They won't be able to. But don't worry too much. They probably will be on a late train. They could even arrive tomorrow morning.

Thursday arrived, and Jack continued to play in the barnyard. His movements became slower and slower as he kept looking for the soldiers to arrive. Then Mom made us get dressed in our best clothes. I even put on my stockings and the Queen Anne heels. Her dyed navy sweater covered my best dress, but I was ready for guests. The farm kitchen was warm, and the aroma of roasted fat stopped any concerns I had ever had about that miserable goose. It lay in a pan surrounded by roasted brown potatoes, carrots and turnips. My bruises were fading. How could we wait any longer for the guests to arrive?

We carried the heavy pan back to our room, being very careful to not spill any juices on our clothing. Louis opened the first beers and invited the Spanish people over. Ellie couldn't really explain our tradition of Thanksgiving to them. They were trying to thank her for the goose, and she was trying to thank them for being her friends. Maria was pregnant again, and she wanted to know what Mom had learned about the special pills from France. Mom was telling her that they would not work when someone was already pregnant.

On Monday Mom arrived at the factory late and a little hung over from the weekend. A co-worker offered her a scarf to cover up the love bites on her neck. The supervisor came by to reprimand her. She exploded. *"Ich bin keine Näherin (seamstress), ich bin eine Leherin (teacher)! Ich kann nicht ein mehr machen, ich bin krank. (I am sick of this.)"* Pallid with grey rings around her eyes, it was evident to the boss that she was useless as a worker. Her clothes hung off the model's figure. This was not fun any more.

The early December days had grown very short and dark. When we got up, there was no promise of dawn or sunlight any time soon. As I walked into town the outdoor markets would be setting up, and the smell of evergreens from the forests began to fill the air.

The shop windows were ready for the coming of the Nicklausmann – St. Nicholas. Candied fruits and chocolates shone through shop windows – little foil wrapped chocolate soldiers, huge glittering displays of candied fruits, even whole watermelons and pineapples – all icy, frozen in sugar. The marzipan displays imitated the shapes and colors of the fresh oranges and lemons in the produce markets. Best of all were the sweet blood oranges from Spain. Families in homes would be decorating for Christmas. Jack could now walk into town by himself, and once a week we each had a mark to spend on a hot meal at the Herti department store cafeteria. That was enough money to buy a nice midday meal with meat, vegetable, and potatoes. Because there were no adults around, our choice was to buy a bowl of chicken broth and a pastry. The chicken broth was my idea. It even had some carrots in it. Jack would have just done two pastries.

Sometimes my long walk after school would include an invitation to stop at a girlfriend's house for the midday meal. By now a few parents had figured out that our mother was really struggling. One day my new friend Jana offered me some dark beer to go with a homemade stew.

"This is malt beer, it's good for you."

Her mother chimed in, "You are too thin and pale. You need beer and some meat."

"Twelve year olds do not drink beer!"

Her mother looked surprised. "Do you mean in America girls don't have beer?" Jana's eyes widened. "But, how do they have babies?"

"Well, first the woman gets married. Then they go away and eat a lot and she gets fat. After a while the doctor takes a baby out of her stomach." There was a detailed conversation with various ideas about how that might work. Jana's suggestion that the baby comes out of the woman's bottom was just gross, and we laughed hysterically over the idea. But according to both Jana and her mother, pregnancy was supposed to involve beer. I was quite sure that grandmother Estelle had never mentioned this, and she had five grown kids plus grandchildren.

December 6 is Nicklaus Day, when St. Nicholas comes to visit children and families. Aunt Monika had shown us what this was. When she came to the US to get married she surprised us. Beside our beds one morning there had been ski boots filled with candies, nuts, and little toys. We were told that the German Santa had come because Moni was in the house. It had been one of those highlight experiences of childhood – completely unexpected because it was not a Christmas surprise, and not part of any familiar tradition.

Now Santa remembered us even though we were thousands of miles from New York. Grandmother and Uncle John had sent money, $10.00 for each of us to have whatever we wanted. That amount was a small fortune. Forty marks was a week's salary for a worker. Mom took us to the bank and went to Herti immediately. By now all the girls at school wore ski slacks and beautiful hand knit sweaters. My unwashed old dresses were a pretty funny sight, since all Americans were supposed to be "rich." A nice pair of Helanca ski slacks cost exactly $10.00, and as I drew the navy trousers up my long legs, I actually admired the image in the mirror. A teenager looked back. Now if I could only knit. I went to look for my brother over in the toy department. He was not there. Instead the little guy was looking through housewares, and then he wandered off into sports. What was he thinking? Finally I saw him touching sleeping bags, one after another. Jack spent his money on a sleeping bag instead of toys. Somehow, the matador cape with mother's old coat on top had lost its novelty for him. The sleeping bag became his fondest possession. He fondled the soft warm fabric like a stuffed toy pet.

The long December nights got colder and darker. The farm was built in the old style with the barns and house connected as one building. That way all living things could share body heat and the benefits of fuel. The barn below us had no heating except that of animals huddled together. The rooms above were even colder. A bare light bulb hung from the ceiling in the rented room. Seven people used the bathroom down the hall as a laundry and scullery. The cold water barely ran in the freezing temperatures, but we had no other option. No one washed any more. Everyone had sniffles. Even the washed handkerchiefs froze on the lines, and thawed to become just slightly cold and damp.

Jack learned a lot of Spanish, and how to tell jokes. But one day, Mom sent him to the bathroom to wash up the lunch dishes because I had helped cook. Carla and Maria came in and immediately pulled his pants down. Maria grabbed the bread knife out of the sink, started yelling, and made cutting motions. Apparently, in Spain men did not wash dishes, and she indicated that if he ever did so again he would turn into a girl. He ran back to the room crying hysterically. Mom tried to explain that American men do help with dishes. She held Jack under her arm, like a mother chicken. I was sent down the hall to finish the washing up, wondering exactly what it was that men did to earn their keep.

Louis was an American man, but he had never said a word about marriage, or being a real dad. He never talked about it with us. It was time to pull out all the stops and show him what a nice family could do to make him happy. Mom decided to make him a sweater. She could not read patterns or instructions in German, but sweaters are basically constructed on a series of rectangles, so it couldn't be that hard. Not an expert at knitting, she worked carefully and slowly, making each stitch even and precise. The knitting went on and on. But, Louis' idea of a sweater was not the same. His idea of a sweater was more like a James Dean T Shirt. He wanted the sweater tightly fitted and tapered from waist to chest, with tight shoulders. He felt that would look the best with his jeans and leather jacket. Never mind the fact that he had more tummy than shoulders. He wanted to look like the men in the magazines. Traditional ski style sweaters were too long, too bulky, and did not show off his muscles. I helped her wind yarn and unravel mistakes. Jack chattered, pressing on with kids' comments.

"Why can't you and Louis just get married? Then we could live together in a real apartment." Apparently, Beatniks didn't get married, and they didn't live in houses. "But Louis lives in the bachelor home. He has an apartment and hot dinners there." Mom swore as she dropped a stitch and then picked it back up. Jack looked worried, and was quiet. Then he said, "Do you think if maybe if you washed your hair and fixed yourself up with some lipstick, he would propose?"

Mom finally explained to the Spanish ladies that the shower was supposed to be kept clean so that people could use it to wash themselves. They had been using it as a urinal. They thought the idea was hilarious, but they cleaned it out. She stripped, jumped in and turned on the faucet. There was no hot running water. There was not even a hot water pipe. There were no soft towels.

"Honey, if we try to wash our hair in this cold, we will die of pneumonia." She was rubbing herself off with a dry cloth.

"Maybe I should get a job. At least I can speak German. I could work in a kitchen after school."

Ellie shook her head and sighed.

*   *   *

Traveling with all your goods in a sack like a real Beatnik was not "cool." I carried home truancy notices from school because I had missed most Saturday classes. Sleeping on trains every weekend had lost its charm. I penned neat letters in German for my mother to sign, explaining things like, "On Friday night we traveled to Munich. We saw the Alps on Saturday and we learned about Romeo and Juliet in Verona. The train was late getting back to Wolfsburg on Monday morning, so we missed school." All the trips were documented in these notes. My journals even recorded the train times. Mom signed the letters. None of this worked. The Director of the school reprimanded me and I was ordered to attend Saturday classes or be discharged to a trade school.

Ellie and Louis seemed to be getting closer to having some kind of a plan. They scheduled a long weekend in Munich to go house and job hunting. Jack and I were secretly hoping that they would elope and make everything good. Mom shared her secrets with us. "Louis has been offered a promotion. If I sell the house in Elmira, we will have enough money to buy a place in Munich." Louis was now a qualified marketing manager for VW and a large distributor was offering him a management position. But Mom's job search was not going well. Her German was incomprehensible and she could not get a work permit without a residence visa. Her applications to US Army schools did not even result in interviews. They didn't need art teachers.

My brother and I were left at the farm while they went to Munich to sort all this out. Christmas was coming, but there were no plans. The Spanish ladies were in the midst of preparations to go and visit their children. A few days before Christmas I was walking through the market places after the booths had cleared out. The Christmas tree lot was empty. I had never stopped to look at the trees. It was best to turn my head away from the shop windows and avoid kid's discussions of the upcoming holiday. There would be no tree for us this year and we had received our gifts already. A few branches lay on the ground. It probably wasn't the right thing to do, but no one seemed to notice a young girl schlepping branches down the street. I was nervous until the signs for the turn out of town. It was the first time I had ever taken anything without asking before.

Families gather on Sunday afternoons in the weeks before Christmas. "Advent Kaffee" is a time to celebrate the season with coffee, sweets, and candlelit wreaths. We had never heard of Advent, but it was a great idea. Jack was delighted with the branches that I had brought back to the room. We set them on a table in the corner. Mom's sewing box yielded some scraps of ribbon and yarn.

We hung her earrings and costume jewelry beads on the branches. There was even a silver medal from Volkswagen to hang on the top – "Fünf millionen VWs" – five million VW Beetles had rolled off the factory lines. Maria and Carla brought beer and oranges. The Bulgarian man brought his accordion. Lively dances and poignant ballads filled the room. Humming holiday songs in German, Spanish, and English, our little group began singing with the accordion.

The door to the room opened. "Look at them! See Louis? I told you the kids would be OK. They're having a party! Chips off the old block."

As the music faded, and the beer ran dry, we began to make plans for the move to Munich and said farewells to Carla and Maria. The plan was that mother and Louis would get things finalized in Munich the week before Christmas. Then, Louis would take us somewhere wonderful to celebrate the holiday. I had a great idea. "Let's go to Spain. It's warm there, and Jack and I can even speak Spanish." Louis loved the cold, and he mentioned that Norway was really fun and interesting. Since Jack had not been to Norway with Mom and me in October, he sided with Louis. They drew straws, and I got the short one. Louis lifted Jack onto his shoulders to begin the victory dance, and the two males started laughing and wrestling on the floor to celebrate their big win. The plan was that the adults would get things settled in Munich and transport their belongings. Jack and I would each have a rucksack, passports and our forged Eurail passes, and instructions about the three train connections that would be required to meet the adults enroute to Oslo on Christmas day. The adults began to pack up and left the farm.

We stayed for a few more days in the cold room above the farmhouse. But, this week Jack could have Ellie's warm bed, and I could use the matador cape to add a layer of warmth to the drafty beach lounger.

On the last night before Heiligen Abend, Christmas Eve, some children invited us to join them at the village church family party. People at church gave us oranges, some nuts, and a chocolate bar each. Then my brother and I walked through Wolfsburg one last time, and caught the night train northward.

# CHAPTER SIXTEEN

## Hopes And Dreams

Mom and Louis had left the farm more than a week before. I had no idea why they had been gone for so many days. We were all excited about moving to Munich. It was so much livelier than our drab little factory town. Even if we didn't have any money, there were things to see in Munich. There would be pretty churches with their golden decorations and jeweled glass, snowy mountains, and of course glittering shop windows with all types of treasure behind their crystal barriers. Louis had a good starting job with Volkswagen, and with our child support we could all finally make a go of it. There were army bases around Munich and mom would be able to teach again somewhere. Finally there would be enough for the four of us.

I didn't really understand the conversations except that apparently Louis could move easily and it might be more difficult for us. Mom didn't understand why there was a problem with moving to Munich. Why did she have to appear before a housing authority? Why did it matter what kind of visa she had? Apparently they had to personally appear at the housing authority and request permission to get an apartment before Louis' work permit was finalized. The funny thing was, without proof of employment you could not get an apartment. Once again, the questions.

*"Your names and passports please."* Louis had produced the requested papers and smiled warmly at the bureaucrat.

*"Date of your marriage."* Ellie looked at Louis. Then she said in English, *"We will be getting married in the spring?"* Louis looked at Ellie, did not blink, and did not raise his eyebrows. He also did not confirm her comment to the housing officer.

*"Employer references and source of income"*
Louis unfolded his work papers.

*"Where were you on September 1, 1939?"*

Why did this question appear on every application for housing or employment? The applications in each office included detailed personal and political questions. What was important about that date, a date that occurred some ten years before I was born? Louis said that the date marked the Nazi invasion of Poland, and that information did not really answer my question.

After a brief review of their application, they were dismissed by the housing office, and told to return in two days for their interviews. The interviews did not go well. Since the two were not married, they would not be allowed to live together. They would have to apply for separate housing, which would mean that our modest child support would have to provide housing and food. By the end of a week, Louis was assigned a single room bachelor apartment based on his proof of employment. We were not assigned housing. Mom did not have work, and clearly an unmarried woman wandering around with two children was not an ideal candidate for German residency. They decided to visit Louis' friends for a couple days to find an unregistered guest place, where the three of us could live on her budget. They sat on the floor of a beatnik apartment drinking wine and talking, but Louis did not propose marriage.

This was not the Christmas that any of us had envisioned. Just eleven months before, Uncle Bill and Uncle Pete had announced their decision to spend the year abroad. Mom's lover was moving to Germany, and she had jumped at the chance to join him. In her mind, we would all be together as an extended family, only in Europe. The day that she received the letter from Bill that he and Monika would be going to Berlin for Christmas she sat down on her bed and turned her face into her pillow. We were not invited. There would be too many people in Berlin. This made sense to me. Mutti Liddy had a two-room apartment in her home and we had no money for hotels or meals. Mom started lashing about "snobs." I looked at our dark clothes and thought about Berlin. Berlin was definitely out in our current state. But I wasn't able to say the right things to make her feel better.

So, on Christmas Eve, Jack and I were to meet them in Bremen in the late evening. We would all be on the way to Oslo. Louis had decided that we should see the famous statue of the four musicians, Donkey, Dog, Cat and Rooster. In the fairy tale, the animals protect themselves by teaming up and protecting each other from danger. Louis and Mom were running and laughing through the streets, sipping a flask of cognac. Jack was quiet and dragging behind, looking at the ground as if he were fascinated by his footprints. As a light snow fell, Mom kept slowing down, looking into the candlelit windows of people's homes. Families were clustered together, just as her family had done each year of her life. I felt like the little Match Girl, only a lot angrier. There were no angels in my story. At least anger keeps you warm.

Finally we were back at the train station and there was just enough layover time for a very important task. On the first trips the past summer, Louis had showed Jack and me how to find money. Train station lockers often drop a coin or two after the person has paid. It was a lot of fun to find 10 and 25 Pfennig coins in the locker returns, and keep them for treats. Now finding the coins was a necessity. We checked every locker, telephone and vending machine for money to buy a holiday meal. We had had no dinner, but I promised Jack that the next day there would be a smorgasbord feast on the way to Oslo. We had found the coins to pay for it.

Tempers were short. Jack was cold and hungry. I did not appreciate the midnight sightseeing expedition. The train was full, so we would not have a compartment for the four of us. Mom and Louis decided to find their own compartment for sleeping. My brother and I had to share a second-class bunk. We stank – from our socks to our breath. One way to share a single bunk is to lie in reverse from your partner, with feet next to heads, but the close contact was disgusting. My pack held clean underwear and socks, a Time Magazine, and a little chess set. Jack had the black bread, and the oranges and nuts from our friends in Sandkamp. At each border my brother and I were accosted by passport control, and an examination of tickets. We had no idea where the adults were, so we pretended to sleep while the officers came by in the dark. A light flashed into my eyes, "It's showtime." Jack opened up the passport case, which conveniently had Christmas cards with commemorative US stamps in the pocket. Train conductors are known for their interest in stamps. I began to babble in Spanish. "Si, si—Oh yes, those are American passports, but we are Mexican. We are from New Mexico. It's a state. Señor, we are from Albuquerque. Shall I spell that for you?" "Are there adults traveling with you?" Jack replied in English. "You may have those stamps if you like. We already have read the letters." He thanked us for the stamps. He did not ask us for our tickets. But, there was more bad news. Since this was Christmas, the smorgasbord was closed.

Throughout that night, I sang every verse of every song we knew, and talked of treats at Grandmother's house. The tears kept coming, quietly, in the dark."

# CHAPTER SEVENTEEN

## Out In The Cold

There is an art to cracking nuts in a sliding steel door. A few hours later Jack and I woke up on Christmas morning, traveling along the coast of Sweden. The morning train change had put us into a beautiful new Swedish coach with the soft blue seats. Somehow, Christmas Day always ends up being special. At the bottom of the rucksack were the nuts, still in their hard shells. The oranges and bread were long gone. Jack, known for taking things apart and making them into something else, looked at the nuts, then looked at the shining new sliding door of the train compartment. He set a hazelnut into the track on the door and slammed it. The nut burst into crumbs. Carefully, we placed nuts in the track and closed the door until we could crack the nuts and not hurt our fingers. The conductor came along the row of first class compartments. He looked at the nutshells in the corridor, and the two dirty children. His face turned white, then red. Neither of us could think of a clever thing to say, in any language. Then, the conductor told us to please make sure that we cleaned up the nutshells when we were done eating. He too forgot to ask for our tickets. Later that morning, he came by again, and brought us some more nuts.

The only thing that gelled that Christmas was the Lutefisk. After washing our faces at the train station and scouring the lockers for spare change, Jack and I met our mother and Louis at the Stationmaster's office. Louis announced that he would be taking us out for a traditional Norwegian Christmas fish dinner. Yum. We loved fried herring, eel, and smoked salmon, and our mouths watered.

Lutefisk is vile. It is gray, it quivers, and it smells rank. The smell of this dish of lutefisk was reminiscent of some cod liver oil that has been stored in the medicine cabinet until it has gone rancid. A codfish is soaked for weeks in lye, and then the gelatinous mass is steamed and served with boiled cabbage and peas. All around us people were eating steaming sausages and roast poultry. Jack asked for water to drink. Someone brought us a black beer called "Wørter" which is probably a cousin to root beer. Except "Wørter" is just the bitter roots with no sugar. It tastes like sour black bread, only wet.

I decided that everything I had learned about table manners in Berlin was now irrelevant. I was furious and decided not to speak at all. After all, grandmother said, "If you can't say something nice, don't say anything." There was nothing nice to say. I just took off my glasses and stared into space. These people did not exist. Jack was just a disgusting little boy anyway, and he chirped on while he smooshed up the gray mess on his dinner plate. Ellie looked at Louis helplessly. He went to pay for dinner and remembered that he had left his wallet in his backpack in the train station lockers. Louis promised to be back within half an hour.

After he left, we began to talk and laugh. Mother thought the idea of us kids cracking the nuts and winning over the conductors was just hilarious. Suddenly, she looked worried. Louis must be lost. He had been gone well over an hour. He must have left her because the children were fighting. Jack started to cry again, and she left the restaurant to go find her missing lover. Once again I tried to get some water. The water in trains is not potable, and we had built up a two-day thirst. The waitress brought another "Wørter." She tried to find out what happened to our parents, and she spoke Norwegian, German, and English. Jack and I answered her politely with nonsense in Spanish.

Across the room, an elderly gentleman was finishing his Christmas night alone. Like Nicholas, the patron saint of sailors he had a white beard but he wore simple dark clothes and boots. Apparently, he had been listening to us for some time. He came to our table with two bottles of lemon soda.

The old man started to tell us stories in English, tales of Oslo and of explorers. He himself was a seaman and had been alone since he was twelve. Fascinated, we listened to tales of West Africa, and of the South Seas – the gentle climates, sunshine and trees. Soon our heads began to nod. Gently, the old man asked us where we were going to spend the night. The restaurant was closed, and we were the only three people there. Jack explained about Louis' wallet, and that mother had left to find him. The old man paid for our dinner. Then, he said that he had no home that he could take us to, but for Christmas, he would put us into a soft bed at the Viking Hotel, the grandest hotel in Oslo.

Jack protested, "But, we need to be with our mother and Louis. We haven't seen them for a long time."

"I doubt they want to see us."

"Kate, I know that mom will come back for us."

"What makes you think so? They hate us, and they want to be alone. Anyway, mom can only speak English, and she gets lost all the time. She isn't clever, and she gets afraid." The old man said it was true that the streets in the area were very close together and that the night's snowfall might make it hard for mother to find the way back. He agreed that we could go to the stationmaster's office and leave a message for our mother. Jack and I were looking forward to soft feather beds at the hotel and promised not to dawdle, not even to check the lockers.

The Stationmaster's Office was a prearranged meeting spot in all cities, a safe place to meet and to leave messages. There was no message from Mom, so I began to write her a note, to tell her the old man was taking us to the hotel to sleep in a white feather bed. Suddenly, we heard her at the front desk. She was just arriving at the railroad office, after having been lost in the snow. The old man invited her to stay at the hotel with us. Just as they were leaving for the Viking Hotel, Ellie turned around, and there was Louis, hurrying toward the office. He had also gotten lost in the snow, returned to the restaurant and found it closed.

"Oh little buddy, I would have never left you." He put his arms around Jack and reassured all of us that we would be safe together now. The old man looked at Mom and asked if she was sure that we would be all right. Then, he turned to my brother and me, wishing us a "God Yul" and a safe sleep before disappearing into the night.

*   *   *

December 26 wasn't really a business day, but the first order of business for the travelers was to get cleaned up. Louis suggested that we all visit the public steam baths. He explained the process and paid for the four of us. Mom and I went into the women's side, and he and Jack to the men's.

For the first time in months, I saw my mother's body: her thin legs, and her full bosom that had turned into "two eggs, fried." In the shower we washed our hair, and then we were led into the steam room. At first the heat felt good, but I began to panic. I couldn't breathe, and the hot air began to stifle. The attendant listened for the signal bell, and then directed us to a sauna, a dry heat bath. Layers and layers of dirty dead skin began to slough off, leaving our skin white and pink underneath. We began to laugh as the sauna and steam alternated. Wouldn't it be nice to be a cat? And just lie in the warm places all day? Suddenly the attendant opened the doors and directed us to an ice-covered swimming pool. "Jump in!" I jumped. Mother was warm for the first time in weeks and wanted to take a nap. The attendant turned and pushed her, screaming, into the pool. Pores open in the steam, and they must be closed quickly so that hairless warm-blooded mammals will not catch cold. A delightful body massage with creams followed the cold dip, and for the first time since August, we were blonde again.

The four of us met up, and Louis located open butcher and bakery shops to buy fresh groceries. He found a comfortable room in a hostel, and Christmas had finally come. Then, he took off for another walk, to see what sightseeing attractions would be open on the holiday. Jack and I were children again, teasing and squealing.

"You should have heard mom scream when the ladies pushed her into the ice water . . . her long legs and arms flying through the air, kind of like a drunken pterodactyl!" Ellie opened the rucksack and removed packets of foods to make beautiful decorated sandwiches, like those she had seen in the shop windows. There was a large red sausage, gjetost, a sweet goat cheese that tastes a little like peanut butter and a little like cream cheese, fresh pickles, and an enormous salami. The aroma of fresh breads filled the air. No codfish anywhere.

Jack sidled up to Ellie and quietly asked, "Mom, how come men's bodies change? Louis really changed in the bath. I asked him, and he said he was just hot. Will I get big like him too someday?"

Kate interrupted, "Oh, women's bodies look different too. We got all puffy and swollen in the sauna, but then we were OK."

Ellie began slicing the sausage. "Damn it, this breadknife is making a mess of the salami, it's just dull."

"But mom, you always say it's not how it looks, it's how it tastes." Jack picked up the large red sausage, something that looked like a hot dog on steroids. "Mom, this kind!" He began to rub the sausage. "Oh, but he hugged me and said he would be OK. Is he OK mom?"

Ellie ignored him. "Kate, give me your Swiss Army knife. I think it's sharper." I handed over my knife, and Mom began to slice the salami into paper-thin pieces. "Gosh mom, it looks like you're trying to flay it! This isn't a torture chamber."

"Kate, shut up and hand me the dill pickle." Ellie continued attacking the sausage and dill pickle, stabbing and slicing pieces for the luncheon plate. Then, she paused, and in a cold even voice explained, "The salami needs to be in very thin slices because it has to last us all week."

"Geez mom, I don't even like salami, and I sure don't want to eat it all week." "Katrine Marie . . ." "Okay, Okay!"

Jack was bouncing like a kitten, pulling at the cords on the rucksack. "Mom, mom, can we have the peanut butter cheese now? We're hungry! Can we have it with jam?" Ellie ignored him, which he took as, well, not as a "no." Jack happily sat down and made himself a big crooked cheese and jam sandwich.

Louis arrived to an attractive cold plate, one of Ellie's kitchen specialties, and dug in. Ellie wasn't hungry, but we opened our beers, served ice cold American style, thanks to the crank handle on the window, and the hanging string bag outside. Jack looked over the list of sightseeing possibilities and decided to go see the highest ski jump in the world. Mom, terrified of heights, laughed nervously, "Why not?" and took our hands as we boarded the tram. Holmenkollen ski jump is so high, that if the skier does not know how to land, he will break every bone in his body.

# CHAPTER EIGHTEEN

## Moving South

It was a three-day train trip to a new home in Munich. Louis had succeeded in getting an apartment in the Leopoldstrasse, a bohemian section of the city. Finally he and Ellie could get back to their ideal of a Beatnik life, only with a home, food, and some money. It even looked like she might have a job opportunity at the US Army base to be a teacher again.

At midnight on December 31 all the church bells began to ring at once, and fireworks exploded across the sky. Brilliant reds and royal blues flashed their pastel counterparts over the snow-covered city which only moments before had been silent. The four of us stood on the balcony in pajamas, and Mom brewed hot chocolate on the new stove. Our little family celebrated the New Year with a toast to warmth and sweetness.

The apartment had its own bath and a kitchen. Mom began to prepare her soups for us. By this time Jack and I had learned to eat whatever and whenever we were commanded. One day Ellie went into the kitchen, took out a skillet, and poured in some rice and fat. Jack went in, watched for a few minutes, and asked, "What is that?" "Fried maggots." "Oh. OK." I snickered at his naivete and chopped an onion for the Spanish rice. Late that afternoon, after our feast, Louis gave us money to take a walk. For two hours we were supposed to go to the park, buy a sweet, and explore the shops. The afternoon was cold and the snow was wet, and but finally it was 4:30 and we could return. The brightly lit apartment was different in some way. I stopped in the entry. "For heavens sake, do we really need to wait outside for hours while you take a damn bath? You might have just closed the bathroom door. We could have waited in the living room." Mom was taking a bubble bath and drinking a glass of wine.

It turned out that we would not be staying in Louis' apartment after all. The three of us needed to leave before the apartment manager found out that we were in the single occupant bachelor apartment. Luckily, no supervisor had been on duty over the New Year's weekend. Our things needed to be out immediately, and Louis had to start his new job. There were garden houses outside of town, near the army base. Louis had found a sweet little cottage that was leased by a Viennese opera singer. It could have been a theatrical set for an operetta. She had painted everything in gypsy colors. The living room had a single bed, a hanging lamp made from a basket, blue carpets, and yellow ruffled curtains. Furniture was painted in red and green with folk designs. An oil-burning stove in the center of the house heated the main room. A makeshift kitchen area contained a hot plate and some open shelves for dishes. A short bathtub stood on a platform in the kitchen, near enough to the oil heater to keep the water warm. Another new adventure was under way.

Louis enjoyed his new job as Assistant Manager for a large VW dealership, and he was working long hours. Although Louis now had a car, he would not be available to help with our weekday move. We would make our way across town on our own. Snow began to fall in the early afternoon. By dusk the trees carried 5-6 inch plumes of fluff, and the new snowfall was already more than a foot deep. Each of us had to carry a suitcase and a bedroll. Mom could barely carry her heavy load. Jack decided to be the little man and shift for himself, but he did not have a camping bed to haul. It was my cot and my responsibility.

Things started well enough. We got everything downstairs from the apartment and caught a tram toward the city center where all bus and train lines circled an enormous plaza. Locating and boarding a bus or streetcar at Karlsplatz had all the drama of facing a circular firing squad. At any point a car could move forward and smack you against a tram or a bus. Bus numbers were obscured in the dark and we skidded along the slippery tracks. Once on the bus, Mom decided to take charge, and she pulled the address out of her pocket while Jack and I waited with our belongings. Her German was not good and the bus driver was not looking forward to the trip in this snowstorm. Mom could not keep the *ie*– sounds like "ee" and the *ei* – sounds like "I" straight.

"Sir, we need to get off at Liebleitner (EE) gasse – or is it Leiber (I) gasse ?

"Sit down. All your things have to go on your seat with you."

"How far is it?"

"Is what?"

"To where we need to go?"

The driver turned away and started up the engine. Not only was Ellie's pronunciation unclear, but she still did not know her German alphabet, or how to read. The bus driver was on his last run of the evening, and the blizzard was getting worse. After several minutes, he dropped us off. We were lost on a snowy night with all our belongings in tow.

After realizing that we had been dumped, Mom once again tried to ask directions and found that the walk would be about three kilometers through the snow. Jack and I were both wearing coats that did not fit. He had on my anorak, and I was once again in Mom's old coat, its wet hem dragging almost to the ground. Mittens didn't keep the wrists warm, and no one had boots for walking in deep snow. The straps from bags and backpacks began to pinch. The cold metal of the camp cot bit into my fingers and I yelped with each nip. Where the hell was Louis? Did he really work this late at night?

"We're going to die. I'm not going to wait around for it. I think I will die right here!" I was done with this exercise and sat down in the snow. I could freeze like the Little Match Girl or I could find the breadknife and slit my wrists. We didn't even have any Aspirin to use for poison, but going on was not an option. Three hours of public transit and walking had gotten us into the middle of nowhere. *"Young lady, get up, pick up that cot, and march!"* Jack quietly trudged ahead with the breadknife in his knapsack as mom and I screamed at each other. My plan was walking away from me.

Suddenly, in the dark, a young man appeared with a bicycle, and he began to shout at us. He had seen the bus driver deliberately put Ellie out at the wrong stop and had hurried home to get a bicycle and to find the children in the blizzard. He loaded the bedrolls onto his bicycle and led the bedraggled parade to the garden house. It was nearly midnight; we had left the apartment more than seven hours earlier.

Frau Burkhardt, the new landlady, had stayed up, fearful that something had happened to us in the storm. A pot of chamomile tea was waiting. Meanwhile the young man disappeared into the blizzard.

\* \* \*

A couple days later Louis visited the garden house and brought his new friend, Ben. Ben was boisterous and funny, a total loudmouth. He was also an American expatriate living in Munich. I cooked a spaghetti dinner, and the adults shared a bottle of Chianti. Louis, Ellie, and Ben laughed loudly into the night, talking of the upcoming celebrations of Fasching, the German equivalent of Carnival. Once again the star of the show, Ellie was flirting with both men.

Frau Burkhardt also had a lover, Herr Komorek. She was an accomplished astrologer, and Herr Komorek came from a gypsy background. She came over daily to cast our charts, and to "tsk, tsk" about some cosmic event or other. She believed that the three fire signs – Ellie, Louis, and Jack – were all compatible, and that the water sign was very unhappy. Mom could have told her that I was a wet blanket without all that.

Herr Komorek taught Jack how to do snuff. How disgusting – the little brother who had once created a mural of boogers on the

wall was now learning to combine mucus and tobacco. I declined.
Tobacco and asthma are a nasty combination. But Herr Komorek
was able to help mom with the endless sweater. Louis had asked
her to tear his Christmas sweater apart over and over, to reknit the
pieces and give the garment a more fitted shape. Apparently, as
a boy, Herr Komorek had learned to wind yarn into balls, how to
hold the needles, and how to keep the stitches even. At last Louis'
sweater was acceptable.

The weekends were calmer. The Eurailpasses were now seven
months old, dirty and frayed around the edges. The ink eradicator
was leaving marks, and there wasn't really enough money to eat or
stay overnight if they did go somewhere. Ben and Louis had all kinds
of great ideas for day trips. Our absolute favorite was the salt mines.

On a frigid day, Louis drove the VW beetle with five passengers
over snow and ice to the salt mines, toward Obersalzberg, a German
word that means "above the salt mountain."

"Oh great, another of Louis' snow expeditions, no ski clothes,
and it is really cold and wet out here."

"Kate, shut up."

At the top of an icy mountain is the entrance to a mine that has
been in use for nearly 500 years. The guide ushered us into a huge
room with lockers and handed everyone a set of clothes. The heavy
white canvas pants would have fit elephants, but the guide showed
us how to tuck the leggings into the big black boots. Now we were
handed black leather aprons, with leather as thick as a horse's
saddle. As Mom started to buckle on her apron, the guide said, "No,
no, it goes on your backside." Over all this went black canvas jackets,
and hats with little lights on them. The guides then led the group to
a little train, like the kind that kids ride on in amusement parks. The
gears engaged and cranked, slowly, down hill into the mine, deep
inside the mountain. The train stopped at a wooden platform. The
platform was the top of a long flight of stairs and the biggest slide
anyone had ever seen. Everyone lined up and shot 100 feet down
into the mountain on the slide, to arrive at a magical sight. The lake
underground was completely rimmed by crystals, and soft blue
lighting illuminated the area just enough to see the edges of the

cave. Salt is retrieved in the water, and left to evaporate on the sides, then brought back up using pails on pulleys. The tour guide began a long and important explanation of the process. Jack and I ran to the top of the stairs and slid down again before taking a rowboat around the twinkling blue lake.

* * *

The colorful little house in Pullach was a warm sweet place. The surface area on the hot oil stove stayed warm, and eventually cooked food that was left in pans on top of it. Frau Burkhardt taught us how to cook ptomaine rice by putting ground meat, rice and onions into a pot before school, and then setting it on top of the heater. That way we could come home to a warm meal. You could place oats and water in the pan at night and wake up to porridge.

The kitchen bathtub didn't afford much privacy, so one day after mopping up the floors, I decided to bathe. No one was home. Dinner was on the oil stove, and it was time to relax. I began to feel odd, and fainted when I climbed out of the tub. Jack came home from a friend's house and ran for Frau Burkhardt and Herr Komorek. They lifted me onto a bed, but I was still unconscious when Mom arrived. I could hear but I couldn't open my eyes or respond. It wasn't like being asleep, because I couldn't even roll over. There were some discussions about a strange color. What was the strange color, and where was it? Someone thought that maybe the problem was carbon monoxide from the oil stove in the kitchen, complicated by anemia. The adults deliberated as to whether they should call a doctor, when there was no money to pay for one. Finally I did roll over and began vomiting. My mother was sitting by the bed, pale and crying.

Meanwhile, Jack was beginning to really struggle in school. The German boys did not like Turks, Spaniards, or any other foreigners. He was an easy target for the bullies. His class was learning about kings and princes, and as a special treat, the teacher took them to a palace. Jack was fascinated by birds, and the palace pond was really interesting, with swans swimming through the unfrozen center. Younger swans, still with their grey down, bumped into the ice, got up to walk, and then slid around until they were able to swim again. It was funny and beautiful at the same time, with a glittering winter sun, icicles, and the young birds on the woodland pond. Jack was just looking off into space, taken in with the pond.

Suddenly Gunther, the class bully, started to tease him. Gunther had a potato face, the kinds with too many eyes and lumps.

"Hey Jack – or are you Johannes today?"

Jack alerted himself to trouble. A Johannes is slang for male genitalia.

"How is your Johannes anyway? And your lovely mama? I see she still can't slice a piece of bread."

By now Jack had listened to adult guidance to not let people bully him. He considered their advice. Then my gentle brother punched Gunther, and pretty soon they went for it right on the thin ice, just kind of slipping all over the place. Nobody really won, but both boys did have to go back to the school and sit in an overheated classroom for an afternoon, just to write some meaningless sentence 100 times. Jack had no idea what the sentence was, but he sure knew he wasn't going to stay in that school very long.

# CHAPTER NINETEEN

## Castles in The Snow

Fasching, the official beginning of the season of carnivals, masks, and deception starts on November 11, at 11:11 PM when all the witches come out of the mountains. By the period of six weeks before Lent, the celebrations are under way, a strange mix of pagan and Christian rituals that have evolved over a millennium. Our witching season began one night in January when Louis and Ben were invited to a dinner party near the Army base, and took Ellie with them. They promised us that they would be home by midnight.

Midnight came and went. Back at the little house, Jack and I played chess until we could not stay awake. We went to our beds in the back room, but kept the front room lit. Mom needed to get home safely. Close to dawn, Louis arrived at the house, bumping against the door while he looked for Mom's keys. Ellie was stumbling behind in the snow, "One, two, cha cha cha." The clumsy Latin dance steps were supposed to be from warm tropical islands that people visited in the winter. Hot-blooded lovers did the tango under the stars. Our starry night of ice and snow was anything but warm.

Right there, in the front room with the curtains open, Louis undressed mom and put her to bed. "I wanna drink."

"Mom, do you need some chamomile tea?"

"No! A real drink. Gimme another Martini!"

The gin reeked from every pore. Jack and I watched in amazement as Louis sat Mom down on the edge of the bed and then undressed her, right down to her black lace underwear. Louis had no business seeing my mother in a bra.

"Ellie, I need to put you to bed."

"Sleep here? Where's Gate 13? Where will Jeff sleep? Waltz me around again, Willie." Now she was singing. Where had she been all night? Didn't she know she was at home with us?

Jack tried to get me to go back to bed. "He can't see her that way!"

"See what?"

"Her bra! Men aren't supposed to see women's underwear."

"I've seen underwear and I'm only 9. Of course Louis has seen a bra; he had a mother, didn't he?"

"Louis, what the heck is Gate 13?" I stood like a guard at the door to our room, with my legs straddling the doorsill and arms akimbo.

"Your mother has had too much to drink. We met up with Jeff Hoffman last night and he took us back to the base through Gate 13. It's not a real gate. It's a hole in the fence. You have seen the real gates with guards. Women are not allowed into the barracks so Jeff had to sneak us in."

Jack did not understand the explanation. "You mean women can't go where men go?"

"The guys all live together without any wives. Women aren't supposed to go there."

"Then why did Mommy go? She says we shouldn't go places unless we are invited."

"Kids, I have to get to work. Take care of your mom, OK?"

I decided to stay home from school that morning. Mom didn't look too well and she might need something. Sure enough, she woke up around lunchtime with a terrible headache. I put the teakettle on.

"Honey, what are you doing here?"

"Louis brought you home this morning. He took off your clothes and put you to bed. You are sick aren't you?" The enamel teakettle began to clank on the hotplate. I found the tea and the spoon to brew it.

"Oh, we had some wine and dinner with Jeff Hoffman. He says hello."

"Mom, why did you go through Gate 13?"

"They had some other drinks at the barracks." Ellie laughed. "I haven't had a Martini like that in a year. Driest Martini ever."

I handed her the mug of tea. "How can a drink be dry? And why were you dancing? Did Louis ask you to dance?"

"You know they can get American things at the PX, so we . . . . you know Kate, this isn't really any of your business."

"It's my business if I have to take care of you." I sat down in the red chair at our little table.

"Touché."

What does that mean?

"It means that you are right – you have struck me in this round of combat. I will tell you what happened and then you will let me go back to sleep." Mom sat up in her bed. I went and got her nightgown from the drawer.

"Jeff's bunkmate in the barracks is Gary, a young soldier from Kansas. Gary said that he didn't know how to dance. So I grabbed him and some others and started to teach them some of the Latin Jazz steps. Is that OK with you?" Mom turned back over onto her stomach and covered her face with her hair. Obviously the headache was no longer going to keep her awake.

It was not OK, but I left her alone and opened a schoolbook. The books had things that I could figure out.

*   *   *

On Friday afternoon when I walked home from school there was a familiar VW in front of the gate. We had guests. Bill and Monika had been on a skiing vacation in the Bavarian Alps, and were dropping by on their way back to Austria. Poor Monika had broken her arm ice-skating on the first night of her vacation, so she didn't even get to ski. She ended up spending her winter vacation knitting. Monika had made mittens for Jack and me – wonderful wooly mittens with blue snowflake patterns that went all the way up to the elbow. For the first time ever our wrists did not hurt when we went outside. Grandmother had been trying to solve the problem for years. In the New York winters, adults bundled children for play in layers of wool. Once the coats and leggings were covered in snow, we were immobilized, frozen stiff and too heavy to move. The fuzzy, itchy armor could stand up by itself after just moments outside. The final defense was mittens. But snow melted when it touched your wrist, pulling the cuff of the mitten down until a soggy little wad of wool fell off, got stuffed in a pocket, and was then lost. In every winter of my life, outdoor play had ended abruptly with frozen wrists and scoldings. Monika's elbow length mittens stayed on. Jack and I could play outside comfortably and throw cold wet snow at each other all afternoon long.

Mom and Uncle Bill had many long talks in the evenings. For months Louis had entertained us with stories of Fasching carnivals, practical jokes, and grand balls. Mom had looked forward to making spectacular costumes and dancing until dawn. Now she was broke and exhausted, not really feeling like a princess about to attend the grand ball. The one costume she had made so far used my black hooded anorak, black tights and blue face makeup. She took a white flower and went as a corpse. It wasn't funny. The serious expression on Bill's face indicated that maybe this party was about to be canceled. Her brother had a way of asking probing questions that challenged her for days.

Instead of partying, Bill suggested that we go with him to Eisenstadt for a few days. We crammed into the VW with Bill and Monika, the brown knapsack of belongings across our laps. Upon arrival, we all took a long nighttime walk through the city, admiring palaces lit with thousands of candles and store windows full of treats. Golden high-heeled shoes that cost as much as a week's groceries were displayed with filmy party dresses and men's black penguin suits. The Viennese ball season was in full swing. A rich dinner of sausages and red cabbage ended the evening as Uncle Bill drove us all to Eisenstadt.

I fell into the comfy bed at Bill and Monika's apartment and was soon sound asleep. Unfortunately indigestion struck again. The last thing I wanted to do was to get up from out of the feathers and trudge across the frozen courtyard to a stinky and unheated outhouse. My pajamas felt funny. When I put my hand down under my bottom I was surprised to find that the flannel pajamas were already moist. "Mom, mom!" "Whuh?" "Mom, I've got my period!" "Whuh – oh my god, I don't have anything with me! Go ask your Aunt Moni." I went to the next bedroom, where Moni and Bill were hugging in bed, took one look at them and fled. There was no way to announce this event in front of my uncle. Jack trotted into our room and I kept my front toward him so that he wouldn't see the bloody pajamas. He shouldn't learn about this either. "Mom, I can't, she's with Uncle Bill." Mom began to laugh. "Go to the outhouse. We will be with you as soon as we can." So, I sat in the cold outhouse until mom and Moni brought some clean rags. There were no supplies in the house, and all stores were closed from noon Saturday until Monday morning. It was Sunday morning.

Over breakfast, Uncle Bill decided to clear the female tension with some incomprehensible dirty joke. Apparently he did know about periods, and he was asking Ellie, "Does that mean that if she gets with a man, she will be able to reproduce? She looks awfully young for that." Oh, for crying out loud. I had grown up in a household of uncles and no one had gotten pregnant. How stupid can men be? But, Bill decided that puberty rites were in order. "What is a puberty rite?" Jack and I were dying to know. At some point in the morning, they had filled Jack in on the details. Great. Apparently the adults had all recently read work by Margaret Mead, an anthropologist, who described elaborate rituals for young women when they first menstruate. "Hmm, we can't really build a menstrual hut in the courtyard." "There is no boy to sacrifice her to." "Sometimes they use wine in ceremonies." "Let's have a . . . . Party!" What a surprise. But, this party was to be different. I was going to stay up and party with the adults.

The Vienna area was home to several of the exchange students who had lived with the Osbornes in Elmira over the past decade. Erich Sokol, the Playboy cartoonist, had been a close friend, along with his twin brother, Fredi. They arrived with their wives, and with a box of elegant chocolates from the shop windows. Helmuth was another of the young men who had stayed with us Elmira. He had apparently heard months of arguments over clothes – the dresses made of men's shirting material and the starched white homemade petticoats, when can-cans were all the rage. He had a tight little bundle under his arm, a gift-wrapped cylinder. Pink, yellow, green, blue, lavender and apricot layers of tulle spilled out of the tightly bound package – a seven layer can-can petticoat with every color of the rainbow! I pulled it on over my ski slacks and began to cha-cha. Helmuth taught me how to waltz. Bill and Monika opened the champagne, and everyone began to talk and sing. I loved singing most of all and knew the words of most of the German folk songs. Life's music was wonderful.

*   *   *

Burgenland, with its vineyard-covered hillsides, is surrounded by the jagged Alpine landscapes that form a band across the face of Europe. This juncture of earth and sky is a land where spirits dwell.

The radiance of a snow covered mountain flashes beams of every color and none, each connecting the earth and the sun in a dance of colors that are too bright to be seen, and so bright that they are felt with every particle of our existence. On the coldest winter days, the earth crackles with excitement and anticipation of its rose colored sunrises, blue white days, and golden sunsets, all mingling through time and space. It is a landscape too cold even for birds, but surely angels can fly there.

At the feet of the mountains is a dark ring of people, inventing ways to survive the clearest days of winter. The rings of people burn coal and cook animal carcasses and roots from the ground, filling the air with smoke and acrid scents of their existence. Outhouses are semi-frozen, and the ground is too hard to bury corpses. The world of people becomes a daily exercise to remain sheltered in place, until they can move freely again.

Jack and I remained in Eisenstadt after Mom went back to Munich. The idea was that I needed to get over the anemia and a bronchial infection. Eisenstadt is a poor city on the eastern point of Austria, with the Hungarian border running through the fields next to the town, Czechoslovakia directly to the north and Bosnia directly to the south. Half the town spoke German, and schools were German language, but the black-shawled women in the marketplace spoke Croatian.

Bill and Moni's apartment was in the back half of a simple countryside villa, complete with courtyards, vineyards, and winemaking sheds. A villa is not really luxurious, even if it is big. Inside the three-room apartment, only two rooms could be used. There was a coal stove in the center room for some heat, and the back room had carpets and feather beds. The front room was used as the refrigerator and freezer, with food stored on top of the grand piano.

On a walk around the property, Bill carefully advised us about the seriousness of the problems between Austria and Hungary, two countries and the same people, who had been part of the same empire less than 100 years earlier. Even though it was their own property, there was a tall fence in the middle of the grape trellises marked with red and white signs, VERMINT. The most recent border conflicts had only been five years before, and the mines had not been cleared yet. The state of Burgenland, including Eisenstadt, had been traded back and forth to the Communist bloc for years. To protect their holdings, they had planted land mines in farming areas. Jack, always curious, was wondering what happens when a landmine blows up. Underneath one of the grapevines lay the frozen remains of an animal, partly decomposed, but with some parts missing where it had stepped in the wrong place.

Mornings in Eisenstadt began with the filling and lighting of the coal stove in the center room. The center disk began to heat, and on it the coffee pot began to steam. As its aroma filled the apartment, the others would wake, and Monika would pour the hot beverage into mugs with milk and sugar. A first vision in the morning was the vapor from your cold breath, mingled with the steam from the coffee. Bill and Jack dressed in the cold, often without washing more than the essentials. Eggs were fried in a skillet on top of the stove, and then Bill would go out to start the VW engine.

As soon as the men left for school, Monika and I agreed that it was too cold to be up until the stove did its work. We reached into the basket for a couple skeins of yarn, and jumped back onto the bed to warm our hands. After being off all night long, the black coal stove began to release heat little by little into the center room. Monika patiently showed me how to use my left hand for knitting, quickly shuttling the yarn between the needles. While I practiced making squares and a simple scarf for Jack, Monika worked designs in her wool, textured cables for warmth, and intricate geometric patterns in mixed colors. She was working on a deeply textured "fisherman" sweater for Bill to wear skiing.

I wanted to become an expert knitter as quickly as possible. Girls my age were already designing and making their own elaborately patterned sweaters and I was knitting like a 6 year old. Knitting may be woman's work, but it is as important as shoveling coal into a stove. Girls discussed types of wool, how to get bigger and smaller stitches, how to shape a garment, and how to build designs into the handwork. They talked of color combinations and located little remnants to work into banded patterns and practice pieces like potholders and simple caps. Girls and women enjoyed talk about the work of keeping a family warm in the winter, and commented on the artistry of friends and neighbors. For weeks we had heard about the talents of Frau Wanjeck, who had designed a gorgeous sweater for her son, in ivory, black, olive green and coral wools. It was apparently the most gorgeous pullover in Eisenstadt, with flowing patterns of leaves and berries, while the rest of the women were working on simple stars and crosses.

This weekend, Werner Wanjeck was going to be joining us to go skiing. I would get to see the most marvelous sweater in Eisenstadt. Because of Ellie's catastrophic love life, I had absolutely no interest in boys. Mom and Monika had already told me that the boys would see nothing in me. After the weird encounters with Louis, I definitely was not interested in any type of masculine contact, ever. So now, I was expected to shake hands and greet a young man when I did not know how to even speak to one. I had never exchanged words or looks with the silly little boys in my classes at school.

In the frozen blackness of early Saturday, after a warm Friday night playing cards, Monika got Bill, Jack and me out of our beds. The electric light in the main room cast yellow shadows on furniture and people as she began to get the group ready. In the dark, she lined us up in the kitchen area, and led calisthenics – deep knee bends, jumping jacks, and stretches. She insisted that this would prevent injuries out on the slopes. Jack and I complied, Bill complained. Then, after hot coffee and rolls, we all piled into the Volkswagen Beetle for a two-hour drive up icy mountain roads. Terrifying slips and skids would be met with "Good job Herzchen – Sweetheart." Bill did not drive on these trips, he advised. His advice to Moni was to steer into a skid as the bug was heading toward the edge of the chasm, and then bring it back onto the road. But, he didn't actually undertake the black ice himself.

What nobody told me to expect was that Werner Wanjeck was the most gorgeous young man in Eisenstadt. He was as tall as me, two years older, with dark curling hair and green eyes. Werner and I were crammed next to my brother in the back seat of the Beetle, and somehow the cold of the morning shifted, first to warmth and then to heat. As I melted we talked about school, teachers, and subjects. Werner tried out some of his English. We talked a little bit about teen life in the States, favorite American music, and astronauts. I flew to the moon from the back seat of the little car. Jack sat in the corner, completely oblivious, and tried not to throw up.

But, there was a problem with spending the day together. Werner had been on skis since he was three years old, and was going to ski on the adult slopes, racing with Monika, curving along the long trails, and jumping across ice patches. Jack and I were beginners, and that combined with my total lack of athleticism was going to be a problem. So, that morning I herringboned my way up the bunny slope, and snowplowed down, over and over, rapidly climbing back up the hill to try and improve my coordination on the long wooden planks. Luckily the years on figure skates helped me get control of the skis in a few hours. I could feel inside and outside edges, balance myself, and stay in motion. I was ready for the tow-rope. The adults came down, and Bill bought tickets for us. We grabbed the line, and I held my legs straight with my back crouched for the trip to the top of the bunny slope. Jack just stood there grinning and wiped his nose. The rope moved, he went down, and of course his long skis caught in mine and pulled me down too. The tow had to be stopped to get the mess of arms, legs, skis and poles pulled out of the way. The brat had done the worst thing possible. I was mortified, with snow in my face and under my glasses, slacks and sweater covered with it, and looking like a complete fool. I wished the pole had a sharper point so that I could run him through. Jack had no sense of how frustrating this was; he wasn't even upset that he had fallen. He was busy dusting himself off. As I began to shuss away from him I hoped for a place to hide, leaving my brother at the base of the tow.

Ice still clouded my glasses. I decided to move diagonally across the bunny slope and then stamped out her herringbone track to the top, planning to rest at the hut. At the top was Werner—could this be any more embarrassing? But instead of mocking me, he offered to share some of his hot chocolate. "You know this is not that easy. I can't believe this is your first day on skis. – Would you like me to show you a few things this afternoon?" The frozen tears were wiped away as I nodded, "yes," and then the two of us walked over to the top of the run to try again.

On the ride home, the three of were again crammed together in the back seat, and Werner and I were talking eagerly of perhaps another skiing weekend soon. That night, the cold of the back bedroom did not exist because of the flame that had been lit in my heart.

Finally I was strong enough to return to school and face the challenges of the Gymnasium classes in Eisenstadt. By now I could understand and read aloud quite well. I had even mastered quite a lot of vocabulary. But, the German language is not friendly. Here for example is an educational story about medieval economy and family values:

*"How he himself now evenings in bed thoughts made and himself in front of worries danced around sighed he and said to his wife, "What shall of us become? How can we our poor children nourish where we for ourselves not more have?" "Know you what husband," answered the*

wife, "we will tomorrow in most early the children outside in the woods lead, where he at the thickest is. There make we them a fire and give each yet a piece bread, then go we at our work and leave them alone. They find the way not again toward house, and we are of them free."

Holy cow. These people were a mess. What was the moral of this story? Was it that they didn't have good jobs because they couldn't tell a story very well? The husband was a total loser, and the wife at least could come up with a plan, but she died. Should I be making a personal connection of some type here? Was Hansel going to be a loser like his father? As long as I was connecting ideas, now that Gretel had been through all this neglect and abuse, what kind of wife would she make? Would she develop a drinking problem? Was she going to live with her father forever? How come she didn't get a handsome prince?

"Fraulein Schloss, please read. Know you even the right page?"

German conversations on academic subjects were like going through the washer and wringer on grandmother's old laundry equipment. The first step was drowning. My thoughts would get swooshed around in some mess of words, mixed in with the grime of other people's words, and the soap of the person who was trying to help by interrupting everyone's thoughts. Once a clean insightful comment assembled, it had to be retrieved from washer without getting torn up. The comment then went through the teacher's wringer, where the adult corrected grammar and paid no attention to what was said, expressing no interest at all in what the learner might have been thinking. The pressure of the disapproval silenced further attempts to respond to the literature. This obviously gummed up the writing process. Dictation sentences were a salvation. There is nothing to understand and nothing to interpret incorrectly. You only needed clean paper and a pen that didn't leak.

But, the most fun class of all was "Religion" when a priest came by for Catholic instruction. I got to be a Protestant. Uncle Bill said that was best, because he didn't want to explain that we really never went to church. All five Protestants in the school were allowed to go out in the hall to do homework. Most of this homework involved snacking on treats, telling dirty jokes, and running up and down the hallways in soccer matches with no ball. The Catholic kids told us that we would all go to hell.

Across the street from the school was the Esterhazy palace. The Esterhazys were the Eastern European arm of the great Hapsburg Empire that dominated Europe for centuries. The Hapsburgs were married into every royal family from Spain to Austria. At war with them for centuries were the Ottomans, a fabulously rich Anatolian empire. The two empires were separated by the Danube River. East and West met up at Eisenstadt and still do. The result of this was that all the Hapsburgs had a great interest in keeping the Esterhazys wealthy and powerful enough to keep the Ottoman Sultans and Russian Czars from invading Europe. One famous story in the lore of the town was that a visiting Russian noble had come to the palace to show off his wealth and power. Among his possessions was a very valuable horse, possibly the most famous horse in the world. The nobleman wouldn't trade this horse for any price. He finally named a price equal to millions of ducats, and the prince paid him in gold. Then Esterhazy turned around and shot the horse.

This fabulously rich kingdom was now boarded up and shuttered, with no remaining heirs. After hearing the story about the horse, I didn't feel particularly sorry for the Esterhazys. No one knew what to do with the shell of a palace. Inside its chapel was still the pipe organ that Franz Josef Haydn had used. It was for sale, but there was no way to transport it to the United States. But this palace and its past glories still brought character to the town.

A favorite walk was through past times, the graveyards above the castle. First in view were the elaborate monuments of the Esterhazys, followed by the graves of townspeople. At the top of the hill, behind the others, was the 13th century Jewish cemetery with its fallen headstones and worn Hebrew letters. Eisenstadt now had only two Jews. The images of death and eternal rest had as many contrasts as the stories of their lives must have had.

One night, Uncle Bill had happened on the open hut near the entrance of the graveyard. The sexton stopped him and the two struck up a conversation. Inside the hut old black iron lanterns lay in heaps with their ornamented crosses and decorative curls suggesting a dance with death. Old cemeteries are not lit, and the lamps were still used during torchlight parades and on the graves. The sexton suggested an appropriate time to return to the graveyard. When Bill returned, the sexton was gone from the hut, and a pair of lanterns was easy to retrieve from the jumble of iron and chains. He proudly brought them home to a wife who refused to sleep with them at the end of her bed like a corpse stretched out on a bier.

This cold dark winter brought daily reminders of death and decay – a deteriorating world wide political situation, palace grounds full of weeds, and an uncertain future. There was a wonderful bright spot. Music feeds the soul, offering unconditional beauty and comfort. Several times a week there were music classes at school, singing and studying the works of Haydn and Mozart. A new world had been opened to me.

# CHAPTER TWENTY

## The Masked Ball

Music and dancing were in the air. Jack and I saw Mom and Louis on the platform before the Munich train even stopped. Hugs and smiles were everywhere. As soon as we entered the busy train station Jack asked, "Is it Fasching yet? Did you go to any nice parties?" The adults exchanged glances and began to laugh. The entire city was bubbling over like a bottle of champagne.

Fasching begins slowly, with a few parades and a masked ball here and there. During the days the cities go about business. Teachers appear a little disheveled, but classes continue. Office workers show up, but it takes a few cups of black coffee to get on task. Louis explained the rules. "No one asks any questions. At a masked ball everyone dances and drinks until dawn. Husbands and wives disappear for days at a time. Then you go home, take a nap and change your costume."

This wasn't as easy as it sounded. Our little village of Pullach was not a party town. It looked like a black and white TV show. The snow-cloud grey of February was repeated over and over in blocks of concrete apartment houses, their window boxes empty and curtains closed. Balconies showed no signs of life. Dark bicycles and jackets rolled through the snow and across train tracks to schools and shops. A complex of stone buildings was completely sealed off from residential areas. Pullach was a good hour by bus into Munich.

The excitement was all in Munich and their new friend Ben had a talent for getting invitations to the parties. Louis had a car and Ben drove an enormous BMW motorcycle, but Mom had to take a bus into town before she could meet them for the evening. The three thirty-something adults had black clothes and no money, but Ellie could put together passable costumes using her black tights and accessories. More than once Louis and Ben showed up in tights, boxer shorts, Tuxedo jackets with dress shirts, and ties – formal menswear but without their pants. Ellie wore a black slip, a shawl and long earrings over the tights, no dress.

They decided to splurge on real costumes for the Artists' Ball and I was allowed to help. My hand-stitched seams were neat and they did not fall apart. Mom was fascinated by old gold coins and we thought that it was time for some good luck. Frau Burkhardt had a pair of gold curtains in a wonderful heavy jacquard. For days Mom and I pleated and stitched the long rectangles into the Grecian Gown that would stay on and keep her warm. Paint, glitter and masks were out of her budget, but leftover gold giftwrap and her skills with paper sculptures offered a way to make a spectacular mask. We had seen ancient Greek theatre masks and were able to construct the oversize paper maché mask with its huge grinning mouth and golden curls. She was pinning up her own blonde hair into elaborate twists and braids. I waved at her as she boarded the bus with her bags and headed across town to meet at Louis' apartment.

Louis had bought himself a new brown bathrobe and shaved his thinning hair into a monk's tonsure. Carrying an enormous bottle of wine, he was ready to party. Ben appeared in his black clothes and a black mask. On his belt were a flashlight and a bag of gold candy coins leftover from Christmas. He was a thief.

At last Mom was going to go to the world famous Alte Pinakothek for a night of partying in the art galleries.

Jack and I got to have our own festivities. Frau Burkhardt cooked goulasch for us, and Herr Komorek began playing one gypsy card trick after another. The red and black symbols and numbers came to life in his hands as he told us stories of the past and future. "Are Mom and Louis going to get married?" He pulled some black card, then put the deck away. "It's time for your sweets." We each got a piece of chocolate and ran back across the yard to the cottage and our beds. When I got home from school the next day, mom was in bed. This was not unusual, except that she didn't move, she didn't greet me, she just kept her face in the pillow. Her eyes were rimmed with old makeup and tears.

"Mom, mom," I shook her awake. "Did you have a nice time at the party? What did Louis and Ben wear? Did they really have fountains of champagne?"

She had taken Louis' arm up the icy steps of the art museum, and they arrived in the brilliantly lit main salon. Louis had explained to her, "At these dances, you kiss your date good night at the door, on the way in." So he kissed her, and disappeared into the crowd with Ben. The thief was already halfway up the stairs, waiting for the monk to follow.

Ellie had stood there, bewildered, staring at the elaborate black and white marbled floor and at the open doors as throngs of artists and socialites poured in. She did not know a soul, but watched groups of friends greet each other. She did not know enough German to carry on a conversation about art or much of anything else. Her German was enough to buy groceries and find toilets. She had arrived, but she did not belong here. What had she been thinking? A year ago she met a man who loved her and the kids. Why wasn't it that simple? The black and white tiles on the floor were making her dizzy. She needed to sit. There were no benches. Even a visit to the ladies room would cost a few pennies. There was no way for her to buy herself a drink.

The tears had started up behind her mask. She pushed it aside to wipe her nose, and looked in the full-length mirrors that surrounded her. Her body in its long golden gown was regal. Her face was not. Dark circles rimmed her puffy swollen eyes, and she looked critically at her teeth, wiping the lipstick off the incisors. She had bitten her lower lip. A very tall figure across the room caught her attention. She slipped the mask back on and turned around.

The chess piece moved across the floor toward her. White knight takes Queen. His face was painted white and the horse's head loomed above the two of them. They began to dance. He was a soldier who now worked for Radio Free Europe. His English was excellent, and he would be delighted to take her on a tour of the galleries.

The art galleries were stripped of all the classics, which were replaced by enormous installations made by art students – theatre flats, outsized furniture, mirrors and lighting effects. Each gallery was serving a different cuisine, with its own orchestra and unique atmosphere. Those who wanted to waltz were in the long gallery with its crystal chandeliers and mirrors. At midnight the White Knight took her to the formal dining room for a light supper. A late night dark room was reserved for bebop and jazz. Just before dawn, they danced slowly to a popular song.

> *Sag beim abschied, leise "servus" – When we part, go with grace*
> *Nicht "lebwohl" und nicht "adieu" – Not farewell nor adieu*
> *Diese Worte tun nur weh . . ." – Those words are for pain*

And so the white knight thanked her for a lovely evening and took off. She had no idea what he really looked like, or how old he was, or even if he was single. In the early hours of the morning, Louis turned up.

"Ellie, where the hell have you been?"

"I was dancing, like you told me to."

"But I looked for you all night. I couldn't find you anywhere."

"Last thing I saw was that you and Ben took off without me. In fact, Ben said something about "shake the fish." Lou, what exactly does that mean?"

Louis's hand went across his mouth, but he stroked his chin calmly.

"Ben left at midnight. Ellie, I was walking those galleries for three hours, and surely I could have found a six foot blonde."

"Not with all the ladies in those tall party get-ups – coiffures, high heels, fancy gowns. I was the plainest one there."

"You are one of the most striking women I have ever seen."

I was listening to her story, but very confused. Why would Louis take her to a party and then drop her off to spend the night with strangers? If Ben was invited to the party why didn't he just bring a date? Four of them would have had a nice time. She wasn't just tired from the Artists Ball. She was tired of everything. She just wanted to sleep.

Is death better than humiliation? To some people it may be. Mom was one of those people. She was so angry that she couldn't wake up. There had been still another problem that morning. She was out of money. Not just little things like bus fare, but completely out. There were no more savings and our landlady was bringing over oranges and colorful hardboiled eggs "for the children." In the spring we would have to give up the little garden house and there were no wedding plans.

Jack and I decided that we had better talk to Louis. I called him at work to say that mother was sick. Could he come over that evening? My brother and I were on our very best behavior. As soon as the spaghetti was served, Jack announced, "I'm going to be ten in April." Mom smiled and Louis looked at him. "So when am I going to be a man? Ten is pretty old."

"Well, yes, you're quite the young man, aren't you? Where shall we go for your birthday?" Instead Jack announced, "I'll give you 100 days to decide if you are going to marry my mom and us."

Louis cleared his throat, and looked straight at the little boy. "Gosh Jack, I don't think I could be a very good dad. But aren't we happy with what we have now? I'm really happy with you kids and your mom."

Ellie looked at him, took out a handkerchief, and blew her nose. Then she picked up her glass of wine and gulped it down. "Yeah, look at us. This is not a home Louis, it is quite an adventure, but not a home. To make it a home I need a job, a career. How free can

I be with no job? I haven't even been out looking for work since we started going to all these Fasching parties."

"Ellie, you will certainly have a job soon and all these doubts will vanish. The kids are fine and you are fine. Tomorrow I will start looking at the Help Wanted ads again. We just got a little lazy during all the holidays. I love you."

Mom refilled his glass.

"Louis, I guess we didn't think this through, casual dating for the long haul. It doesn't work if you need a home because it's snowing outside. It doesn't work if you can't feed your kids. I'm not a kit, and you are not a hep cat. I'm an art teacher and you are a car salesman. I guess, uhh, what if I was looking for something different in spite of all this?"

"Ellie honey, now you're talking crazy. I think you are just tired from too many late nights. Let's make this an early evening."

"Is it?" asked Ellie, "is it that crazy? Even in Leopoldstrasse some people are married." Suddenly she sat straight up in her chair and pulled her sweater so that there were no rumples at all. She looked at us, then she looked directly at Louis. He took off his glasses and began to fiddle with his napkin.

"Oh my god Louis, you really don't understand this, do you? Here I am crazy in love with you, but I love my kids too. And what is the deal with Ben? How come he is with us on every family outing, joining the two of us for every party? Is there something I should know? What really happened to your marriage? Why did you really quit teaching?"

"Ellie, that's just not fair. Ben doesn't have a family. He enjoys everything we do. Look at how the kids laugh with him."

"Yes, I know. You let Jack take apart the broken alarm clock. Ben showed him how to put it back together, sort of. They left off the ringer, because we hate it."

She froze and then tried to look him in the eye. He had folded his napkin into a bird. "Louis, wake up!"

"Come on, are you telling me Ben doesn't have other friends? That he can't make friends? And yes, I am worried. Jack is a little boy, and even he plans to grow up to be a man. I sure don't want him to grow up like Ben, some motorcycle riding ne'er do well, without a thought as to his own safety or others. I hope that Jack will be like dad or Bill. There are men all around, but I don't see Jack becoming a man like the men in my family. At least not the way things are now."

I was watching the two of them intently. My little brother was beginning to play with the noodles. For the first time in months, my mother was showing some strength. "You don't understand. I don't have a job, I don't have a home, I don't have a husband."

I suddenly noticed that her fingertips were bluish, even in the heated room. She was so mad she was freezing. She did not move a muscle; she did not blink. Mom was as frozen as any piece of Alpine ice that we had ever seen. She made the ice swans at the palace look alive. She was fighting for her life.

Louis took her hand. "My god! You are so cold. Ellie, you really are sick." "Honey, you have a home now. Your kids are sweet and they love you. We have lived our dream of leaving Elmira. We talked about being free of all the small town gossip. Now look at us." She looked at him. "I need to know who we are and where we are going, or even if there is a 'we'."

Louis turned to me, "Kate, Jack, Bedtime. I want to say good night to your mother alone."

# CHAPTER TWENTY-ONE

## The Unmasked Ball

We were visiting Louis. He and mom had planned a nice weekend expedition to Italy. Leopoldstrasse was quiet in the morning. The Beatniks and Bohemians were not early risers. Louis had gone out to purchase bread, cheese and fruit. Mom was washing up several days of bachelor dishes, mostly egg cups and toast crumbs. "Kate, can you find the folder with the Eurailpasses and put them in my purse?" The folder didn't seem to be on the desk near the window or the bookshelves. But the bookshelves were a mess. Volumes of poetry, magazines, VW brochures, and loose papers were jumbled in piles. It was time to tidy up this little rat's nest, but that was not my job.

I began to shuffle through the papers, and mom's name jumped off the page. The words said "tell Ellie." Tell Ellie what? So I handed mom the lengthy letter. The light blue airmail paper fluttered in the breezy room. There were other letters like it on the shelf, light blue paper and dense text. Mom began to read the letter and then she froze. The letters were from a psychiatrist in New York City. The psychiatrist was advising Louis to "tell Ellie." She read on.

. . . . *relapse for homosexuals, even after they have been through conversion therapy, will always be a significant factor. You must tell Ellie that there may be no hope of a lasting relationship or successful marriage. Honesty may be the best way to resolve your feelings for her.*

*As a mother, it will probably be best if she and the children return to
their home in the U.S.*

Mom knew that Louis had been a teacher in San Francisco. His
love for learning and for children was one of the first things that had
sealed her love for him. He had been so patient with us kids, and had
shown Jack and me things that we would have never seen without
him. The tears began to fall as mom continued to read through
the folder. Louis had been arrested for child molestation, but not
convicted. He had lost his teaching credential, but because he was
homosexual, there would be no opportunities for reinstatement
even though the charges had not been proven. That was why he had
begun traveling from city to city as a salesman until he ended up at a
party upstate in Elmira, New York with a bunch of guys he had met
in a Greenwich Village bar.

Louis came home from the store, and found Ellie crying on the
bed. Putting his arms around her, he said, "I am glad you found the
letters. I hadn't found a way to tell you about my problems. I love
you, I love the kids, and I want to work things out. Think about the
glow in their eyes when we went to Neuschwanstein last weekend,
Jack looking at solid lapis lazuli pillars, and Kate's awe at the hand
embroidered silk draperies that took 700 seamstresses seven years
to sew. There is so much to learn, and I would like to be here for
them. If you want me to marry you, I will. But, the Dr. doesn't think
that it is a good idea." Then he looked at me.

"Kate, can you leave us alone for a bit? It looks like it may
rain, but I brought you something from the PX. I opened up the
long bundle. In it was a daffodil yellow umbrella. Munich would be
thawing out soon.

The trip to Italy was not to be. Instead mom asked for paper and
a pen and she wrote Grandmother Estelle.

\*   \*   \*

The boat to New York left from Rotterdam, and the four of us
said our goodbyes at the harbor, after one last Eurail ride. Crossing
the North Atlantic in March is a rough proposition, and Ellie spent
the ten days lying in bed, alternately crying and fighting nausea.

Jack and I found games to play and new friends. He tagged along behind the officers in their uniforms until he was finally invited up to the bridge where they let him steer the boat for 5 minutes. It was a long time, but we didn't run into any icebergs. I won the teen chess competition on the ship. The food on the ship was plentiful and delicious, and the sea air brought back some color to our faces. We ate ravenously, trying everything that was put on our plates. As long as Captain Nemo didn't prepare the food, we were going to eat it.

The rich treats had their price. As I lay in my bunk on Day 10 of the voyage I couldn't tell if my stomach was rolling, or if the world around me was turning. Late that night I listened to mom's snore and Jack's gentle breathing. I got up. Mom and Jack were deep asleep. Up on the decks I watched as they pulled off the heavy wooded hatch covers, opened up the deck, and began to lift things out of the hold. Huge wooden crates were lifted on cranes, entire VW Beetles hung in the air. The machinery and men were everywhere.

The starry night began to turn a deep violet gray, the deepest twilight. As dawn rose, I could begin to see the outline of the Statue of Liberty and began to cry. In just a few hours we would be with Grandmother and Uncle John, who were driving down to the city to pick us up. The tugboats came out as the islands of New York City were coming into view. Grandmother Estelle had always talked about the "cute little tugboats." Good grief. The hawsers, huge ropes that are on the tugboats, are each as thick as a muscle man's arm. Somehow they tossed these enormous heavy cables up onto the deck to men who then secured them. The ship went silent as it cut the engines. The smaller boats then towed the great ship into the harbor, and we somehow arrived at one of more than 50 docks without knocking everything over.

As gangplanks were attached, Jack and I anxiously scoured the crowd looking for grandmother and Uncle John. Finally, the three of us gathered our belongings and went through customs with 11 bags and a bicycle. Mom had also purchased a case of fine imported liqueurs for Uncle John. Little Jack was already a fan of Advocaat, a rich Dutch egg liqueur. He gulped it at every opportunity.

Uncle John and Grandmother looked at the pile as they headed toward the Hoboken parking lot. "Holy smokes, Ellie! I thought you traveled light. How in heck will we get all this into my car?" So, in the early April bluster of New York, John took the top off the convertible for the six-hour drive back upstate. Five people and the luggage made the car look like an old fashioned sleigh.

Grandmother pointed her hand back for a final view of the Statue of Liberty and the harbor, and began to recite.

> "*Keep, ancient lands, your storied pomp!*" *cries she with*
> *silent lips.* "*Give me your tired, your poor,*
> *Your huddled masses yearning to breathe free,*
> *The wretched refuse of your teeming shore.*
> *Send these, the homeless, tempest-tost to me,*
> *I lift my lamp beside the golden door!*"
>
> E. Lazarus

Uncle John lit a cigarette and started up the car. A case of excellent liqueurs sat in the parking lot as we pulled away.

# AFTERWORD

*6 January 1965*

*Dear Ellie, Kate and Jack,*

*Thanks so much for your Christmas card—you know I was planning to write you all this Christmas but I have just now gotten around to sending out all my cards — today is a German holiday. In fact, I tried to call you Christmas Eve of 1963 but the telephone lines were so overloaded that I couldn't get through. Do you remember our crazy Christmas in Oslo? And New Years Eve watching the fireworks from my tiny apartment in Leopoldstrasse? I so often think of our mad weekend trips to and from Wolfsburg. Any many, many other things like the house in Pullach and Fasching. Life has been very good to me here and I think sometimes I will stay here indefinitely. Please write to me sometime this year even if you don't get an answer right away. Believe me, I miss you all very much, even though we haven't seen each other for almost three years. Good Lord, has it been that long already? How time flies!*

*Love,*
*Louis*

# PUBLISHED REVIEWS

OFF THE TRACK: A Beatnik Family Journey *formerly published* as NIGHT TRAIN: A Beatnik Family Odyssey

"Night Train is funny, entertaining and captivating. It's story is fast and intense with characters that feel real as if they were right in front of you and feelings that come through sometimes with light humor, other times through heartbreaking events." Magy, age 17

"Connie Hood's Night Train is a probing and poignant tale of an American family living outside the box. This merry troupe never allows language, customs or authority to detain them throughout their "Beatnik Odyssey". Max

"This book follows how a mother's attempt to fit into the Beatnik culture at all costs affected her children. In a larger sense, it epitomizes why following any cult or using a movement to justify ones actions or to keep from accepting responsibility can have dehumanizing, devastating effects. It is also a testament to the ability of children to gain maturity and purpose in spite of early challenges that appear overwhelming."
Barbara, poet

"The author uses words like a camera, and to reverse a folk-saying, they are more revealing—and potentially instructive—than pictures. There is much to ponder here regarding the benefits and pitfalls of emotional vs. reasoned decision making. A detailed look at how to—or not—experience "growing up" for both children and adults." Danica, educator

"Night Train is a thoughtful and profoundly moving examination of the beatnik generation and post-war Europe. Told through the lens of an awkward adolescent, this story is both tender and irreverent. Kate is a protagonist that is simultaneously trapped within the prison of her family dynamics while unleashed on an adventure without borders. Her journey is completely relatable, even though the circumstances would be hard to believe if they weren't based on the author's own experiences." Joseph, writer

"I did not want to put this book down. The story is grounded in world-shaking events from the early 60's and takes the reader through situations that are, in turn, hilarious, heartwarming and harrowing." Kay

Edwards Brothers
Oxnard, CA USA
September 21, 201